"So, just so I'm clear, you're staying, right?"

Erin sealed her fate with a nod. "I'll stay and help you with what I can, but I'm not doing it for Charlie. He made his bed, and he can lie in it for all I care."

It sounded convincing. Too bad it wasn't entirely true. Foreign feelings assaulted her when she thought of her father and his condition, confusing and frustrating her. But what bothered her more was that somehow Colin had seen through the layers she piled around herself to the bare truth underneath. His keen sense made him both dangerous and alluring.

"Who else are you doing this for?"

"Aunt Caroline, of course," she answered. "If this was deliberate, I want that person to pay for what he or she did. Caroline was the best, and she didn't deserve to die. When it was her time to go, it should've been peaceful and preferably in her bed."

Something akin to admiration lit up his face and Erin had to bite back a smile. "Stop that."

"Stop what?"

"Stop looking at me like I'm something special."

Colin's grin widened and he almost looked boyish. "Sorry, no can do."

Dear Reader,

As a native of a rural town in Northern California, I suppose you could say the inspiration for this book sprang from real-life experiences. I understand how reputations can be hard to live down and gossip in concentrated amounts can be toxic to the soul.

With that said, I think some of the best people reside in small towns and I'm thankful my roots are firmly grounded within small-town soil. In my experience, life in a fishbowl encourages character growth and fosters accountability. There's nothing like thinking you've gotten away with something, only to learn your mom heard hours ago thanks to a large and tangled network of friends and family.

Both Erin McNulty and Colin Barrett are plagued by the past, but together they find the strength to confront old issues, freeing up space in their hearts to embrace a bright future. Their story is one of courage and discovery, but ultimately of hope.

Over the years I've found I'm most drawn to characters who use a prickly personality as protection against anyone getting too close. I enjoy the transformation that occurs when two people who are meant to be together finally overcome their individual obstacles to discover their personal happily ever after. That's the best part about writing romance. No matter what I do to these poor people, I know in the end... everything will work out.

Like my firstborn, my first novel will always hold a special place in my heart. I hope you enjoy reading Erin and Colin's story as much as I enjoyed writing it. I love hearing from readers. Please feel free to drop me a line either through snail mail at P.O. Box 2210, Oakdale, CA 95361 or through e-mail at author@kimberlyvanmeter.com.

Enjoy!

Warmly,

Kimberly Van Meter

THE TRUTH
ABOUT FAMILY
Kimberly Van Meter

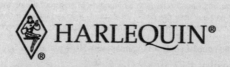

TORONTO • NEW YORK • LONDON
AMSTERDAM • PARIS • SYDNEY • HAMBURG
STOCKHOLM • ATHENS • TOKYO • MILAN • MADRID
PRAGUE • WARSAW • BUDAPEST • AUCKLAND

ISBN-13: 978-0-373-71391-2
ISBN-10:   0-373-71391-6

THE TRUTH ABOUT FAMILY

This edition published by arrangement with Harlequin Books S.A.

® and TM are trademarks of the publisher. Trademarks indicated with
® are registered in the United States Patent and Trademark Office, the
Canadian Trade Marks Office and in other countries.

www.eHarlequin.com

Printed in U.S.A.

ABOUT THE AUTHOR

An avid reader since before she can remember, Kimberly Van Meter started her writing career at the age of sixteen when she finished her first novel, typing late nights and early mornings, on her mother's old portable typewriter. Although that first novel was nothing short of literary mud, with each successive piece of work her writing improved to the point of reaching that coveted published status.

A journalist (who during college swore she'd never write news), Kimberly has worked for both daily and weekly newspapers, covering multiple beats, including education, health and crime, but she always dreamed of writing novels and someday saying goodbye to her nonfiction roots.

Born and raised in scenic Mariposa, California, Kimberly knows a thing or two about small towns—preferring the quiet, rural atmosphere to the hustle and bustle of a busy city any day—but she and her husband make their home in Oakdale, which represents a compromise between the two worlds. Kimberly and her husband, John, met and fell in love while filming a college production. He was the camera operator and she the lead actress. Her husband often jokes that he fell in love with his wife through the lens of a camera. A year later they were married, and have been together ever since.

In addition to writing, reading and drinking hot chocolate by the windowsill when it rains, Kimberly enjoys photography and is the resident photographer for every family event, including weddings and new babies. The photographs gracing the walls of their home are comprised almost entirely of shots Kimberly has captured, whether on the job or just playing around with the camera. The oldest of four siblings and the mother of three children, Kimberly divides her time between soccer games, swim meets, bottle feedings and deadlines.

To my husband, John, for ten-second kisses, our three beautiful children and everything in between.

To Kamrin for being my dedicated reader—you never let me down, no matter how inconvenient the request.

To my parents for always believing I had the talent to achieve my loftiest aspirations.

To Trudy and Kevin for always being the wonderful people you are.

To my mentor Debra Salonen for believing I had what it took to be a "Super" author, and my critique partner Theresa Ragan for being brutal.

To all the other friends and family (you know who you are) that are too numerous to mention individually but without whose constant encouragement I might have failed.

To my editor Johanna Raisanen for showing me in the kindest way possible how to make a good story even better than I imagined.

And, finally, to my grandmothers. Pat—for passing on the dream; and Doris—for cookies and homemade pickles… I love you both immeasurably.

Special thanks:

Special thanks must go to Detective Sergeant Michael Eggener with the Oakdale Police Department for his invaluable advice on the inner workings of a real police station. Any deviations from correct procedure are completely my own and no reflection on the professionalism exhibited by most law enforcement agencies.

CHAPTER ONE

"ERIN MCNULTY, line three, please." A disembodied voice sounded above the din of the newsroom just as Harvey Wallace, editor-in-chief of *American Photographic* magazine, poked his head out from his office and bellowed.

"Erin! I need those proofs, like yesterday! Marshal," Harvey shouted at the reed-thin reporter who was trying to scuttle past without drawing attention to himself, "that piece on corporate America was pure crap! College graduate, my ass! I want a rewrite by tomorrow or else I'm placing a listing for a features reporter in JournalismJobs.com first thing in the morning. You got me?"

Erin looked up long enough to watch the color leach from Marshal's face. She spared the young man a compassionate thought but quickly returned to the latest proofs scattered about the light table. She didn't have time for much else—they were all on deadline for the February issue and Harvey was riding her just as hard as he rode everyone else, possibly even harder since she announced her interest in the recently vacant position of senior photographic editor. Every assignment felt like a test, every successful campaign felt like a step closer to her goal. And as she surveyed the photos before her, she was sure she'd just taken a giant leap forward. They were, without a doubt, the best of her career thus far. If Harvey didn't at the very least wet himself when he saw them he was a blind man and she was wasting her time.

"Erin!"

Despite the near growl he'd ended her name with, she held up a hand, halting Harvey's tirade in mid-breath. "Two minutes, Harv. Two minutes and you'll have the proofs on your desk." *So, shut your yap, you cantankerous old fart.* If only she could actually say that. She scooped the three best and headed for the lion's den.

"It's about time," he said once they were in his hands.

"You upped my deadline by two days," Erin reminded him, silently chafing at his tone. "You're lucky I didn't cut it close to my actual deadline."

"No—" he glanced up, the look in his eyes combative "—you're lucky." When she failed to snap at the bait, he returned to the photos. His sharp blue eyes scanned the photos for the minutest of flaws, but Erin knew he wouldn't find any. They were almost textbook perfect in composition, lighting and subject. She'd really outdone herself this time.

"Erin McNulty, line three, please." The voice over the intercom sounded again, this time more urgently, but Erin ignored it. Not even the opportunity to photograph God himself could have torn Erin away. The longer Harvey studied, the more tense her stomach muscles became. Her confidence level dipped ever so slightly until Harvey leaned back and tossed the photos to the desk. "Not bad," he finally grunted, making Erin want to climb over the desk and choke him until his eyes bulged from their sockets.

"I happen to think they're my best," she countered.

Harvey grunted again but didn't comment further, which led her to believe he felt the same but wouldn't give her the satisfaction of voicing it. If he weren't the best in the business, she'd have told him to take a flying leap a long time ago. Sometimes she thought it was a miracle she'd lasted this long.

Figuring there was no time like the present to broach the subject of her promotion she opened her mouth to start, but Harvey had already moved on. "I've pulled Michael from the Hometown America spread and I'm putting you on it," he announced as if he didn't know that Erin hated happy-sappy photo spreads. "Deadline's three weeks from now."

Disappointment at being thwarted drowned in the rush of anger that flooded her veins at the knowledge that he was deliberately provoking her.

"Problem?"

"No problem," she answered, taking great effort not to clench her teeth as she said it. "Just surprised."

"Why's that?" he said, growl returning.

Sensing she was treading on dangerous ground, she proceeded with as much caution as her temper would allow. "Harvey, I've been working at *American Photographic* for three years full-time, and two years freelance. The last time you sent me to take pictures of hometown hoedowns was when I was freelancing and you figured even a novice couldn't screw up that easy of an assignment. The only reason you're putting me on this one is to see how much that promotion means to me. Well, I'll tell you right now...that promotion means everything."

Half expecting his marble pen holder to go whizzing past her head, she was relieved when all he did was snort.

"You've got a lotta nerve, McNulty," he finally said. "I've fired better photographers than you for less."

She didn't doubt that, but it was too late to pull back. Either he'd toss her out or not. She met his stare. "But you know I'm right."

The silence stretched between them until Erin thought she'd pass out from the breath she was holding. Finally, Harvey shrugged but the look in his eyes was shrewd. "Deliver this assignment and I'll give it some serious thought."

He'd give it some thought?

"See you in a few weeks, then," Harvey said, finished with the conversation. His dismissive tone was meant to push buttons. The old man was notorious for driving people to their breaking point, which was why only a select few remained on staff for more than a year. She doubted poor Marshal had much of a chance. He was already sprouting gray hairs and the kid hadn't even hit twenty-five yet.

She returned to the assignment. So, he wanted happy-sappy? *I'll give him a Norman Rockwell overdose,* she thought as she scooped up the folder and turned her back on him. "In a few weeks then," she said over her shoulder, equally dismissive.

Pompous windbag! She deserved that promotion, probably more so than anyone who'd ever had the misfortune to work under Harvey Wallace. Yet he continued to dangle the promise of that coveted position like a juicy carrot to a starving horse if only to see if it could take one more step before collapsing. Well, she was *this* close to telling him to stick his carrot up his ass, promotion be damned. *Whoa there,* a voice reasoned, putting a quick stop to her inner diatribe. *Don't throw away everything you've worked so hard for.*

Breathe. She exhaled slowly. Right, she reminded herself, taking another slow breath. Creative freedom and the power to delegate—not to mention a pretty sharp addition to her resume. That's why she put up with his crap.

Feeling only marginally better, but certainly less likely to rip the last remaining hairs from Harvey's head, she detoured toward human resources to grab some mileage forms, when she was nearly bowled over by Molly, the harried receptionist whose voice she'd heard over the intercom.

"Ms. McNulty! I'm so sorry," she exclaimed, reaching out with a manicured hand to steady herself. "But I've been paging you for the past ten minutes. You have an urgent call on line three."

It took a moment for Molly's words to sink in. Erin's mind was stubbornly refusing to let it slide that she was being sent like a cub photographer on her first assignment to shoot some bucolic country scene because her boss was on a power trip.

"Ms. McNulty?" Molly ventured hesitantly when Erin failed to answer.

Erin shook her head, realizing she was being rude. "I'm sorry… What were you saying? A phone call?"

"Not just any call," Molly said with a worried frown. "He said he was with the Granite Hills Police Department."

At the mention of her former hometown, Erin stilled. She rarely received phone calls from home. "Did he say what he wanted?"

Molly shook her head, her expression concerned. "He said it was personal…sounds serious. Isn't that where your family's from?" At Erin's barely perceptible nod, the little worry lines that seemed a permanent fixture on Molly's middle-aged face deepened. "I'll transfer the call to your office," she said and quickly disappeared down the hallway to the reception desk before Erin could say anything else.

Granite Hills. Aside from her Aunt Caroline, there was nothing of interest to Erin in that place. Her father included.

Closing the door behind her, she stared at the blinking red light on her phone and wished she didn't have to take that call. There could only be one reason the police were calling her at work. *Charlie.* The urge to simply ignore the call and let it go to voice mail almost had her finger on the button to do exactly that, but a small seed of doubt laced with fear made her hesitate.

Dropping the assignment folder to the center of her desk, she sank into the leather chair and reluctantly picked up the line. "This is Erin McNulty," she answered, hoping the reason for the call was innocuous, or better yet, a mistake.

"Ma'am, this is Officer Barrett with the Granite Hills Police Department," a voice with a subtle New York accent said, his solemn tone trapping the air in her lungs and causing a bad feeling in her gut. "I'm sorry to have to tell you this over the phone but there's been an accident."

An accident? The image of Charlie weaving his beat-up truck down the highway, heedless of the danger he posed to others, popped into her mind and she had to force her voice to remain level when anger quickly replaced her fear. The drunken old fool probably drove off a cliff.

"What kind of accident?" she asked, though she sounded the exact opposite of someone who cared. Assuming her theory was correct, she returned her attention to her assignment folder. "Is he all right?"

He was probably fine. The man, despite the fact that his liver had been pickled nearly every single day of his adult life, was surprisingly healthy.

Erin, impatient for an answer yet not entirely interested in the details, rolled her eyes at the photographic drivel Harvey was sending her to capture and pushed the folder away. Boring as hell.

"Ms. McNulty…there's no easy way to tell you this…"

"What?" She heard him drag a deep breath and knot of foreboding returned to her chest.

"I'm sorry but Caroline Walker died in a single-vehicle car accident earlier this morning."

CHAPTER TWO

AUNT CAROLINE?

"Are you sure?" she asked, the words breaking like glass in her mouth. A snapshot of Caroline's plump, beloved face flashed in Erin's memory and a choking sound followed as she tried to form the right words. "What happened?"

"Your aunt was thrown from the vehicle when the truck hit a tree—"

The sound of the officer's voice continued, providing details that were lost on her at the moment. Her mind had gone quickly and terrifyingly numb, yet it felt like something heavy and cruel had caved in her sternum. She sucked a ragged breath and realized she couldn't get enough air.

Gone. Her aunt was gone? There had to be a mistake. Caroline was the most cautious driver ever issued a license. She was the type of person who personified the term Sunday driver. In fact, she once received a warning from a state trooper for driving *under* the speed limit on the highway. At the time it'd been really funny and Erin had teased her mercilessly, but Caroline had sworn the cruise control had been set on the speed limit and she hadn't a clue as to what had happened.

"My little Toyota must have a mind of its own," she'd joked.

Erin paused, her brain suddenly working again.

"Wait a minute…my aunt doesn't own a truck," she said, clinging to the hope that perhaps there *was* a mistake. That her aunt was fine and more than likely baking something.

"No, she was a passenger in an old, beat-up Ford," the officer said, the sound of paperwork shuffling in the background. "It was registered to Charles William McNulty…I assume that's your father?" When Erin didn't answer, he obviously took that as an affirmative. Swallowing, she realized that the officer wasn't finished and she squeezed her eyes shut. "Your father—"

"Is he dead?" Erin cut in, her voice tight. "Please don't drag it out, just tell me…is he dead or not?"

The knowledge Charlie had been driving in the accident that had killed Caroline made her chest burn with an emotion a lot like hatred, but it was side by side with something else that felt like fear at the realization her entire family might have been wiped out in a single blow.

"Is he dead?"

"No," he answered slowly. "But he's in pretty bad shape. He went straight to surgery as soon as they got to the hospital but there was a lot of damage. I'm sorry. I wish I had better news."

Her father was alive, yet Caroline was dead. The

injustice of it made her nauseous. If anyone had to die, why couldn't it have been Charlie? She heard Caroline's voice chastise her for the desperate thought and she sagged against the back of the chair, tears tickling the back of her throat.

"Tell me she didn't suffer," she said, the sound strangled.

"It was instantaneous."

Thank God. The thought of Caroline dying in pain was more than she could handle at the moment.

Her mouth trembled and she nodded, even though she knew the man on the other end couldn't see her.

"There are some details that need to be attended to…." the officer said in an apologetic fashion, leaving the rest unsaid. She knew what he was expecting to hear, what she was supposed to say, but the words were stuck in her mouth.

The sound of Caroline's voice, mildly reproachful for Erin's continued refusal to come home to visit, echoed in her head and caused fresh tears to collect in her eyes. Every holiday, Caroline had called, asking her to come home, and every time Erin had found a reason not to. Most times she'd blamed work, which wasn't hard since she maintained a hellish schedule, but there were times when Erin had simply lied to get out of going back to Granite Hills. And now Caroline was gone.

"Ms. McNulty?"

The soft query dragged her back to the phone in her hand. She swallowed and took a shuddering breath. "Yes?"

"About your father…"

A muscle twitched in her jaw and she realized she had clenched her teeth. She made an effort to relax but she couldn't keep the tone of her voice from reflecting how she felt about the man at that moment. "What about him?"

"He might not make it," he answered gravely.

Her stomach churning, she snuffed out the flicker of concern that had the gall to flare to life and pressed her lips together. She'd be damned if she were going to care one iota for that man. Her Aunt Caroline was dead and it was all Charlie's fault.

"There's nothing I can do for him. I'm sure he's in the best of hands," she said, nearly choking on the toxic mixture of grief and regret clogging her throat. She fastened her gaze on the folder lying on her desk in an attempt to keep from collapsing in on herself. "I appreciate your call, Officer Barrett. I'll take care of the necessary arrangements," she said, her voice sounding as if it were coming from someone else, someone who hadn't just lost the one person who had truly loved her. "I have to go now," she said, wiping at her nose with the back of her hand when she realized her tissue box was empty.

"Wait!" he exclaimed, catching her before she hung up the phone.

"What?"

"I know your father had a bit of a drinking problem," he said, trying for tact but he needn't have bothered.

"No, actually, he didn't have any problems

drinking. If it'd been an Olympic sport he would've won a gold medal," she retorted bitterly. "My father was a drunk who took advantage of his family and never took responsibility for his actions. I'm sure last night was just the inevitable conclusion of his reck- lessness." Her breath caught in her chest and she forced herself to continue. "Unfortunately, it was my Aunt Caroline who paid the price."

"Well, we don't know for sure if he was drinking and I'm not about to make that assumption," he said. "We'll know when the blood alcohol content comes back from the lab."

Erin shrugged. She didn't need a piece of paper to tell her what she already knew. "Suit yourself."

"I'll call you when I get the results," he said.

It was on the tip of her tongue to say don't bother but she was quickly losing her fire. All she wanted to do was cradle her head in her arms and cry. "Fine," she finally answered. "I'm usually here until nine p.m. After that, you're out of luck."

The officer paused and Erin could almost feel his censure at her cold attitude toward her sole surviv- ing kin. She knew how she must look to someone who didn't know their history, but she'd long since stopped trying to defend herself to total strangers. It was easier to let them assume what they pleased. No doubt, the officer judging her on the other end of the line was no exception.

"I'll try to get back to you before then…in case you change your mind and want to book a flight home," he said.

The flesh on her arms suddenly puckered and popped as a chill raced down her spine. Granite Hills, Michigan, hadn't been her home for a long time. San Francisco was her home now. "That's not necessary," she said, rubbing the skin on her arms. There was no way she was going back there. Especially not now. "I'm sorry, it's just not—" Possible. If she went back to Granite Hills the memories would destroy what little hold she had on her sanity. "I have deadlines."

"Right. I understand," he said, but his tone told her he didn't understand at all. He probably had two loving parents who hadn't left him to fend for himself at the age of six so they could drink themselves into a blind stupor. And most certainly, probably hadn't beaten him so badly that he'd lost consciousness. Bitterness flooded her mouth along with the bad memories, but she held her tongue. No. He probably didn't understand at all. "Is there anything else?"

"No, I suppose not," he answered slowly, seeming reluctant to let her go, as if he could sense she was holding it together by a thread. Erin swallowed, wishing for a fleeting moment someone, perhaps even Officer Barrett, was here with her. She remained quiet, not quite trusting her voice any longer. The silence stretched and Erin was grateful when, after offering his condolences, he said goodbye.

Another memory popped into her mind, unwelcome and very recent.

"Please come home for Christmas, love. It's been so long since we've seen you," Caroline had pleaded, pulling at Erin's conscience. "I'll make all your favorite dishes…candied yams, mincemeat pie, fresh cranberry sauce…you name it. The sky's the limit, if you'll just come home, at least for a visit."

Caroline's insistence had coaxed a small smile, but Erin had shaken her head as she rolled a pencil back and forth on the surface of her desk. "I can't, I'm shooting a holiday spread for the magazine. I'll be booked before and after Christmas."

That much had been true but Erin could have scheduled a few days in Granite Hills if she'd wanted to. Even Harvey Wallace had family. He would have granted her at least a weekend.

"Are you going to invite Charlie?" she asked after Caroline refused to let the subject go even after she'd politely declined the offer. There was a telltale pause on the other end. "Well?" Erin prompted, yet already knowing the answer. "Because you know if he shows up, I leave, and frankly, that's a waste of airfare."

Caroline let out a sigh. "Erin Mallory, why must you be so hard-headed? He's your father for goodness sakes! And he deserves a second chance. He's changed, really he has, and if you'd talk to him you'd see that," she said, her tone openly disappointed. When Erin remained stubbornly quiet, Caroline changed tactics. "Erin, I know things were bad, Lord, how I know, but people change. Why won't you give him a chance to show you he's not the man you remember."

Because men like Charlie didn't deserve second chances. Men like Charlie were the human equivalent of a black cloud of doom hanging over a person's head. He destroyed everything he touched. He was probably the reason Erin's mother killed herself before Erin was even out of diapers. Of course, she didn't know that for certain because Caroline refused to talk about it but Erin wasn't stupid or blind. It hadn't taken long for her to piece together that pathetic puzzle.

Erin had ended the conversation with an empty promise to call again but they'd both known she probably wouldn't. As it turned out, Erin had spent Christmas Day in the same place she'd spent it last year—in her apartment alone. She didn't even have a cat, unlike her Aunt Caroline, who thought it was unnatural to live without the company of a good animal or two.

Staring at the far wall, half-lost in memories, she sniffed back the tears that seemed to flow no matter how hard she tried to hold them back and bit her lip to keep from wailing. Why did bad things happen to good people? How could fate be so cruel a second time around? Hadn't her family suffered enough? She closed her eyes but the action was useless. The dialogue in her head continued to rant with the single-minded purpose of a spoiled child. It just wasn't fair.

Caroline was all she had. No mother, no father to speak of…no other family. She was *alone*. Cradling her head in her arms she sobbed until the tears had soaked the silky softness of her cashmere turtleneck. Finally, the sobs racking her body slowed to a trickle and she lifted her head with a watery hiccup. Arrangements…she had to make arrangements. What did that entail?

She dragged a fresh notebook from her desk and attempted to start a list, though her fingers felt stiff and useless. Where did she start? It was damn near overwhelming. Caroline had mentioned something about a living trust during one of their conversations, but truthfully, Erin hadn't been interested in pursuing the details. Somehow it had seemed morbid talking about arrangements for the estate when her aunt was still alive.

"Oh, God." Her eyes widened in alarm as she remembered Butterscotch, Caroline's dog of thirteen years, midway through her list. "What am I going to do with the dog?"

She dropped the pen and ground her knuckles into her eyes, trying to stop the tears from flowing. *Focus, damn it.* You can fall apart later, she promised herself, sniffing back another wave of moisture that was gathering like an ocean swell after a big storm.

She supposed she'd have to call someone to go over to the house and pick her up, but who? Erin had long since lost contact with the people she'd once known in Granite Hills. Someone was bound to realize Butterscotch was alone at the house, right?

Perhaps. Then again, perhaps not.

Visions of a half-frozen dog waiting pitifully for her master to come home made her shudder, the very thought weighing like a two-ton bulldozer on her conscience. After all Caroline had done for her, she couldn't possibly let her aunt's favored companion die forgotten like day-old trash. But what was she supposed to do if she couldn't get hold of anyone?

Her gaze returned to the assignment folder and she contemplated telling Harvey that she wasn't going to do it. He'd no doubt spit bullets but there was nothing he could do if she chose to take time off under these circumstances. Of course, if she did that she could probably kiss off any chance of landing the senior photographic editor job. She drew a deep breath and leaned back to stare at the ceiling, her grief-numbed brain reminding her sharply to get her priorities straight. The promotion was the least of her worries.

Yet, she realized with a groan, time off with nothing but her grief to occupy her mind would probably drive her crazy. Photography had always been her form of therapy. Losing herself in the process of capturing a sliver in time enabled her to stay sane when the moment proved too much to handle. It was what had kept her on track those first few years after leaving Granite Hills; what had kept her from self-medicating with drugs or alcohol. Closing her eyes as another wave of anguish rolled over her, she knew with resigned certainty that she wasn't going to pull out of the assignment, no matter the circumstance or her personal feelings on the subject matter. Once again, she would cling to her photography like a life raft in the hopes that she wouldn't drown.

A fat tear slid down her cheek and she wiped it away, almost absently, her mind already attempting to work in some sort of productive direction. She glanced at the folder on her desk.

Hometown America—the fantasy of small-town life.

Granite Hills—the reality of what small-town life was all about.

Quaint pictures of cobbled streets and gabled churches didn't always tell the story straight. Most of the time, the pretty picture was simply that—a nice illusion. Which was why she hated these types of spreads. She preferred urban settings—gritty and real.

But, as she soon realized, most people weren't like her. They wanted the fairy tale, which was why *American Photographic* was going to give it to them in full Technicolor.

"Happy-sappy sells magazines," Harvey had snapped when she'd tried to talk him out of a similar spread last year.

And that's what mattered.

Ironically, Granite Hills was probably the place of Harvey's photographic dreams. On the surface it was chock full of Mayberry goodness; almost enough to give a person a cavity if they stuck around too long. It was the kind of place that Erin distrusted. She'd always felt apart from the shiny, happy people around her; always felt afraid that someone might judge her by the actions of her father. It hadn't been easy being the only child of the town drunk. It probably hadn't been any easier to be his sister but Caroline was one of a kind; she never gave up hope that things might change for the better. Unlike Erin, who'd given up on that pipe dream the day she left Granite Hills.

"Erin McNulty, line two."

Erin stared at the sudden appearance of the blinking red light on her phone and wondered what more bad news could be waiting for her on the other end. She was half-tempted to let it blink for all eternity. Not possible, a derisive voice answered back. Besides, whoever it was would probably just call back anyway. She scrubbed the last of her tears from her face, and made an attempt to appear as if her world hadn't just crumbled around her feet, before picking up the phone.

The officer with the New York accent spoke and the corners of her mouth turned down as fresh tears threatened to ruin her mask of composure. *What now?*

"I thought you should know the results of the BAC tests," he said, pausing ever so slightly. "Aside from a little Robitussin for a cough, he was totally sober. I just thought you should know that before you made your decision."

Sober? Impossible. "How accurate are those tests?" she asked.

"One hundred percent."

Erin recalled Caroline trying to tell her that he'd stopped drinking a while ago but she hadn't believed her. Actually, she hadn't given Caroline much of a chance to convince her either. The thought of a sober Charlie was too fantastical to entertain and it tugged too hard on a childish dream that Erin had let die the night he beat her nearly senseless.

"You must have caught him on an off-night," Erin retorted, a different sort of bitterness flooding her chest. "Ironic. The night he ends up killing someone with his driving is the night that he's, according to your tests, quite sober." A mirthless chuckle broke free. "Fate is a fickle bitch, isn't she?"

Knowing there wasn't an appropriate response to her acidic comment, she let him off the hook and changed subjects. She didn't want to talk or think about Charlie. Ever again.

"My aunt had a dog," she began, focusing on keeping her voice strong. "Her name's Butterscotch. Can you send someone to get her? She'll freeze out there by herself."

"Sure thing," he answered. He paused, then said, "We can hold her for three days, but if no one adopts her, I gotta be honest with you...she'll be put down. Shelter policy. It's a terrible thing but there's just not enough space to hold all the animals we pick up."

Of course. "Are you sure there's no way the shelter could keep her until someone adopted her? I'd be willing to pay for her room and board," she offered, yet, she knew that finding a family for an older dog was difficult at best. Most families wanted puppies or at least adolescent dogs who still had the energy to romp and play and fetch a stupid stick. She tried sweetening the deal. "I could even make a donation to the shelter, if need be."

Money was one thing she had. If she had to she'd pay room and board for the dog until she died. If she had to empty her savings to build another wing for the animal shelter, she'd do that, too. But the man's hesitation told her it wasn't going to be that easy.

She could almost hear the man shake his head. "Sorry, ma'am, it doesn't work that way. If the shelter ran like that it'd be a kennel," he said, adding in a tone that was meant to soothe…or rile, she wasn't quite sure. "But don't worry, we'll send someone out to get her. She'll sleep warm tonight."

But after that? Who knows. Criminy, what was she supposed to do? Fly to Michigan for a dog? She wasn't a dog person. She wasn't a pet person *period*. What was she supposed to do with the dog if she went and picked her up? Her apartment wasn't conducive to other living things. The dog was probably better off taking her chances at the shelter. Someone was bound to adopt her. Judging by the pictures that Caroline always sent around Christmastime, she was fairly cute, as far as dogs went. A mutt of indeterminate parentage, but cute nonetheless.

And what if no one adopts her? a small voice shot back.

Then she'll be put to sleep.

Can you live with that?

Don't all dogs go to heaven?

Don't be flip. This time the voice sounded a lot like Caroline's and Erin actually flinched.

Caroline loved that dog. And Erin owed Caroline at least that much for all the times she stood by her, protected her, treated her like the daughter she never had the opportunity to have.

Once again her eyes strayed to the folder lying on her desk and she realized if she could manage it emotionally, this was an opportunity to hand Harvey his precious Hometown America wrapped with a gingham-print ribbon. But could she handle it?

She'd have to.

"Fine." Erin closed her eyes and heard herself say the words that she never imagined herself uttering in this lifetime. "I'll take the next flight out. I should be in Michigan by tomorrow afternoon."

CHAPTER THREE

COLIN BARRETT'S SUV lumbered through puddles of slushy mud as he made his way carefully to Caroline Walker's house. It was near nightfall and the rain had quickly turned to sleet with the promise of a full-blown, nasty snowstorm on the wind, but his wipers were doing a valiant job trying to keep his windshield clear and as long as he could still see, he wasn't turning back.

A woman was coming all the way from San Francisco for this dog; the least he could do was make sure it hadn't caught pneumonia by the time she got here.

He pulled onto the long, dirt driveway, his tires slipping a little in the mud, and turned the spotlight on. The dog, eyes reflecting the light, rose painfully to her feet from her place on the porch but managed to wag her tail in welcome.

"Poor thing," he murmured, knowing from the dog's stiff gait it wasn't accustomed to staying outside for long periods of time. Caroline had probably let the dog out while she went with Charlie, figuring she'd only be gone for about an hour.

Colin pulled his slicker over his head and climbed out of the vehicle, narrowly missing a puddle that looked as if the Loch Ness monster could easily take a few laps in, and reached behind his seat for the control pole he'd borrowed from the animal control officer.

He walked slowly, offering soothing words of welcome until the old girl sniffed his hand and then gave him a warm lick with her tongue. Smoothing her damp fur, he started to slip the nylon loop around her neck but thought better of it. This dog was no Cujo, that was for sure.

"We don't need this, do we, girl?"

She licked her chops and stared up at him expectantly. She was probably wondering where her master was, and if her dinner was coming, Colin realized.

"She's on her way," he said, feeling only slightly ridiculous for trying to make a dog feel better.

Suddenly his radio crackled to life.

"SR4, ten-nineteen."

Return to station?

"This is SR4, ten-four." Holstering his radio, he made quick work of getting the dog settled in the vehicle and jumped in himself.

Once inside, he switched to his Nextel for privacy.

"Hey, Joe, this is Colin. What's going on?" he asked the dispatcher.

"Sorry, Colin, but Danni was hauled in while you were heading out to the Walker place. Thought you'd want to know right away."

As soon as he heard his daughter's name he felt a flush travel up his neck that was surely a result of his blood pressure hitting the ceiling. He bit back an oath, needing a moment before he was able to speak again without clenching his teeth. "I'm on my way."

Twenty minutes later he was sliding his ID card into the back door of the police station, silently fuming. It had taken every ounce of training he possessed not to speed down the snow-covered streets of the quiet town as he drove to pick up his only child. This was becoming an all-too frequent occurrence and he didn't know what to do about it.

"Hey, Col." Joe Boland waved and gestured toward the holding cell. But before he could enter, Joe stopped him, his face grave. "They had to book her this time. I'm sorry."

Colin pressed his lips together but nodded in understanding. "With what?"

"Possession," he answered. When Colin swore and shook his head, Joe tried lessening the blow. "It was just a bit of weed—a misdemeanor—but she's going to have to go to court. I think Marty's already processed the citation, you can probably take her home."

Colin thanked Joe for his help. This wasn't the first time Danni had been caught hanging with a group of kids with a shady reputation, but the officers had let her off with a warning. This time, Colin knew, she'd gone too far. He couldn't expect his buddies to keep covering for her. It wasn't right. The law was the law.

A sense of loss filled him as he pushed open the holding cell door. Where was his little girl? And was she ever coming back?

Colin's heart contracted at the sight of Danni slumped in the metal-backed chair, chewing at the cuticle on her index finger as she stared glumly at the dull metal table. She looked up as he entered the room, her expression changing quickly to the picture of defiance but not before he saw the relief in her eyes. Colin ignored the pain that lanced through him and made a curt gesture for them to leave. "Let's go. You're supposed to be at your Aunt Sara's. She's probably worried sick."

"Yeah, right." Danni shoved away from the table, the legs scraping against the old tile floor, as she shouldered her backpack and stalked past Colin with more attitude than an MTV diva on concert night.

"An attitude like that won't land you anywhere but more trouble, young lady," he said to her back as they walked out of the station and into the biting cold. He hit the automatic door lock on his key ring and both locks popped up in unison. "You're in enough trouble as it is. Do you have any idea what could have happened to you out there? The weather alone made it dangerous, never mind the company you've recently taken up with. And what about your homework? Or the fact that you have school tomorrow?"

"Whatever." Danni jerked the door open and slid in, noticing after she took her seat that there was a dog in the back. Startled, she dropped her scowl long enough to give him a questioning look. "What's with the dog?"

"The shelter's closed and, as you can tell, there's a bad storm. I didn't want her to freeze to death," he answered, amazed he was able to keep from yelling. He was so mad he was shaking.

"How sweet," she said, reverting back to the sour-faced teen that he'd found sitting at the station. She gave the dog a long look then wrinkled her nose. "It smells like wet dog in here."

"And you smell like cigarettes and stale beer," he returned. "Frankly, I think I prefer the smell of the dog."

The black look he received was completely out of place on the face of his thirteen-year-old daughter and made him wish that he could turn back time—to change what had gone so horribly wrong between them.

But he couldn't and because of that he could feel her slipping further and further away from him with each sullen glare, each angry exchange. Lately, she seemed to hate him.

They drove home in silence, the endless swish of the wipers the only sound between them. Colin risked a glance at his daughter as she leaned against the window frame, her cheek resting against the cool glass. Her profile, so much like her mother's, made him ache. Danielle had been classically beautiful, yet her delicate features could not have hinted at the vulnerability hiding in her fragile mind. Years ago, geneticists had warned him that Danielle may have handed down her condition to their only daughter. Colin swallowed against the lump that had risen in his throat. All he could do was hope that Danni had dodged that bullet.

Putting the SUV into Park, he turned to tell Danni to go straight to bed, but she hadn't waited for instruction. She was already out of the truck and stomping her way through the snow to the front door. By the time Colin made it to the house she was already ensconced in her bedroom with the door closed firmly behind her.

"Well, girl," he said to the dog, which to his best guess looked to be some kind of yellow lab cross, her face nearly white with age. "It's just you and me. How about something to eat?"

The dog looked up at him with big brown eyes that were sweet and trusting and he found himself hoping that Erin McNulty didn't flake on the poor thing. He didn't know her from Adam but she made it pretty clear that coming home to Granite Hills was as appealing as having a nail pounded into her foot.

He went to the fridge and pulled out some ground beef he'd planned to make into burgers tomorrow and crumbled some into a bowl for the dog. He'd hate to have to put her into the shelter. By the way she moved, stiff and slow, it looked as if she had some level of hip dysplasia. If the McNulty woman pulled a no-show and he had to check her into the shelter, the odds were slim that she'd find a home. He wasn't a bleeding heart, by any means, but he didn't like the thought of putting the old girl down.

"It ain't steak but it's better than nothing," he murmured, giving the dog a gentle pat on the head as she bent down to eat what was offered. A small smile lifted the corners of his mouth. At least someone would go to bed happy. His gaze strayed to his daughter's closed door, knowing that he was, no doubt, playing center stage as the villain in his little girl's dreams, and his brief moment of satisfaction evaporated. After placing a bowl of water on the kitchen floor, he retired to the small room he'd converted to an office, wishing he could sleep but knowing that he couldn't. Despite the late hour, he sighed as he picked up the phone and made a quick call to his sister so that she wouldn't worry. With Sara's husband in Iraq and a six-month-old to care for, she certainly didn't need the grief Danni was dishing out on a daily basis to everyone she felt had betrayed her.

A box of chamomile tea sat unopened on his desk, part of a care package his mother had sent. He wasn't much interested in it, but his mother swore by chamomile when things looked rough. She said it had a soothing touch. He eyed the box without much hope. He knew what he needed wasn't in that box but at this point he was starting to feel a little desperate.

God, he missed his parents. They'd bought a condo in Florida last year in search of warmer climates. With her arthritis getting worse each year, Ma said she couldn't take the winters here anymore. They were coming back for the summer, but it just wasn't the same without them. Although his sisters lived close by, they were busy with their own lives and he hated to bother them with the problems he was having with Danni. Turning to face the large bay window, he watched as Mother Nature did her level best to ensure that Granite Hills was buried under a soft layer of snow come morning. Colin thought of the McNulty woman and wondered if her flight would be delayed due to the weather.

He closed his eyes to relieve the burning behind them and briefly thought about giving that damn tea a shot. He needed sleep but he knew that if he went to bed he'd just end up tossing and turning, punching his pillow in frustration or staring at the ceiling. He was only thirty-six but he felt one hundred. The last few weeks with Danni had been hell.

And he blamed himself. He should've told Danni the truth a long time ago but he'd chickened out. Now, the secret was out and his daughter hated him for it.

A seemingly innocuous slip of paper, he mused bitterly, had driven a wedge between him and his only child.

How many times since that afternoon had he wished he'd burned it the moment it'd been put in his hands? A dozen, a hundred, a million? Countless. But he hadn't. Like an idiot he'd put it in his file cabinet and forgotten about it.

Until he came home one day three weeks ago to find Danni standing in his office, holding it in her hand, her eyes full of wounded disbelief, demanding an answer.

"What is this!" Danni had screeched, tears streaming down her cheeks, jerking the paper away just as he'd reached for it—no, grabbed at it—in horror. "You lied! You said she died in a car accident when I was a baby but she didn't!" She thrust the document at him, the broken-hearted look reflecting back at him nearly sent him to his knees apologizing. "This says she died five years ago—" her voice dropped and wavered, suddenly sounding much younger "—of a drug overdose."

He'd tried grasping the death certificate she'd waved under his nose but she'd jerked it away, scanning it as if it would somehow reveal the truth to her as he had not.

"Danni, you don't understand…it's complicated," Colin tried explaining, but Danni wasn't interested in the reasons. "I was going to tell you when you got older, but the time never seemed right…I'm so sorry you had to find out this way."

"But you lied," Danni wailed, the tears falling unchecked to splash down the front of her shirt in wet splotches. "All that time…I could have known her. I *wanted* to know her! You didn't have the right!"

The rise in Danni's voice bordered on hysteria, reminding him of Danielle for a split second and panic fueled his reaction. "Like hell I didn't!" he roared, his hands curling in his vehemence. His heart thundered in his chest and he fought for control but it was too late.

Face pale and lower lip trembling, Danni pulled away when he tried reaching for her and fled the room.

The echoed slam of her bedroom door reverberated in his memory. Lately, the sound of a slamming door was just about the only communication between them. Colin understood her rage, the sense of betrayal, but he'd had no choice.

He stared grimly at the gently falling snow out his bay window. That saying "the road to hell was paved with good intentions" could be tattooed across his forehead. His intentions *had* been good. He'd wanted to tell Danni the truth when she were older. Old enough to handle it. Instead, fate had different plans and here he was up to his eyeballs in misery because of it.

Colin dropped his head into his hands and drew a painful breath. The fact of the matter was it had been easier to tell Danni that her mama had died from a car accident than a drug overdose. And it sure was a lot easier than telling his little girl that her mother had tried to kill her.

CHAPTER FOUR

TEN HOURS LATER, after hopping a red-eye, Erin's plane was touching down in Ironwood at the Gogebic-Iron County Airport on time, despite the storm that had the snow-removing equipment busy on the runway between flights. She rubbed at her eyes, blaming the constant burn she felt on the lack of sleep due to two lengthy layovers, one in Denver the other in Chicago. She tried not to think of the fact that she was actually returning to the place that she'd gratefully said goodbye to long ago.

For a dog.

Not just any dog, her conscience whispered. Caroline's dog. Her breath hitched in her throat and she forced herself to ignore the pain in her heart and the fatigue that dragged on her heels. *Let's just get this over with,* she thought, winding her woolen scarf around her face as she prepared to leave the warmth of the crowded terminal to find the Chevy Tahoe she'd reserved.

Although Erin wasn't religious, she sent a prayer skyward as she got in the SUV that the cop was true to his word and Butterscotch was not frozen to her aunt's porch.

Caroline had gotten the dog right after Erin had left, saying the house was too empty without her, and Erin had been glad that she did. It made her feel less guilty for practically abandoning her the way she did. A sudden prick at the back of her nose warned of impending tears and she sniffed them back. A part of her was screaming *turn around, go back,* but somehow, she kept on course and an hour later she was pulling into Granite Hills, a surreal fog surrounding her senses as she drove past landmarks that seemed locked in time.

Nothing had changed.

When she left fourteen years ago, the place where her heart should have been felt filled with broken shards of glass that cut and scratched each time she breathed; today, it felt much the same. Except, this time she wouldn't have Caroline's soothing voice to get her through the rough spots.

The weather forced her to drive slowly but her foot itched to press the gas pedal harder, if only to escape the flood of memories that were already pushing at her mind.

Dulcich Hardware—the only place in town to buy nails, paint and plumbing supplies.

Gottaleri's Pizza—her first real job.

The *Granite Hills Tribune*—the only newspaper in town worth reading and the first place she'd nervously look after Charlie went on a binge, hoping—no, praying—that he wasn't listed in the cop log.

Erin swallowed and purposefully dragged her

gaze away from the shops lining the main street, grateful for the anonymity of the rental car. She wasn't stupid enough to think that she could escape without someone recognizing her but if she could prolong it, she certainly would.

Going by memory, she turned down a side street and headed for the police station. Moments later, she was there. Aside from subtle changes to the building, it looked the same. Charlie had spent many a night sleeping off a drunk in one of the three holding facilities. She'd gone with Caroline—once when she was too young to realize what was going on—to pick him up. Her nose twitched at the memory of whiskey on his breath and she clamped down on a wave of nausea.

To this day, the smell of alcohol made her skittish.

Two officers sharply clad in blue uniforms erupted from the side door reserved for employees and Erin's heart leapt into her mouth. She waited for them to climb into their squad car before exiting her own vehicle. She'd been crazy to board that plane. She should've listened to her instincts and refused to come.

But, she hadn't. *So, quit whining and get it over with.*

The sooner she found a home for the dog, made arrangements for the…funeral…

Suddenly her chest felt tight and it hurt to breathe.

Funeral. She'd have to make arrangements for her aunt's funeral. She squeezed her eyes shut and tersely ordered the tears to stop. Now was not the time to start blubbering. She was being brutal with herself but she didn't have a choice. She blinked to clear her vision and then opened the front door. First things first...

COLIN GLANCED UP AT the wall clock and wondered what time the woman's plane was scheduled to arrive. He'd thought she would have called to let him know, but she hadn't so he was left to guess. He thought of Charlie McNulty, laying broken and battered, in the hospital ICU, and he couldn't help but wonder what had caused such animosity between father and daughter. His thoughts shifted to his relationship with Danni and a cold chill entered his heart. What if Danni never forgave him? Was he doomed to spend the next few years chasing after an angry teen, only to lose her forever when she finally moved away?

This morning he'd tried to talk to her about the events of last night, but Danni had stonewalled him, choosing instead to chew her oatmeal in silence. Only occasionally did her gaze stray to the dog that had commandeered a spot by the fireplace.

As a last-ditch effort, he tried offering to give her a ride to school, but all he received in response was a withering stare, which told him that she'd rather freeze to death than spend more than five minutes in his company.

How much longer was she going to punish him for trying to protect her? Surely, she couldn't hold it against him for the rest of their lives? He grimaced at the sour feeling lodged in his gut. Of course, she could. And at this point, it was probably exactly what she planned on doing.

Ah, hell…

Realizing that he'd been staring at the same piece of paperwork for the last ten minutes, he was almost relieved when the dispatcher called his name over the paging system.

"Officer Barrett to the front desk. Officer Barrett to the front desk."

Dropping the paper in his in-tray, he went to answer his page.

He peered through the window in the lobby door and saw a tall, lithe woman with a startling contrast between skin so pale it looked almost translucent and shoulder-length, jet-black hair. She removed a pair of stylish glasses, and quickly folded them into a case while she waited. *Erin McNulty.* There was no doubt in his mind. For someone who grew up in Granite Hills, she couldn't look more foreign to her surroundings. She had *big city* written all over her, from the black cashmere scarf wound around her neck to the leather gloves she was pulling from her fingertips as she glanced around in an impatient gesture. He shook his head at the realization that she was nothing like he'd expected, though, to be honest, he hadn't thought he'd be so off the mark. In this case, it seemed the apple had catapulted from the proverbial tree and landed somewhere on another continent.

Pushing open the door, he found himself staring

into a pair of blue eyes that were almost unreal in their brilliance. He nearly said something stupid but, fortunately, he caught himself in time. The woman's family was in shambles. The last thing she needed was some yahoo babbling about the color of her eyes.

"You must be Erin McNulty," he said, extending his hand with professional courtesy, which she accepted with a nod. "I'm sorry to meet under such circumstances," he said, watching as she made a concentrated effort to hold back tears. "I knew Caroline from her volunteer work at the Winter Festival. She could make a mean cup of cocoa."

Her head jerked in a nod. "She said the secret was using fresh cream instead of milk." Her voice was husky with emotion. "Makes it smooth as silk and twice as fattening."

"Twice as good in my book," he countered, wondering when she'd last eaten a good meal. She was so skinny he could almost count her ribs through the turtleneck sweater she wore.

"Yes, that's what people said," she added, offering a brief smile that was clearly for his benefit before drawing a deep, halting breath. "But then again, there wasn't much that Caroline couldn't make taste good," she murmured, dropping her gaze in an attempt to hide the sudden glistening in her eyes. A rueful smile touched her lips. "She was always trying to get me in the kitchen, one way or another. I tried telling her I didn't inherit her talents but she wouldn't listen and invariably, every Christmas I'd get the newest Betty Crocker cookbook in the mail. I have everything from *Crock-pot Creations* to *Delicious Desserts* and I've never cracked open a one. But she never quit trying...." She frowned as if embarrassed at her personal comments to a total stranger.

"It's okay—"

"I'm sorry—" she cut in tightly, shaking her head before clearing her throat. "My aunt's dog...were you able to go get her last night?"

"Yes," he answered, feeling oddly guilty for catching a glimpse of her personal pain when she had no desire to share such intimate details about herself. There was a brittle quality to her rigidly held composure, like someone whose hold on the fabric of life as she'd known it was slipping as it tore in two.

"Have you gone to see your father yet?" he asked, the question springing from his lips without conscious thought.

An iron curtain slammed behind her eyes and he had his answer. Disappointment welled in his chest but he couldn't explain why. If the woman had no interest in seeing her father before he died, it was none of his business. Sure, it seemed heartless, but why should he care? His utmost concern was relieving his home of the dog that had seemed quite comfortable this morning laying beside his hearth. "Your dog is at my house. If you want to follow me I'll take you to her."

"She's not my dog," she corrected him.

"She is now."

She conceded that small point, adding, "Well, only until I can find a suitable home for her. My life isn't conducive to pets."

He knew she worked for a magazine but he wasn't sure in what capacity. Before he could ask, she answered what must've been the question in his eyes.

"I'm a photographer. I travel. A lot."

"That's right, *American Photographic*," he said, recalling how difficult it had been tracking her down. "Real nice magazine."

She accepted his compliment with a reluctant smile and he was struck by how she looked every inch the part of a sophisticated traveler. She could probably navigate a crowded airport terminal with ease and sleep just as comfortably in a hotel bed as her own. In her world, the word *home* was probably a relative term. He couldn't imagine a life like that. "So, how long are you staying?"

She seemed startled by his question and she fumbled a little, causing a momentary break in her carefully held composure. "N-not long," she answered, quickly regaining her equilibrium. "Um…the dog?"

In other words: Butt out of my business.

"I'll get my coat," he answered, prickling just a little at her subtle hint to back off, yet at the same time reluctantly intrigued by the questions that came to mind when he considered her attitude toward her father. He was smart enough to know that it was foolish to draw parallels between his problems with Danni and the damaged relationship Erin had with her father. The situations were likely not the same but he couldn't help but wonder if there would ever come a time when Danni would refuse to see him at his darkest hour. The pain that went straight to his heart almost made him make a plea for Charlie's case, but a quick reminder that it was none of his business kept him from making a fool out of himself.

Five minutes later Colin was pulling into his driveway while Erin's sleek, black rented Tahoe came to a stop directly behind him. The storm had kicked up again, sending flurries of snow drifting to the ground, making him wonder whether or not Danni had remembered to take her woolen hat when she stomped off to school this morning. Probably not, which was why he decided at that moment, despite the glares he'd no doubt receive, to pick her up after school.

"Dog's pretty easygoing," he called over his shoulder as he trudged his way through the freshly fallen snow to his front door. "She might be a little hungry, though. I gave her some hamburger to tide her over." He unlocked the door and waited for Erin to catch up. "She also seems to have some sort of hip dysplasia. You might want to have a vet check that out."

"Hip dysplasia? Wonderful," she said with a touch of frustration. She rubbed her arms for warmth despite her thick woolen peacoat. "Old and crippled. What are the chances of finding her a home within a few days?"

Not good, he communicated with a look.

"That's what I thought," she said, following him into the house. At the sound of the door opening, the dog raised her head and peered expectantly into the hallway. As if believing it was her job to greet guests, she struggled to her feet and walked over to them. Erin's forehead furrowed and her gaze softened ever so slightly. She cast a worried glance his way. "She does seem a bit stiff…is there a vet in town who could look at her?"

Ridiculously relieved, he nodded. "Doc Archer can probably take a look at her first thing in the morning." At her glance, he explained. "Doc closes shop at noon, and he's the only vet in town."

She accepted his answer, but from her expression he could tell she wasn't pleased. It was clear she wanted her stay in Granite Hills to be as brief as possible and a crippled dog only hindered that plan.

"I figure you'll be staying out at Caroline's place?" he said, leaning down to gently click the leash into place and handing it to her.

"No," she answered, the tone of her voice suggesting the thought was too much to bear. She added hastily, "There's bound to be a hotel that has a room available. It'll be easier if I stay in town."

He frowned and she queried sharply, "What?"

"I don't know how long you've been gone but around this time of year the hotels are all full. Winter Festival. It's one of our biggest tourist attractions," he said.

She swore under her breath. Obviously, she hadn't

taken that into consideration. Her voice took on an incredulous tone. "All the hotels? Even Buttercreek?"

"No, that one closed about a year ago. Mr. Grogan died from congestive heart failure and his wife went to live with their daughter over in Ironwood," he answered, surprised by her stricken expression.

"I hadn't heard," she murmured, something, regret perhaps, catching in her throat. "The Grogans were nice people. They used to let me swim in their pool during the summer and Mrs. Grogan always had a small something for me at Christmastime. Well, that's too bad about the hotel closing. It was a special place."

He didn't disagree with her. Danni had learned to swim in the Grogans' pool. When Cappy Grogan died, he'd been one of the pallbearers.

Eyes suddenly clearing, Erin looked down at the dog, who was watching the exchange with a soft intelligence that was almost startling, and reluctantly relented, though he could tell it was the least desirable option. "I guess it's back to Caroline's then…for the time being," she said, focusing for a moment on the leash in her hand before meeting his gaze again. "Thanks…for taking care of her."

"No problem," he answered, noting that the brief smile she offered was pained around the edges. "She's a good dog. I hope you can find her a good home."

"Me, too," she said, sincerity evident in her tone, as she headed toward the door. Suddenly, she paused and twisted to face him wearing a drawn and pinched expression, as if whatever she was about to say tasted bitter on her tongue. "When I used to live here, the Barstow family owned the mortuary…is that still the place to go to make…funeral arrangements?"

He answered her with a short nod, his gut reacting to the almost palpable sense of sorrow that surrounded her like a cloud. She drew a deep breath, as if she needed the extra oxygen for strength, and offered her thanks in a husky murmur before turning and leading the old dog carefully down the snow-covered steps to the front walk. Within minutes they were gone.

He stared after the retreating back end of the Tahoe and pressed his lips together in silent commiseration. He didn't envy her homecoming.

What had gone wrong between her and her father? He only knew Charlie McNulty in a peripheral fashion but the man seemed harmless enough. He'd picked him up a few times when Charlie had had one too many, but it'd been a while since he'd had to do that. Someone had said something about Charlie finally joining AA. He chewed absentmindedly on his lower lip. After years of more than likely driving drunk, Charlie McNulty got in a wreck stone-cold sober. The irony was tragic.

Locking up quickly, he returned to the station, detouring briefly to grab a cup of coffee from the carafe that some blessed, probably underpaid, junior officer kept gurgling at all hours of the night, before making his way back to his desk.

"Sorry to hear about Danni," he heard Max Stubberd, a patrol officer, call out as he walked by. Colin acknowledged the man with a nod. He was sorry, too.

Sipping his coffee, he winced just a little as his muscles protested his early-morning snow shovel duty. He supposed he could pay someone to do it but it seemed like throwing away good money when he was just as capable. He rotated his shoulder and stretched the muscle. As much as he hated to admit it, paying someone was beginning to have some appeal. Reaching in his bottom drawer for a bottle of aspirin, the voice of Detective Leslie O'Bannon, a native of Granite Hills and one of his good friends, sounded at his shoulder.

"Here's that supplemental from the state trooper, Col," Leslie said, handing him the two-page report. Crossing her arms, she leaned against the partition separating their desks, her expression solemn. "So, you were the first on the scene, huh? Pretty bad, I take it?"

He nodded. "One of the worst I've seen in a long time. Caroline Walker died on scene, poor gal, and Charlie's over in the ICU at GH Medical."

"Think he's going to make it?"

"Hard to say. He's pretty banged up."

"Man, can you imagine going sober after all those years only to have *this* happen? Doesn't seem fair." She shook her head. "Caroline was about the sweetest person I'd ever known, too. I remember she used to volunteer at the schools when I went to

Granite Hills Elementary, always brought homemade cookies for the holidays. Every kid went home with a small bag of goodies." Leslie frowned at the memory. "Geez, she must've been baking for days, but she never complained. In fact, she always seemed to enjoy doing something for everyone." She was quiet for a moment, her expression full of sorrow. "What a crying shame...."

Colin nodded in agreement. Caroline would surely be missed in this town. Leslie sighed, the sound echoing the emotion he felt in his chest at the tragedy. "So, is Erin coming back for the funeral and to take care of her dad?"

Leslie's inquiry summoned the image of Erin's shuttered expression when it came to the subject of her father and the corners of his lips twisted. "She's already in town, but I get the impression that as soon as the funeral is over, she'll be on the first plane out of here. Seems she and her dad don't get along so well."

"Yeah, that family's had it rough. I guess you can't blame Erin for wanting to get the hell out of here."

Leslie's tone suggested that she knew what Colin was referring to but before he could prompt her for more details, she was paged to the front desk and she turned to leave. "Well, let me know if you need any help," she said, gesturing to the paperwork before hurrying down the hall.

He knew the offer was made in light of Danni's escapade and, although he appreciated everyone's concern, it chafed more than a little that everyone knew his business. He couldn't hold it against anyone, though. Colin had moved to Granite Hills when Danni had still been in diapers. As a single father, sometimes without daycare to fall back on, Danni had been a frequent visitor to the station. This recent turn of events probably had everyone alarmed, he realized.

Returning to the case in his hand, he grabbed the hospital report to attach to the file and his eyes focused on the BAC levels.

Totally sober.

He had to admit, he'd been surprised. The discovery certainly begged a few questions.

If the man hadn't been impaired and, as evidenced by the supplemental report, the roads had been clear, what had sent the old Ford into that tree? He flipped through the medical evaluation, but there was no indication that Charlie had had a stroke or heart attack, no medical reason for him to lose control. Then he thumbed through the state trooper's report, looking for the skid-mark pattern, but came up empty. Puzzled, he checked again, thinking he might have missed it, until he realized with a perplexed frown that there weren't any to find. Charlie McNulty had plowed headlong into that birch…for no apparent reason.

What was he looking at?

Something didn't sit right with Colin about this accident. His mind was moving in circles, but he couldn't put a voice to his suspicions.

The unanswered questions prevented him from filing the case as closed.

He needed more information, preferably background, to see if he had cause to dig a little deeper. A pair of vivid blue eyes appeared in his mind and an electric thrill followed that was both unexpected and startling. If he hadn't been annoyed at his own reaction, he might've chuckled at the absurdity. Erin McNulty? She was about as warm as the waters in Lake Superior at this time of year. Anyone willing to walk out on family like she was itching to do could use a little help in the compassion department. He'd do well to nip that attraction in the bud. He had enough problems.

From what he could gather from people who'd known Erin's family, he found that while the McNulty side had been hard workers, they played equally as hard. Erin's mother Rose had come from an upper middle class family. Rose Rawlins's father had been a businessman, and her mother a homemaker, but both had perished in a house fire when Rose had been seventeen. Rose had been sleeping over at a friend's house when it happened. It seems that family was a magnet for trouble.

Colin sat back in his chair, his thoughts returning to Erin. He supposed he was still caught off guard by how different she was. Though he had to admit his assumptions had been ridiculous. What had he expected? A wild-haired, younger version of Charlie? He snorted—well, she was anything but that. She was sleek and refined, whereas Charlie was coarse and crabby. The differences raised more questions than they answered.

Another officer walked by, offering a quick goodbye before heading out the door. Shaking himself out of the useless direction of his thoughts, he proofread his official report of the accident, reviving the memory of that night.

He'd been heading down Old Copper Road when he saw the vapor spiraling from the ruptured radiator into the frigid air. The front end of the older model Ford was wrapped around the solid trunk of an old yellow birch while a fresh drift of snow had started to fall on the wreckage. As Colin picked up speed toward the accident, he radioed for emergency crews and prayed whoever was in that mess was still alive. He glanced at his report again.

Driver #1, 58-year-old male, head lacerations, multiple injuries.

Passenger #1, 54-year-old female, severe head trauma. Dead on arrival.

The sterile report in his hands did little to communicate the horror of the fatal accident. Colin could smell the tang of copper drifting on the wind and mingling with the scent of wintergreen from the injured tree as emergency crews worked to save Charlie, knowing that Caroline was long gone.

Thank God no one else had been traveling that same stretch of highway that night. Colin shifted in his chair and let the paper slip out of his hands.

Tomorrow he'd have to stop by the hospital and check Charlie's status. He couldn't help but feel bad for the old guy, seeing as he was broken all to hell without a soul in the world to care if he lived or died. The one person who had cared was dead; and the one who should care would rather walk the other way.

Colin could hear the night shift arriving, their voices rising in playful banter with one another. He recognized the voice of Mark Sporlan and the newest officer to join the small department, Missy Reznick. Then, he heard the voice of Roger Hampton, the chief of Granite Hills P.D.

"Got a minute?"

Surprised, Colin swiveled in his chair. "Sure, Chief," he answered, following him to his office. Normally, the chief left before the night shift came in. The fact that he was still here and wanted a private audience gave Colin pause. Something was up.

"Take a seat, detective."

"Something wrong?"

"I was hoping you could tell me." He fixed Colin with a sharp stare that was piercing, yet showed concern. "I'm not one to meddle in personal affairs but I couldn't help but notice that Danni got hauled in last night on a misdemeanor drug charge. What's that all about?"

Colin tensed, immediately on the defensive. "Nothing I can't handle. Just your run-of-the-mill teenage rebellion."

"I'm sure you've got things well in hand, Colin. Look, I know I'm treading on dangerous ground here. No parent likes a meddler. So, I'm not going to do that. But if my officers are having personal problems that might affect their job performance, I like to know ahead of time what I'm dealing with."

"The problems I'm having with Danni won't affect my job," he assured the chief. "She's a good kid. This is just a phase."

"What if it isn't?"

The chief's blunt question zeroed in on Colin's worst fear. "Then, I'll deal with it," he answered with more confidence than he felt. How he was going to deal with it, he hadn't a clue, but that was just one more problem he'd work through. If he could handle midnight feedings, diapers and daycare issues as a single father, he could handle this.

"Listen, Colin." The chief drew himself up as far as his round belly would allow, his finger tapping his desk. "You're a good cop. I'm only saying this to you because I don't want to lose you. I'd rather authorize some personal time now so you can figure things out than lose you permanently because the problems have spun out of your control. I already had Bruce look at the books and you have plenty of vacation time banked. If you need it, just say the word and I'll sign the paperwork."

At a loss for an appropriate response, he gave the chief a curt nod. "Thanks," he said. "I'll keep your offer in mind. If things continue to go downhill…" God, he hoped it didn't go that way. "Then I'll take your advice and cash in some of that vacation time."

"Good. Glad to hear it." The chief stood and

grabbed his jacket. As Colin approached the door, his mind returning to the situation with Danni, the chief's voice stopped him.

"I heard Charlie McNulty was banged up pretty bad in that fatal accident with Caroline Walker on Old Copper. Is he going to make it?"

Colin stopped and turned. "Not sure," he answered truthfully. "Did you know them?"

His expression guarded, the chief answered with a slow nod. "We used to be buddies. But we had a falling out years ago. Haven't seen much of either one of them lately. It's a shame about Caroline, though. She was quite a woman."

Surprised at this admission, Colin started to ask him some more questions about Charlie, but suddenly Roger winced and rubbed at his breastbone. "You okay?" he asked, not quite liking what he saw.

The chief stopped the motion and waved away Colin's concern. "Just a little bit of heartburn, is all." Then, in a characteristic move, he winked. "Had hot sausage for lunch—don't tell Vera or she'll have my head."

Relieved, Colin returned the conspiratorial grin. There wasn't much he wouldn't do for Roger Hampton. He was a great guy and a mentor to his officers. "Your secret's safe with me Chief."

"I knew I could count on you," the chief answered, his lips twisting in a smile that was probably meant to be appreciative yet seemed ragged on the edges. A flutter of unease returned to his gut.

He had no choice but to shelve it for the time being. The chief had already stayed later than usual on account of Colin and he didn't want to keep him any longer.

He glanced at his watch and drew a deep breath. It was time to pick up Danni from school. Gathering his coat, he waved goodbye to the night shift and prepared to endure another emotional assault at the hands of his daughter.

CHAPTER FIVE

BY THE TIME ERIN PULLED into Caroline's driveway, she was bone-tired, but even the fatigue wasn't enough to dull the shaft of pain that went straight to her heart as she stared at the old house. Shutting off the ignition she pressed herself against the soft seat and fought against the well of tears that sprang to her eyes with the knowledge that Caroline wasn't coming out to greet her, nor would she ever again. Despite her best efforts, a tear snaked its way down her cheek, and before she knew it, she was holding her face in her hands and sobbing.

Why were you with him, Caroline? What were you doing?

Erin stared into the darkness as the tears continued to fall unchecked. The questions were as endless as they were pointless. Butterscotch whined from the back seat, and Erin realized she was shaking from the cold. Logic dictated that she go inside, but she wasn't sure if she could. Another whine from Butterscotch sounded, this time more urgent, and Erin reluctantly pocketed her keys. Drawing a deep breath, she ruthlessly shoved her heartbreak into a dark corner of her mind and focused on the situation. If she stayed much longer in the car, someone— more than likely Colin Barrett—would find them frozen to their seats, and dying from hypothermia with an old dog for a companion was not the way she envisioned going out.

A bright porch light illuminated the familiar house against the snow-topped forest and even through the milky light she could see signs of decay that tore at her heart. The house wasn't what anyone would call fancy, but at one time it had been quite lovely. A frown crossed her face as more guilt pricked her conscience. If she'd known the house was in need of repair she would've sent the money. Of course, Erin couldn't have known because she never came home to visit and Caroline, darn her stubborn soul, would never ask.

Without conscious thought she inhaled deeply the scent of fresh water on the air from Lake Superior as her breath plumed in frosty clouds. The crescent moon sheathed the wooded backdrop in pale light, giving the snow a luminescent glow, like something out of a fairy tale. The quiet stillness was soothing to her ragged nerves and for a moment she just stood and listened. She couldn't remember the last time she'd felt such peace. In the city, the constant cacophony of busy streets, honking horns and loud pedestrians filled her apartment despite the windows that she kept closed and locked.

Erin shook her head free of the melancholy that had enveloped her and went to grab her gear. Obvi-

ously, jet lag was doing more than tiring her out—
it was making her downright loopy. She did *not* miss
this place. Opening the back hatch, she grabbed her
suitcase along with her camera bag.

Glancing down at Butterscotch, who was waiting
patiently by her side, she shook her head in disgust
at herself and made her way to the front door.

She was here to take care of business, not wallow
in useless nostalgia. Yet, when she came to the porch
steps, she stopped and cast one last look at the
wooded shoreline, hating it for its beauty and its
ability to move her in spite of everything. She shut
her eyes against the ghostly light of the moon and
focused on getting through the door without collapsing.

Don't think of it as Caroline's house, she told
herself fiercely when her breath hitched in her throat
as she slid the key into the lock.

It's just a bed and a place to shower.

No, it was more than that, a voice argued with the
same vehemence. Caroline's house had been the one
place she'd felt loved, cherished and safe. The place
where she could sleep an entire night without
waking in a cold sweat, terrified of the agonizing,
drunken bellows that echoed in the still night air. The
place that Caroline had insisted she consider home—
no matter how old she was.

Erin closed her eyes and swallowed, knowing
with a fatal certainty that walking through that door
would crack her heart in two, yet also knowing that
the pain was inevitable.

She swore softly at the situation. *Congratulations. You've made it as far as the porch before falling to pieces. Open the damn door already before you and the dog freeze your asses off.*

Wiping the residual tears from her eyes, she opened the door and stepped inside as Butterscotch nosed her way past, intent on finding her own bed for the evening. Erin didn't bother with the hall light. Despite the years that had passed since she'd been back, Erin knew her way around as if she'd never left. The fatigue that had been a constant companion as she drove returned with a vengeance and, for once, she welcomed it.

Walking like a zombie to the bedroom that had once been hers, she stepped over the threshold, flipped the light and sucked in a breath as memories assailed her.

It was exactly as she remembered, as if time had stopped or Caroline had been loath to change anything. It was both oddly comforting and disturbing. She crossed to the wrought-iron bed and sank onto the sturdy mattress, a small smile lifting her lips as the old springs squeaked from disuse.

Erin's fingers skimmed the soft fabric of the quilt covering the bed, remembering how her aunt had patched it together especially for her from old odds and ends that'd been collected over the years. Erin had spent many a night snuggled into its protective warmth.

The hardwood floor still had a bare spot by the entryway from the many comings and goings throughout the years and the antique armoire that had once been part of a glorious collection of hand-crafted Victorian furniture stood sentinel against the wall near the bed. Caroline had inherited the piece from her mother, who had inherited it from her husband's family before that. Erin had loved having something with such history. It'd made her feel as if she were someone important instead of always feeling forgotten.

Spurred by the flash of a memory, Erin rose, despite her fatigue, and walked to the armoire. Bracing her hand against the opposite door, she gently opened it and peered inside. The sharp smell of aged wood and dust motes tickled her nose but her gaze immediately fell to the far left corner. She knelt, a pained smile curving her lips, as she traced her fingers over the tiny scratched initials of a lost, scared little girl whose tears were locked deep inside so that no one would know just how much it hurt to feel alone.

E.M.McN.

Erin rocked back on her heels. If it hadn't been for her Aunt Caroline, she'd often wondered if anyone would have noticed or cared if she'd disappeared. Her father certainly wouldn't have. An old familiar ache crept into her chest. She groaned when she realized she was doing exactly what she'd sought to avoid for the past fourteen years. Rising, she shut the armoire doors and wearily dusted her knees. She needed sleep, not a trip down memory lane.

After quickly changing, she burrowed under the

thick quilt and closed her eyes as she gratefully sur-
rendered to a deep, dark, dreamless exhaustion.

A RESPECTFUL MURMUR FILLED THE AIR from the
crowd that mingled beneath slate-gray skies outside
Barstow's Mortuary as mourners made their way
out of the funeral home following Caroline Walker's
services two days later.

The dreary weather seemed to fit the occasion as
Caroline had been well-liked within the community
despite her brother's wild reputation and often un-
predictable nature, and everyone had come to pay
their respects.

As Colin searched the line of mourners for a
familiar face, he realized there was only one face he
was looking for.

He spotted Erin standing outside the mortuary
doors, looking brittle in her stylish, black pantsuit,
and nearly frozen to the bone as she accepted hushed
words of kindness from virtual strangers. She had
grace despite the grief that dragged on her slight shoulders and he was reluctantly drawn to the aura of
sadness and vulnerability that she was struggling to
hide. As he approached, he noted the quick flare of
relief that followed recognition and he was glad he
came.

"Quite a turnout," he acknowledged once he
was by her side, his voice low. She nodded, the
motion so filled with sorrow he hastened to say
something soothing. "Your aunt will be missed in
this community."

Her chin wobbled in a subtle motion but she managed to hold it together. "Did you catch the ceremony?"

He gave a short nod. "It was beautiful. Caroline would've been proud, I'm sure."

The shine in her eyes told him that his comment hit a nerve that was particularly sensitive but he wasn't sure why. Before he had the chance to ask, she looked away, her gaze wandering over the assembled crowd. "I had no idea she had so many friends." Her voice caught and she cleared her throat a moment later. She tried again. "I didn't get home very often. My schedule—" She stopped, as if an internal alarm had warned that she was in danger of sharing too much, and the smile that followed was short-lived. "Well, as I said before…my schedule didn't allow for much visiting," she finished, her stare dropping to the frozen ground.

Feeling useless in the face of such heartache, yet knowing that there was little he could do to ease her suffering, Colin merely stood by her side as she received the long line of mourners offering their condolences. He caught a few questioning glances but Caroline's friends had the good grace to leave it be for the time being. He didn't blame their curiosity, he hardly knew her; that much was true. But it didn't seem right to leave her alone.

He watched as she received a warm handshake from an elderly gentleman and weighed the measure of her apparent grief against the magnitude of a past transgression. Whatever Charlie did, it must have been a doozy to keep her away from her Aunt Caroline. The love she'd had for her aunt was almost palpable; as was her anguish for not being able to say goodbye.

He considered his major screwup with Danni and inwardly flinched. For all he knew, he was catching a firsthand glimpse of what his own future held with *his* daughter.

"Thanks for coming," she said, once she had a free moment, jerking him out of his troubled thoughts. "I know we just met but it feels good to see someone I recognize."

Her comment startled him. "I thought you grew up here."

"I did. I used to think I knew everyone there was to know in this town. I figured I would recognize at least a few people," she admitted almost to herself as tears welled in her eyes despite her attempt to blink them back. "But, just when I think I know who they are I can't seem to remember their names and I feel like I'm losing my mind."

The last part came out sounding like a confession and the force of her statement hit him like a punch to the gut.

There was little he could do to stop the grief but he could help in one small way. He turned to survey the crowd, looking for people he knew. He nudged her gently.

"The lady with the weird purple hat is Mrs. Sanderson," he whispered without drawing attention to himself or embarrassing her. "She and my mother

used to play bridge before my mom moved to
Florida for the winter. Caroline was part of the same
bridge club." With his peripheral vision he caught the
quick motion of Erin's gloved hand rising to wipe at
the corner of her eye before peering in the direction
he was discretely pointing. "See the lady wearing
what looks like a parka and mukluks?" Erin almost
smiled as her eyes locked on the target. "That's Ms.
Mathel, she owns Pedigree Pets, the local animal
supply store. It's the best place to buy dog food if
you want more than just kibble."

"She probably knows Caroline through Butterscotch," surmised Erin, nodding in agreement. "I
think I remember Caroline saying something about
Butterscotch's special diet."

"Well, that would be the place you'd be finding
that special blend of dog food," he said.

She turned to him as he started to point out
another person, a reluctant smile curving her lips.
"You don't have to do this...."

He acknowledged her comment with a shrug. "I
know."

"Then why are you?"

He paused, giving it some thought. "Because it's
the right thing to do, I suppose." Plus, he could only
imagine the private hell she was going through. If he
could lessen the strain somehow, he was more than
willing. She seemed caught between appreciating his
concern and the instinct to keep her distance, but as
she gave him a slow nod she seemed to accept the
fact that without his help she'd end up wandering

through a sea of unknown faces. He resumed his covert introductions until nearly all the major players in Caroline's life had been identified. Just as Colin was finishing, a matronly woman made her way toward them.

She barely had time to take a step back before Mrs. Gottaleri, wife of Paul Gottaleri, the owner of the pizza joint, grasped her gloved hand and patted it warmly.

"You must be Erin," she said, sorrow in her voice. "Lovely service, darling, your aunt would've been proud and that's a fact." Erin visibly flinched at such praise but Mrs. Gottaleri didn't seem to notice as she continued. "It's always the good ones that get taken much too early. But God has a plan, you know. Trust in that. God has a plan."

Erin stiffened and Colin knew that was the last thing a grieving person wanted to hear, no matter how earnest the sentiment. He smiled at Mrs. Gottaleri. "How did you know Mrs. Walker?" he asked, politely sending the conversation in a different direction.

Mrs. Gottaleri pursed her lips and shook her head. "Oh, she and I go way back. Caroline and I have been on the Winter Festival committee since I can't even remember when. I'm the only one she trusted her cocoa recipe with, and that's a fact, I promise you." She leaned toward Erin and whispered as if sharing a great confidence. "It's the fresh cream brought over the night before from Roanin Farms. Fresh as fresh can be. Makes it smooth as silk."

And twice as fattening, he recalled Erin's wry comment and nearly smiled at the memory.

Mrs. Gottaleri went on, sighing heavily. "Yes, right shame. I suppose if it's your time to go, it's your time, but I wish I'd known what had been bothering Caroline so much the last time I saw her. She was in quite a dither...very distracted, if you ask me and that's just not like Caroline. She always had a smile for everyone. In fact, I don't think I'd ever heard her utter a cross word as long as I'd known her. Sweet as her own mincemeat pie. Sweeter even."

Colin knew no one was that perfect, but death had a way of bringing out the best in people. Still, the praise wasn't that far off the mark. He'd be hard-pressed to find anyone who'd offer an unkind word about the woman. He looked to Erin to gauge her reaction and noted a troubled expression on her face.

"What did you mean...something was bothering her?" Erin asked.

Mrs. Gottaleri nodded vigorously, obviously tickled to have something of importance to share. "Distracted is the word. In fact, she missed our last committee meeting. We were supposed to discuss strategy for recruiting new volunteers for the cocoa booth. It's just been a handful of us for years and I'm not as young as I used to be." She shook her head, frowning. "And, of all the bad timing, not that it could be controlled, because as I said, God has a plan, but we *are* short-handed at the festival tonight." She turned a speculative eye toward Erin. "Of course, you wouldn't be interested in filling Caroline's spot, would you?"

Erin was saved from making any comment as another woman came barreling over to them, a stern look of annoyance in her eyes.

"Delores Gottaleri, land's sake, stop badgering the poor girl!"

Delores managed to look offended and hurt at the same time as she bracketed her generous hips with both hands. "I was doing no such thing! I was merely—"

"Merely pressuring her about things she could care less about in her time of grief," the woman said huffily before turning to Erin with a sad smile. "I'm Vera Hampton, dear. I was friends with your Aunt Caroline, too, and I can't tell you how much she'll be missed."

Tears pricked Erin's eyes and she couldn't hold them back this time. "Thank you," she managed to choke out, the emotion rolling over her, causing her cheeks to flame in embarrassment. "How did you know my aunt?"

"I met her through various committees, the Winter Festival being one of them, but I like to think that we became friends…as much as Caroline would allow, of course. For all her generosity, she was a private person, after all. But I do know you were the light of her life," Vera said, her comment making Erin's gut pitch as if she might lose the coffee she'd gulped down earlier that morning. "She used to talk about how talented you were and how prestigious the magazine you work for is. Her face would plumb shine with pride when she talked about you. Always talked about how she hoped someday you might come back home."

Erin managed to shake her head, feeling undeserved of such praise. She was too ashamed to admit that she never once followed through on her promise to send Caroline a subscription. It wasn't that she hadn't planned to, it was only that time had always seemed of short supply and frankly, other things had seemed more important. A hiccup of grief burned under her breastbone and she had to look away for fear of what the women might read in her eyes. A wave of vertigo followed and as she reached a hand out to steady herself, she felt the strength of Colin's arm close around her shoulder for support.

"Are you okay?" he asked, allowing her to pull free only once he was sure she was steady on her feet again. Despite her embarrassed assurances, he continued to eye her with concern, causing an unexpected warmth to heat her body. It wasn't her style to act like a fluttery woman who needed a man by her side to function, but she hated to admit that leaning, even for an instance, on someone stronger than she, made her hunger for a solid shoulder to rest her head against.

Disconcerted by her own reaction, she avoided his eyes as she fended off an immediate attack from Vera, who had at that moment taken it upon herself to be Erin's caretaker despite having been a complete stranger only moments before.

"Oh, dear!" exclaimed Vera as she gestured toward the awning overlooking the funeral home.

"Get her out of this wind. She needs to rest, not catch pneumonia standing out here with the likes of us."

"It's all right—" Erin started to say, but Vera was not to be deterred and before Erin knew it she was being herded under the shelter of the awning like a lost chick needing a safe place to roost.

"I'm fine…really," she cut in quickly, trying not to be rude as the two older ladies fussed over her, arguing with one another over the best course of action. Just as Delores suggested she see a doctor for a prescription to help her sleep, Erin rushed to ease their worries for fear of ending up medicated or hospitalized. "Ladies, I appreciate your concern, really, but it's just too much coffee and not enough sleep."

"And more than likely not enough food," added Delores, her keen gaze making Erin acutely aware of her sparse curves. "Colin Barrett, promise me that you'll see to it that this girl gets some food in her stomach before the next storm blows her to Canada. It's the least that we can do for Caroline," she added staunchly, leaving little room for disagreement, but Erin tried anyway.

"Really, I appreciate your concern but—"

"How about Sammi's for some chowder?" Vera said to Colin, ignoring Erin's protests, causing her to stiffen just a little.

Vera turned, smiling despite Erin's guarded expression. "Trust me, it's just the thing to warm you up and put some meat on your bones at the same time. Colin, I won't take no for an answer. Tell Roger I said that you were to personally see to it that this girl get some food. I'm sure he'll understand. Now—" she drew herself up with a satisfied expression, pinning Erin with her sharp gaze "—that's settled and I don't want to hear another word about it. It's what Caroline would've wanted, I'm sure."

Erin closed her mouth, further protest dying on her lips. How could she argue with something like that? She could almost feel Caroline's approving smile at the woman's clever manipulation. She suppressed a sigh and sent Colin an apologetic look for being thrust upon him without warning or invitation, but he didn't look like a man being pushed into anything that he didn't want to do.

She frowned. Were his actions merely professional courtesy, or was he motivated by something else? *Don't make a federal case out of it,* the voice of what couldn't possibly be her better judgment argued in her head. Grabbing a bite to eat after a funeral was hardly a social occasion. It was simply fulfilling a basic need—hunger.

"I guess I could eat something," she admitted, looking quickly to gauge his reaction. He nodded in agreement, as if her answer were just plain good sense and she was confused by her disappointment. "I mean, if you were planning to grab a bite anyway, I could tag along," she clarified.

"That's the spirit," Vera said, satisfied. She gestured to Delores, who was adjusting her belt loop and looking decidedly uncomfortable in her outfit. "Quit fiddling with that thing," she admonished as they turned to leave. "That's what you get for insisting on wearing clothes that stopped fitting during the Reagan era!"

Erin let out a pent-up breath as the two well-meaning ladies followed the dispersing crowd. She turned to Colin with every intention of letting him off the hook, but her stomach took that opportunity to yowl like a cat in heat and she knew saying something like *she really wasn't hungry* would come out sounding ludicrous. Still, she hated the idea that his actions might be purely motivated by the older women's comments.

"Please don't feel obligated—"

"I don't," he assured her, the serious look in his dark eyes giving Erin pause. There was something unreadable reflecting back at her, something that almost looked like concern and that wobbly feeling returned to her knees. He continued, pointing at a small deli directly across the street, and gestured for her to follow. "That's Sammi's right over there. Follow me."

Her stomach growled again, reminding her that the last thing she ate was a few stale red licorice strips washed down with a steady stream of coffee, and she hustled to catch up.

Annoyed at herself, she quickened her pace until she was just outside the deli and hastened to get inside before he tried to do something like open the door for her. It wasn't that she didn't enjoy a man who acted like a gentleman, it was that she didn't want *him* to act that way with *her*. It made her feel…off-center. She stole a quick glance while he was reading the menu on the wall. So, he was attractive. Big deal. So are half the men on her block. *Of course, half of those men are also gay,* she countered in the next breath, causing her to wonder whose side her inner voice was on.

"Know what you want?" he asked, gesturing to the menu.

My life back the way it was. Wasn't that the truth? She wanted to be back in San Francisco, running herself ragged on an endless stream of assignments, and she wanted Caroline on the other end of the phone telling her in detail about things that had stopped interesting Erin years ago. For goodness sake, forget all that other stuff, she just wanted Caroline back.

She looked away before the shine in her eyes became obvious. "Turkey on rye," she croaked, nearly shoving a crumpled five-dollar bill into his hand before escaping to a table. As she slumped into a chair, she wondered if she was ever going to feel normal again.

Of course, normal was a relative term. She was sure the word *normal* had never really applied to her, but at least under average circumstances she didn't break down in front of total strangers. Wiping away at the tears that betrayed her at every turn, she heard Colin's voice lighten as he gave the boy behind the counter a firm pat on the shoulder.

"Hey, Brian, how's your mom doing these days?" he asked, his expression dimming appropriately as

Brian divulged details about his mother's current battle with ovarian cancer. "Well, you tell her to listen to the doctors and hurry up and get better. We need her around here." He patted his midsection with a wink. "Tell her no one makes corn chowder like she does and my shrinking waistline is proof."

Erin caught herself glancing at his waist to check the validity of his statement but averted her eyes when she felt she'd been staring a tad longer than necessary.

"She'll like to hear that, Officer Barrett," Brian said, offering a smile with a mouth full of braces. "What'll it be today? The usual?"

A feeling of envy invaded her system as she realized that she wished she had that kind of familiarity with someone. If she tried that back in San Francisco the person behind the counter would probably just stare at her like she'd grown another head. She used to love that about the city. The anonymity had been a salve to her wounded psyche. Now, it just felt cold and impersonal.

Colin approached and Erin was startled to find her thoughts reverting to his midsection. She'd read somewhere that extreme grief often created a magnet for misplaced attraction. Well, she could certainly attest to that.

"So, what's the 'usual'?" she asked in an attempt to put her thoughts on more stable ground.

"Clam chowder in a sourdough bowl," he answered with relish, sitting down across from her. "Just like Vera said, it's the best thing to warm a person up.

With this storm coming in, I feel like my insides are frozen."

"Sounds good," she murmured with a nod.

"I took the liberty of ordering your turkey on rye toasted. I hope that's all right with you." He looked apologetic as he added, "You looked like you could use a little warming up, too. How long were you standing out there?"

Erin didn't want to tell him that she had fled the receiving room as soon as she was able, because the thought of Caroline lying in that box had made her nauseous. "Not long," she lied. "Probably about ten minutes or so, but I'd forgotten how cold it gets here."

A server came by offering to fill their coffee cups and both obliged. Erin wrapped her hands around the mug, closing her eyes as the warm liquid heated her hands. She'd been wearing gloves but they were more for show than actual warmth.

"Thanks for coming with me," she said, suddenly very grateful she hadn't backed out on lunch. Her stomach was truly growling and having something warm in her hands was doing wonders for her disposition. She wasn't ready to do somersaults but she didn't feel like bawling, either. That was progress.

"No problem," he said, offering her a genuine smile that made her wish they had met under different circumstances.

What difference would that make? the voice in her head challenged. Although the question caused a subtle frown to pull on her eyebrows, she knew where it was coming from. She didn't date often. It was one of the many lamentable situations that Caroline had been itching to change. First, the zip code; then, the love life. Trying to explain her usual table-for-one status had only illuminated one clear fact about herself: she wasn't cut out for relationships. It wasn't that she didn't enjoy the idea of having one, it was that the reality of sharing your future with someone also meant revealing your past and Erin never felt compelled to do that.

"Have you had much luck in finding Butterscotch a home?" Colin asked, breaking into her turbulent thoughts and dragging her back to the present. She shook her head and blew out a frustrated breath. Honestly, she hadn't been able to give the search much of her time. Right about now, the dog seemed the least of her problems. If it hadn't been for the fact that she'd been exhausted beyond coherent thought the first night, and she'd spent much of yesterday on the phone making arrangements, being surrounded by memories of her childhood might've cost her the tenuous hold she had on her ability to keep it together. Now, another night loomed ahead of her and she wasn't sure how well she'd handle it.

"No," she answered, pausing long enough for the server to set down their food. For a moment hunger overrode anything else and it was several bites before she was ready to talk again.

"I've barely had time to do much more than make sure she's fed and walked at fairly regular intervals." She swallowed a mouthful, absently wondering if she should order one to go since she wasn't much of a cook. "Plus, I have to admit, I can't let the poor girl go with just anyone. She deserves a good home. Caroline wouldn't have it any other way."

"It's good of you to see that she gets that," Colin said, tearing away a piece of his bread bowl to dip in his chowder. "Most people would just dump the dog off at the nearest shelter and let the dog take her chances."

Yeah...people like me, she reminded herself when she began to warm under his praise. The next swallow of sandwich seemed to stick in her throat. "That dog was my aunt's world. I wouldn't put it past Caroline to come back and scold me from the grave if I did anything less," she said, trying for levity despite the sadness that seemed her constant companion. She wiped her mouth with her napkin and leaned back to watch the snow as it drifted lazily to the ground.

"Well, I don't doubt Butterscotch held an esteemed spot in Caroline's life, but by the sounds of it, you were her world," Colin observed. "At least if what those ladies said was true."

"I suppose," she said, feeling low because she knew it *was* true. Caroline had never remarried after her husband had died and Erin had become her surrogate daughter due to circumstance.

"What kept you away from Granite Hills for so long?"

It was an innocent question, but her nerves were stretched to the point of snapping and that particular spot was always sensitive even under the best of times. She avoided his gaze and attempted a flippant shrug but her shoulders were too tight. "My work," she managed to finally answer, wishing that being a workaholic had been the sole reason she'd stayed away for so long.

"Your work," he repeated slowly, obviously disappointed in her answer. "Anything else?"

She gave a shaky laugh and fidgeted with her napkin. "Boy, you're full of questions. What about you? I don't remember you growing up here. What's your story?"

"I moved here from upstate New York shortly after I graduated from the academy with my daughter, Danni, when she was still in diapers." He pushed his empty bread bowl away and leaned forward, resting his arms on the table.

"What made you pick Granite Hills?" she asked, despite the warning bells that had rung in her head at her interest. If she delved too deeply into his personal life, he'd no doubt feel entitled to do the same.

"I see I'm not the only one who values their privacy," she murmured, when Colin hesitated to answer. He smiled and nodded as if to say *touché,* but when he actually started to explain she found herself eager to listen.

"My parents moved here when they retired," he said, brushing away the small flakes of bread that had fallen from his bread bowl. "My sisters followed and shortly after, I did, too."

"An entire family transplanted. Who knew Granite Hills was such a huge draw?" Her smile was vaguely sardonic but she couldn't help it. She'd spent the last fourteen years avoiding this place, yet Colin's family had flocked to it. "How old is your daughter?"

"Thirteen going on sixteen," he answered grimly.

"Ah. Do you guys have a good relationship?" she asked, unable to resist catching a glimpse of this man as a father.

The heavy silence that followed made her wish she hadn't asked. She hastened to change the subject when he gave a short, mirthless chuckle, the sound something Erin could certainly recognize.

"We used to," he answered, his mouth pulling into a tight line.

"And?" she asked, ignoring her better judgment to let the conversation end. She had nothing to gain by getting to know this man. Her life was complicated enough.

"And now we don't."

The bitter retort was at odds with the sadness in his eyes and Erin knew she should have listened to that nagging little voice at the back of her brain. "If you don't want to talk about it, I understand." If anyone could, it was her. "I shouldn't have pried, anyway."

"No, it's fine. I didn't mean to snap," he apologized, continuing with a rueful shake of his head. "The truth is, we've hit a rough patch and I'm having a hard time dealing with it. I'm kind of out of my element."

"What? You never fight?" What was that like? She bit down on her lip in retribution for her sarcasm. Now it was her turn to apologize. "Sorry. That was uncalled for. I guess you could say I'm out of my element as well."

He laughed softly yet there were subtle lines bracketing his eyes. She pulled her gaze away from the wealth of concern she saw there but couldn't help but wonder what was causing it. "Listen," he started, leaning back in his chair. "I know this isn't going to go over very well but I have to ask you something...."

"What?"

"It's about your dad."

Erin stiffened. "What about him?" Then, she thought better of it. "On second thought, I really wish you wouldn't."

"Wait—"

"No!" Her heart rate accelerated and she had to make a concentrated effort not to press her fingers to the pulse point at her neck. "I don't want to talk about my father. I know you think I'm being a cold-hearted bitch for refusing to see him but there are some things that just can't be forgiven, all right?"

Colin blanched and Erin stopped, wondering why he cared so much. Flustered, she just shook her head. "Nothing can change that, okay?"

But for some reason it wasn't okay and it wasn't just because the man sitting across from her thought she was wrong; somehow it felt as if she were leaving unfinished business, which made no sense because she had tied up any loose ends she might have had with her father years ago. Hadn't she? She glared at Colin, willing to believe whatever confusion she was having was directly attributed to his influence. "If there isn't anything else, I really ought to get going," she said, making a move to leave but a hand on her arm made her stop.

"What if someone had tried to kill him?"

CHAPTER SIX

"WHAT?" ERIN'S EYES WIDENED IN SHOCK.

Colin knew he should've prefaced the question better but he hadn't been thinking clearly. Although his first inclination in attending the funeral had been professional, once he saw Erin, stunned by the sea of people swarming around her, he'd felt a need to protect her that had nothing to do with his job. The unwelcome reaction had thrown him off-center and his mouth had started moving of its own accord.

"I'm sorry, I don't think I heard you correctly...."

"No," he assured her, "you heard me right. I asked if you knew of anyone who might have it in for your dad."

She sat back, stunned, and Colin cursed himself for acting like a rookie just because he was sitting in front of a woman that intrigued him, despite her prickly nature at times.

"Do you have proof of this?" she asked, her tone disbelieving.

"Not exactly."

She did a double take. "Then what are you saying?"

"Probably something sounding pretty melodramatic—"

"You got that right."

"But I'm following up on something that's been bothering me about the accident and I thought you should know."

"So what is it that made you believe someone tried to kill Charlie?" she asked, shaking her head as if the motion might clear up her confusion.

The brittle quality he'd seen earlier returned as she awaited his answer, but he sensed there was more going on beneath the surface of her stony expression than she was comfortable letting on. It was this hidden vulnerability that gentled his voice as he tried for more finesse this time around. "I didn't mean to upset you. But, when I was going over the report I realized something I'd missed the first time around."

"Which was?"

He eyed her intently to gauge her reaction. "There were no skid marks."

"So?"

"So, usually in an accident there are skid marks. From the looks of it, he just plowed headlong into that tree like he had his foot pressed to the floor. Granted, it's not a lot to go on but you have to admit, it doesn't sound normal. Unless, he was trying to commit suicide, which doesn't make sense either since Caroline was in the truck with him. But does that sound like something your dad would do?"

"How should I know? I haven't seen the man in

fourteen years," Erin returned, but there was something aside from just irritation in her voice. Uncertainty? Fear? The unknown quotient caused him to press a little harder.

"Listen, I get that you guys didn't get along—" he paused as she gave him a look that said *understatement of the year* "—but I don't have anyone else I can ask. Your dad was a bit of a lone wolf from what I know of him. With Caroline gone…you're the last person, aside from Charlie, who might have some answers."

"Unbelievable," she muttered, closing her eyes. When she opened them again, her expression was wary. "What kind of questions do you have?"

"Well, personal history for one," he answered. "Who were his friends? Where did he go for fun? What did he do for a living? Things like that."

"Then I'm certainly not the right person to ask," Erin answered, with an indelicate snort. "In case you weren't listening, I haven't seen or talked to my father in *fourteen years*. I wouldn't have a clue what his life was like. All I can tell you is that I wasn't in it."

She looked away but not before Colin caught the hidden hurt couched inside her declaration.

"What happened? To keep you guys apart like that."

"I'd rather not talk about it." She met his gaze squarely, almost in challenge. "It's personal."

"In my experience, everything turns out to be personal in some way or another," he said. He hadn't planned on going down this road just yet, but it was too late to pull back now. "But perhaps there's something in the past that might shed some light on the accident."

Her fingers twitched with her napkin until she became conscious of the telling gesture and withdrew both hands under the table. "Nothing that happened between my father and me has any bearing on what happened out on Old Copper Road," she said, her voice carefully modulated despite the anger he felt coming from her in waves. "Please drop it."

"I can't."

"It was an *accident*," she said, her voice rising emphatically until she noted that her sudden outburst had attracted attention from the other patrons. Lowering her voice, she continued. "Why do you have to read anything into it? For God's sake, it could've been anything. The weather was bad, the roads could've been icy, or maybe a deer jumped out in front of him. I don't know…there are a million different possible explanations, none of which include some conspiracy theory. So there were no skid marks…big deal. I don't see the relevance."

She cast a quick glance around to see if anyone was still watching them, then leaned back in her chair. "The truth is…Charlie was just a drunk. He was a sorry son of a bitch but I doubt anyone cared enough about him to want him dead."

She was probably right. "Perhaps," he conceded, yet he still wanted to know what had happened between them. The problem was, he wasn't sure whether he wanted to know for completely professional reasons. He shifted uncomfortably and uncertainty roughened his voice. "Perhaps not. But why don't you let me be the judge of what's relevant to my case."

He met her stare head-on, and after a tense moment, Erin gave a short exasperated sound that clearly communicated that she thought he was wasting his time and grabbed the small handbag at her feet. "Fine," she said, standing. "Thanks for the company. It was nice talking to you and good luck on your wild-goose chase."

She gave him a smile that was nearly as plastic as the chair he was sitting on and left, leaving Colin to stare after her in surprise. He hadn't thought she'd react that way, though he wasn't sure what he'd expected after deliberately pushing her buttons like that. But, as he watched her hurry across the street, he realized he didn't want to let the conversation end as it did.

"Not so fast, shutterbug," he muttered to himself as he quickly followed her outside, his voice rising. "Erin, wait up a minute!"

For a half second he thought she was going to keep on going, regardless of what he said, but just as he caught up with her, she turned and they nearly collided. Her eyes widened and her hands flew up in an instinctive motion. She leaned into his chest, electrifying his skin despite the layers of clothing between them, until she jerked away as if she'd been scalded.

"What are you doing?" she asked, the question

coming out with a gasp, as she took a quick glance around to see if anyone had caught their near mishap. "You almost knocked me into a snowbank."

"Well, if you hadn't run off like a scared bunny, I wouldn't have had to chase after you," he said defensively, his breathing a little erratic from the sizzle still warming his body. Her jaw hardened and he almost chuckled despite the glare directed toward him. Well, he could've called her something less cute and cuddly but she didn't seem to take that into consideration as her expression became downright hostile. "As I was saying—" he returned her narrowed stare "—you're the only one who can answer certain questions pertaining to your family. I'm sorry if you don't like it, but there's nothing I can do about that."

Erin opened her mouth, but as he shifted on the balls of his feet, moving subtly to reveal the badge partially hidden by his overcoat, she snapped it shut. He was willing to bet that he'd just been christened a name a person couldn't repeat in polite company and, though it shouldn't matter, the thought didn't sit well.

"Ask your questions but don't be surprised if I don't know the answers."

Fat flakes of snow landed on her head as the storm started to worsen and Colin gestured toward the deli. "Let's go back inside," he said, assuming she'd follow.

"No," she answered, causing him to turn in surprise. "We can finish right here."

Another flake landed on her cheek and slowly

melted, looking like a tear as the moisture slid down her face. He ought to give her a break. The woman had been through hell and he was only adding to what was surely a very bad day, but he had a sinking suspicion that if he didn't keep pushing for answers while he had her here, the moment he turned his back she'd hop a plane and he'd be screwed. He gave her a stern look and pointed at the darkened sky.

"I know it's been a while since you've been home but in case you've forgotten, the stuff that's falling from the sky is called snow and we're about to get a lot of it. I, for one, don't want to catch pneumonia." He jerked his thumb toward the deli. "It's either the deli or the station, make your choice."

She gave him a look that pretty much said that any conversation from this point forward would be unpleasant and stalked past him.

As Colin followed he heard his mother's voice in his head, reminding him that he could catch more flies with honey than vinegar. But he realized with a regretful sigh, he may have just tangled with the equivalent of an emotional diabetic.

ERIN LEFT THE DELI A SHORT time later still angry and more than a little conflicted. Who would want to kill Charlie? If anyone had a right to feel that way about the man, it was her, not some stranger who hadn't lived with him. Her gaze strayed in the direction of Granite Hills Medical, where her father remained in critical condition and the unwelcome sensation of fear pierced her heart. What if it were true? It was hard to fathom but she sensed that Colin wasn't the type to make something out of nothing, which was why she'd reluctantly agreed to take him out to Charlie's cabin tomorrow to search for possible clues.

At first, his heavy-handed tactics had enabled her to convince herself that whatever she'd been feeling earlier had been exactly what she'd been afraid of—misplaced attraction—but once they'd returned to the deli he'd gone and offered an apology and she'd relented. He was, after all, just doing his job. No, she countered fiercely as she stalked to the Tahoe, he was opening up a closet that held more than its share of skeletons. And if he knew how long she'd kept that door locked and bolted perhaps he'd understand why she had no interest whatsoever in opening it again.

Her cell phone jangled to life and she reached with clumsy fingers into her purse to retrieve it. She smothered a groan as the name *Harvey Wallace* flashed on the screen. Knowing that if she let the call go to voice mail he'd just keep calling, she answered with an attempt at keeping the edge from her voice, but Harvey's bark in her ear sent her blood pressure skyrocketing.

"McNulty!"

"What?" She snapped back before she could help it. *Watch it, girl. Don't let him get to you.* She cleared her voice, trying for a more professional tone. "What is it, Harvey?"

"How's the assignment going?"

She frowned. "Seeing as I just got here the day before yesterday, I'd say it's not going at all yet. Why?"

"Deadline's been moved. I need the proofs by Monday."

Erin gasped. She was good but not that good. "Impossible. That's only five days from now."

"And?"

She pressed her lips together and prayed for restraint, though in her present state of mind, she wasn't entirely sure she'd make it. Counting silently to five, she tried for calm. "And…I'm not sure I can get the shots you're looking for in that short amount of time. When you gave me the assignment I was given three weeks. Now, you're cutting it down to barely a week. If you want shoddy pictures send someone else because I'm not putting my name, and reputation, on a spread that's half-ass."

There was a long pause and Erin checked her phone to see if the connection had been dropped. She brought the phone back to her ear just as Harvey started talking again. "Fine," he said tersely. "Two weeks. No longer…or I *will* replace you."

The line died and Erin almost tossed the phone into a snowbank. *Jackass.* She rubbed at her nose, which had started tingling from the cold, and climbed into the Tahoe.

Despite Colin's prediction, the snow had actually slowed, which meant good news for the festival. The words of Dolores Gottileri rang in her head and she found herself half considering volunteering at the cocoa booth—if only to avoid spending too much time at the house. A group of kids walked by, laughing and chattering, dressed like an ad out of L.L. Bean, and Erin felt a smile wanting to form. On the outside, Granite Hills was the very picture of hometown America. Historic churches, cobblestone streets, quaint storefronts placed on foundations that had been standing since the 1800s and ice-skating in the town square—it was something off a postcard. Her smile faded with the knowledge that places such as the ones Harvey wanted on his pages didn't really exist—no matter how hard you wished they did.

DANNI IGNORED EVERY ATTEMPT her dad made at conversation as they drove to the Winter Festival. She'd tried getting out of it but he wouldn't budge. Two can play at that game, she thought spitefully, tightening her lips together.

When he finally gave up and continued the drive in silence, Danni was relieved. She'd never admit it but this fight with her dad was killing her. Before she'd found out that her dad was a liar, Danni would've defended him against anyone. But that was before she'd learned that he'd kept not only the truth from her, but he'd kept her from knowing her mother. There wasn't an excuse he could offer that she would understand. If her dad weren't a cop, she'd swear he'd done something illegal. But, even as the mean thought entered her mind, she had to discard it. Her father was the epitome of a good cop. He didn't bend the rules or allow anyone else to, either. She frowned. So, why had her mother allowed him to just take her away? She shot a look at her dad. He was the only one who could give her the answers, but she couldn't trust him anymore.

She looked away before her dad caught her staring. An awful queasy feeling made her mouth water, as if she were going to throw up and tears welled in her eyes. Life sucks, she thought, giving in to the self-pity that threatened to swallow her whole.

The old truck lumbered to a stop and her dad put it into Park. "Let's get that wood to Henry," he said as he climbed out. "We're running a little behind and the bonfire should already be started."

Danni gave him a caustic stare for his reference to their tardiness but it was lost in the dark. He was blaming her for their being late when it was his fault. If he hadn't insisted on dragging her here against her will, he could have delivered his stupid wood on time.

Usually, Danni didn't mind hauling a few pieces of seasoned oak from their own personal stack but tonight it was just one more thing she didn't want to do. She'd rather spend the evening with her new friends or at home listening to music. She smiled as she remembered the expression on her dad's face when he'd heard her new hip-hop CD. It'd been somewhere between appalled and frightened. *Good.*

"See? I told you once we got here, you'd have fun," her father said, mistaking her smile for something else. "Let's get that wood to Henry so we can get some hot cocoa."

Danni quickly replaced her smile with a sour expression as they trudged through the snow toward the brightly lit festival, the sounds of laughter, quartet singers and horses clip-clopping down the square filling the air between them.

"Whatever you say," she answered, hoping the acid in her tone was enough to convey how much she couldn't stand to be around him anymore. She was rewarded with a brief flash of wounded feelings, which made her feel worse, but she refused to acknowledge it. "Just because you dragged me out here doesn't mean I have to enjoy it. I've always thought this was dumb, anyway," Danni lied, wishing that were true. She *loved* the Winter Festival. Sleigh rides, hay bale jumps, fresh cream cocoa…it was almost something out of a movie set. But instead of giving in to the delighted tingle in her stomach she glowered. "How long are we going to be here?"

"Is this going to be your attitude all night?"

"What do you think?" Danni shot back.

"I don't appreciate your tone, young lady," he warned.

"And I don't appreciate being lied to."

"Danni—" he started, looking as if she'd just sucker punched him but she cut him off before he could say anything.

"Don't bother," she answered sharply. "Just leave me alone."

She threw down the few pieces of wood she was carrying and broke into a run, nearly stumbling in her haste to get away from him. Her heart felt as if it were beating right in her throat and tears filled her eyes. Misery at her father's betrayal threatened to swallow any joy the Winter Festival may have created.

"Danni!"

The sound of her father's voice at her back only made her run faster. People went by in a blur as she pushed her way through the crowds, seeking only to get away before he could see her tears.

Sparing a quick look behind her, she was relieved to find that she'd managed to lose her dad in the crowd. As she turned, she ran smack into a warm body carrying something wet. Something that was now trickling down both their fronts.

"Oh, gross!" Danni exclaimed, forgetting that the accident had been her fault. "What is this stuff?"

"That would be fresh cream," the woman answered, shaking her hand free of the white coating. She gestured toward a booth manned by Vera Hampton and surrounded by the longest line Danni had ever seen at the Winter Festival. "For the infamous Granite Hills hot cocoa. Apparently, it's what makes the stuff good enough to travel all the way from New York for a cup. And now, thanks to you we're both wearing it."

Danni grimaced. "Sorry, I didn't see you."

The woman sighed, then shrugged. "Don't worry about it. It's kind of fitting for the day I've had." She extended a hand, cream and all to Danni. "Name's Erin. What's yours, kid?"

"Danni," she answered, grimacing as their hands

connected and made squishy sounds. "Do you have a towel or something?"

"Yeah, I think there's a roll of paper towels tucked away somewhere at the booth. Come with me. This stuff might freeze and then we'll be in a whole lot of trouble."

Edging past the long line, Danni followed Erin around the booth to the back where bags of supplies were within easy grasp. Erin tore into the plastic of a new paper-towel roll and handed Danni several sheets. "It's not a shower but it'll have to do," she said, wiping her hands and the front of her sweater. "Unfortunately, by the end of the night we're both going to smell like sour milk. Hope you don't have a hot date or anything like that."

Danni cracked a smile. Like her dad would let her date. Although the thought had potential in terms of freaking him out. She'd have to give it some serious consideration later.

"Erin, where's that cream?" a voice called from the front of the booth. Danni looked at Erin and mouthed another apology.

"Don't worry about it," Erin said. "To run the risk of using a cliché, there's really no sense in crying over spilled milk, right?"

"I guess." Danni chewed the side of her cheek, not quite sure what to make of Erin, but suspecting that she was pretty cool.

The flap separating them from the operating side of the booth parted and Mrs. Hampton poked her head out. "Erin? The cream?"

Before Erin could answer, the woman's gaze dropped to the obviously soiled fronts of their tops to the wad of paper towels at their feet, and her expression changed from annoyance to concern as she immediately recognized her. "Oh! Danni, what happened?"

"A minor traffic accident," Erin answered for them. "Fortunately, your cream was the only victim." Taking a final scrub at the front of her sweater, she noted with a wry grin, "I see you two know each other?"

Stupid small towns. A person couldn't sneeze without someone on the other side of town knowing about it. "She works with my dad," Danni acknowledged sullenly.

"That's right. Known her since she was this high." Mrs. Hampton motioned to her knee, then took in the state of Danni's sweatshirt and exclaimed, "You're soaked through! If you stay like that you'll catch your death out here and your poor father will be beside himself. Where is Colin, by the way?"

For a second, Danni thought Erin hadn't caught that last part until her eyes widened in recognition.

"You're not by any chance Colin Barrett's daughter, are you?"

Danni's face fell and she answered glumly, "Yeah." Then, she added under her breath, *"Unfortunately."*

Erin and Mrs. Hampton exchanged perplexed glances and Danni took that as her cue to leave but Mrs. Hampton was faster.

"Oh, Erin, you've got to help Danni find her dad. She'll freeze for sure with all that milk on her or at the very least catch a cold and I couldn't live with myself knowing that. Would you mind?"

Erin nodded but seemed concerned about leaving the older woman in the lurch. "You sure you can handle the booth for a while?"

"If you can get me another batch of cream I'll be fine for an hour or so. Danni can help you."

"Sound all right with you, kid?" Erin turned to Danni, but it wasn't as if Danni were really expected to disagree.

Grown-ups. Why did they ask questions you aren't supposed to answer? She wanted to say no but she was raised to be polite and couldn't bring herself to be rude. Besides, Erin seemed cool enough for an adult. She figured she could hang out for a while. It wasn't like she could hide from her dad forever, anyway.

ERIN STOLE A LOOK AT THE TEEN beside her and wondered at the cosmic irony. Of all the kids to run into, it had to be Colin Barrett's daughter.

"Alright, let's go get that cream for Vera so that we can find your dad," she said, shouldering her camera bag.

"What's that?" Danni asked.

"My camera and all the lenses," she explained as they walked out of the booth and into the small throng of people. "I'm a photographer for a magazine called *American Photographic.* Ever heard of it?"

Danni shook her head and Erin shrugged. "Well, I'm not surprised. It's a magazine geared toward a more mature age group."

"I'm not a baby," Danni retorted, obviously stung by Erin's remark.

"Oh, I don't mean that," Erin said. "When I say 'mature' I mean more like retired. You know, *old* people."

Danni cracked a smile and answered with a sheepish "oh." "So are you on assignment or something?"

"Something like that." She drew a deep breath. "My aunt and father were in a bad car accident and I came back to make arrangements for the funeral."

"I heard something about an accident on Old Copper Road," she admitted, then asked solemnly, "Who died?"

"My aunt. Caroline Walker. Did you know her?"

Danni's eyes widened. "Yes, she used to deliver cookies to the school around Christmas."

Erin's eyes misted even as she chuckled. "Yeah, she used to do that when I was a kid, too."

"Even though it's against the rules to send treats to school unless they're made at a bakery or sealed, they made an exception for Ms. Walker. I guess they figured she'd never put anything bad in the cookies like some people."

Erin nodded. "I suppose so."

"She was real nice," Danni offered, biting her lip. "I'm sorry."

Erin accepted her condolences and they walked

in relative silence, each checking out the sights before Danni returned to the subject of Erin's work.

"So, they're making you work even though your aunt died? Don't you get some kind of leave?"

"Oh, the decision to work was my own," Erin answered. "I know it seems weird to actually want to work at a time like this but photography has always been my outlet for everything…even grief." She risked a smile. "It's cheaper than a shrink."

Danni giggled. "I'll bet."

"And, I'm up for this really big promotion and it would've been a bad idea to take time off if I want to be seriously considered."

"That sucks," Danni said, her nose wrinkling. "Sounds like your boss is mean."

"He is." *Kid, you have no idea.* "But he's the best in the business and I'm going to write my ticket with his name on my resume."

Danni looked confused. "What does that mean?"

Erin laughed. "It means if I can survive everything Harvey Wallace can throw at me then I will walk away from *American Photographic* with the credentials to open the door to any magazine in the business."

"Are you any good?"

Danni's blunt question startled her. "Of course, I'm good."

"Then why do you need some old mean guy to write you a ticket to someplace that you can get to yourself?"

Erin did a double take. "Are you sure you're only thirteen?"

"Yeah, but I'm in all advanced classes." Danni grinned.

"I'll bet."

"So, what's your assignment about?"

"It's a spread called Hometown America," she answered, surprised at the girl's interest. "I figure the Winter Festival is a perfect fit for what my editor is looking for."

"Have you found anything yet?"

Erin shrugged. "Nothing really but I've been busy helping Vera at the booth." She gave Danni an assessing look. "Maybe you could help me out."

Danni's face lit up at the prospect and Erin smiled at her enthusiasm. "Yeah? How?"

"Well, if you see something that seems particularly pretty or interesting, let me know and I'll shoot it. Sound good?"

Danni nodded and a deal was struck. They made quick work of getting another batch of cream for Vera and then they set off through the festival.

They'd only been walking a few moments when Danni ventured a possibility.

"You know my dad said that the Winter Festival is one of the last places you can find a real true bonfire at a public function because of the liability or something like that." She turned to gauge Erin's reaction to her suggestion and Erin rewarded her with a thoughtful nod.

"You know you may be onto something, kid," she said. "Let's check it out."

As they approached the area cordoned off for the

bonfire, Erin only had to take one look around to know that Danni had good instincts. People from all ages enjoyed the welcome heat from the massive blaze, while sparks of hot embers floated into the night sky before expiring in a flash like doomed fire-flies. The glow from the fire gave everything a peachy tint that softened and diffused, and the sound of laughter carried on the subtle breeze. She knelt and carefully pulled her high-end Nikon digital from the bag and selected an appropriate lens for the low light. She knew without having to look that Danni was watching her carefully, totally absorbed in what Erin was going to do next. She smiled to herself and lifted the camera to her eye. She'd snapped two or three shots when her eye fell on the scene that sent her photography senses twittering.

It was old man Henry. A face, though half-hidden in shadow, she recognized. Despite the years, his craggy, yet surprisingly gentle features hadn't changed all that much. Swallowing the lump that had inexplicably risen in her throat, she focused on her subject.

As if sensing her direction, Danni trained her gaze on the old man. "You almost can't see his face…." she whispered.

"That's okay," Erin whispered back, taking a quick moment to adjust her f-stop. "I'm more inter-ested in his profile and his hands."

Henry was resting his hands atop the long-handled shovel he used to keep the logs in place as they burned. The light from the fire softened the lines on his face but there was no mistaking the quiet contented expression. This was a job he did every year and it gave him purpose. She swallowed and snapped another picture, immortalizing old man Henry with megapixels and digital bits. She lowered her camera and shot a quick smile at Danni.

"You think it's gonna be a good picture?" Danni asked, her tone hopeful.

"Probably one of the best," she answered truthfully. In one of his rare moments of generosity, Harv had once said she had a knack for knowing what was going to stand out to make a good photograph. It was her gift. Old man Henry reminded her of a brick building she'd photographed in Illinois that everyone had taken for granted until it was torn down. Tears pricked her eyes suddenly and Erin had to blink hard to force them back. Time to move on. She turned to Danni with a bright smile. "Want to get something to eat?"

Later, as they were finishing their fish and chips, Erin knew it was time to broach the subject of Danni's father. It'd been nearly an hour and they still hadn't found Colin. Nor did it seem as if Danni were in a hurry to be found. Tossing her trash in the bin nearest them, Erin leveled with her.

"Your dad is probably worried sick right about now. I figured we'd run into him, but seeing as we didn't, does your dad by any chance have a cell phone so that we could call him?"

Danni's formerly contented expression fell sour but she gave a short nod.

Perplexed by Danni's obvious reluctance to find her dad, Erin held off making the phone call. "What's going on? Anything you want to talk about?"

Danni gave her a look that was probably meant to appear rebellious but for someone who was a pro at projecting an attitude to hide something else entirely, she knew the kid was hurting. "I take it you and your dad aren't getting along right now." When Danni failed to answer, she ventured a little further. "What's the fight about?"

"Nothing you'd want to hear about," she answered darkly.

"Let me fill you in on a little secret. If I didn't want to know I wouldn't ask. I don't do things out of courtesy. My aunt used to say it was one of my most enduring character flaws. So, if I ask, it's genuine."

Danni's eyes widened at Erin's frank tone but she seemed to loosen up a bit.

"I don't know your dad that well but I've got to say he seems—" *strong, reliable, even caring* "—pretty nice. Am I wrong?"

"Oh, yeah? Well, he's a liar," Danni shot back.

A liar? Erin hadn't expected that one. "How so?"

"I don't want to talk about it," she answered glumly and Erin knew enough to back off. The kid would talk when she was ready.

"Okay, let's call your dad before he has the entire Granite Hills P.D. out looking for you."

"He would, too," Danni mumbled.

Any good father would. Erin smiled and dialed the number Danni had given her. She took a discreet, steadying breath and braced herself for another encounter with Colin.

Five minutes following the quick phone call, Colin strode into view. It took extreme effort to keep her facial expression from betraying the unexpected flutter that had begun in her belly the moment he appeared, but she did it.

"Thank God, you're all right," he said in one breath and thanked Erin in the next. "I was out of my mind worried when I couldn't find her. I didn't think it was possible to lose someone in a place so small but I was wrong. Thank you for finding her."

Erin nodded but waved away his thanks. "I didn't actually find her. We ran into each other." When he didn't understand, she pointed to her soiled shirt. "We both got cream down our fronts, which is actually the reason why we were looking for you. She needs to change or else she's going to catch a cold or something."

As if on cue, Danni sneezed and Colin agreed with Erin's logic. He turned to Danni, placing a hand on her shoulder. "Let's get you home, then." He looked at Erin. "How about you? Do you have something to change into?"

Erin sighed, wishing she had time to go home and change, but knew she didn't. Vera was probably wondering what was taking her so long. "I'll be fine." When he didn't seem convinced, she tried making light of his concern. "Don't worry, I'm a big girl. I can handle a sniffle or two. Really. Don't worry about it."

Despite her assurances, he did seem worried. Finally, he gestured for her to follow. "Come with me, I've got a sweatshirt in the truck that you can borrow."

Erin started to protest but Danni stopped her. "He's right, Erin. It's pretty cold out here. Just take the sweatshirt."

It was hard to refute logic, especially when it felt as if ice crystals were starting to form on her chest. She grudgingly relented but tried not to put too much value into the gesture.

They arrived at Colin's truck and Danni volunteered to get the sweatshirt.

"Thanks," she said, feeling suddenly awkward. She hugged herself for warmth. "I'll get it back to you as soon as possible."

"Don't worry about it. I just threw it in there last weekend for a fishing trip that never actually materialized." Danni hollered that she found it and Colin turned to her. "Listen," he said, his voice rushed as if he didn't want Danni to hear what he had to say. "I just want to thank you again for keeping Danni safe. Right now I'm on her hit list and I was afraid she might do something rash just to get back at me." He placed a hand on her arm and gave it a gentle squeeze. "Thanks."

She swallowed hard in the hopes of untwisting her tongue but all she could manage was a short nod. The flesh on her arm tingled with warmth and if she hadn't witnessed him dropping his hand she would've sworn they were still touching.

"She's a great kid," she said, hoping he realized the compliment was a reflection of his parenting skills.

"Yeah, she is," he acknowledged but his smile was sad.

"I just wish…"

Colin stopped as Danni appeared with a bundle in her hands and Erin was almost desperate to hear what he'd been ready to say.

"Here's the sweatshirt, Erin," Danni said, tossing the garment her way. "It doesn't stink so it must be clean."

Erin raised the sweatshirt to her nose and gave it an assessing sniff. Colin rolled his eyes and she smiled. "All clear. Thanks, I appreciate the loaner. I'll get it back to you tomorrow."

"No rush. I know where to find you."

It was an innocent statement but it sent her heart to racing. *Don't be ridiculous,* she gave herself a stiff reprimand before acknowledging his words with a quick nod. "I'll see you later, then."

She held out her hand to Danni and thanked her for helping her find some great shots. The beaming smile she received in return caused something to blossom in her chest that was not unwelcome but she wasn't sure what to do with it. She gave a short wave and hurried back to the festival, deliberately squelching the attraction to Colin Barrett that continued to grow the more she came into contact with him.

Hanging out with his daughter certainly hadn't helped in that department, but she sensed a kindred soul in the young girl, creating a pull that was hard to ignore.

CHAPTER SEVEN

KNOWING THAT ERIN was the one who'd found Danni had sent Colin's mind moving in strange directions. When he'd come upon them, Erin was showing Danni the mechanism of her camera. The rapt attention on his daughter's face had illuminated a dark place in his heart. The picture of the two, heads almost touching, sent a wistful yearning twisting through his body that nearly stole his breath away. He hadn't realized that he was ready for someone to come into their lives but seeing Erin perched next to his daughter awakened a desire he'd long thought dead.

He risked a quick look at Danni in the darkness and breathed a silent prayer of gratitude that none of the horrifying scenarios his mind had obligingly provided had actually come to fruition. He returned his attention to the road, content to let the lecture that was coming to her die on his lips. There'd been enough excitement for one night.

"How do you know Erin?"

Surprise over the fact that his daughter had initiated conversation momentarily took him off guard.

When he realized the window between them might slam shut with too pregnant of a pause, he recovered to offer the safest answer he could think of within such a short time frame. "I'm investigating her father's accident, the one on Old Copper."

"I know. That's the one that Ms. Walker died in."

He nodded gravely, the sad tone of Danni's voice tugging at his heart. "Well, Ms. Walker was Erin's aunt."

"I know, she told me."

He was embarrassed to admit that he wished Erin had been as forthcoming with personal information with him as she had Danni, but he knew confiding in a preteen was wholly different than opening up to an adult.

"Did she tell you where she's from?"

"No, but she told me she works for a really big magazine. That's what she was doing at the festival. Do you know where she's from?"

"Well, she's from here but she lives in San Francisco now."

"Figures." Danni snorted. "Nobody with that kind of talent would hang around this dull place if they didn't have to."

"I wouldn't say that," he countered, frowning. "There are plenty of talented people who chose to stay."

Except for whatever reasons, Erin hadn't been one of them. Colin couldn't help but wonder what might have been if they'd met when he moved here years ago. Realizing he was wandering into dangerous territory, he forced a chuckle. "But you're probably right in Erin's case. Granite Hills must seem dull in comparison to the life she leads in San Francisco."

"That's the understatement of the year," she said, the derision in her young voice hard to miss. "She's a big-time magazine photographer who travels all around the world taking pictures of famous people and places. She told me she took a picture of Johnny Depp for a special Oscars issue but it wasn't half as cool as shooting some famous mountain in Tanzania."

"Mount Kilimanjaro?" He guessed and she snapped her fingers in recognition.

"Yeah, that's it." She slumped in her seat. "So, why would she want to stay here? Nothing exciting ever happens in this tiny place. I'll bet we're not even on the map."

"We're on the map," he assured her but was rewarded with a heavy sigh. "So, you think Erin's pretty cool, huh?"

"She's the coolest person in Granite Hills, that's for sure," Danni said, letting her gaze fall to the passing scenery out her window.

I would agree, he answered silently as they pulled onto their street. He wished he'd made some excuse to go around the block a few times just to keep Danni talking. This was the first time she'd opened up to him since the big blow-up and he was reluctant to sever the moment. But their driveway was soon in sight and he knew his opportunity had passed.

"Here we are," he announced unnecessarily as he put the truck into Park, wondering if this were a start to a grudging truce between them. "Danni…" he began, stopping her as she moved to open the door. She waited, watching him warily.

"What?"

"I…nothing. I'm just glad you're all right."

She swallowed then gave the slightest of nods to indicate that she'd heard him. Two seconds later she was out of the car and heading toward the front door.

Colin leaned back against the headrest, hating the ache in his chest at the rift between them. He tried not making a habit of playing the what-if game but he'd do anything right about now to rewrite the moment Danni had found that damn death certificate. A part of him wanted to just sit down and spill the whole sad story but the knowledge of how much the truth would hurt held him in check. If she were to know the whole truth would she forgive him? Would she understand? His thoughts turned to Erin. What would she think if she knew? Would she condemn him as Danni had? Too many questions. Not enough answers. Sighing, he grabbed the keys and locked up.

ERIN PULLED UP TO THE CABIN she'd spent half her childhood trying to escape and fought the urge to turn around. Much like Caroline's house, the cabin wasn't much to look at, but unlike the rambling farmhouse, her father's cabin had started out that way. It was basically a two-bedroom shack with barely enough square footage to support the bedroom space. Looking back, Erin was surprised her father had thought to put in indoor plumbing.

Coming face-to-face with yet another piece of her childhood made the gooseflesh pop along her forearms. Her gaze roamed the mud-slicked yard where an abandoned chicken coop leaned dispiritedly against a sturdy elm. The entire place seemed dejected and forgotten. Much like she'd been.

Shaking her head at the useless direction of her thoughts, she jerked the door open and got out. Colin was bound to show up any minute and she wanted to get this over with.

The snow had stopped but the air was so cold any hint of moisture would freeze instantly. Shivering, Erin wound her woolen scarf tighter around her neck and slipped her shaking hands into the lined leather gloves that were all but useless in this type of weather. As her breath plumed in frosty curls before her, she vowed to pick up a pair of North Face gloves while she was still here and made her way toward the front door. Careful to avoid the worst of the icy mud puddles, she climbed the steps to the porch and let herself in.

The dim interior was dank and cold. The practical side in her immediately questioned the roof's integrity. An image of her father shivering under a thin blanket, listening to the steady drip of water invading the small cabin, filled her mind and an unexpected pang of worry pierced her chest. Shrugging it off, she reminded herself that her father's comfort level was none of her concern. It wasn't as if he'd cared much about her comfort when she'd been young, left alone frozen and starving so that he could go on a bender.

A knock from behind jerked her back to the present. She turned and motioned for Colin to enter.

"Have you been waiting long?"

Define "long," she wanted to quip. Two seconds was too long in this dump. "No," she answered, turning to survey the room. "So, what are we looking for?"

The sound of Colin's booted footsteps followed until he was standing beside her. "Anything that looks out of place."

Erin made a rude noise. She wouldn't have a clue as to what was normal in her father's life. The only out-of-place thing she could immediately identify was herself. She tried stifling her sense of frustration but a little seeped out in the tone of her voice. "Could you be a bit more specific? I'm not accustomed to digging around in other people's stuff."

To his credit, instead of ruffling at her openly derisive comment, as she would have done if the situation had been reversed, he gestured toward the small desk against the living room wall, directly beneath the window. "Start there. Look for papers that may have been rifled through or anything that looks like it's missing something," he said.

Like my manners. Erin almost sent a guilty look skyward just in case Caroline was watching—no, frowning—from her perch in heaven and made a mental note to be less touchy. It was a wonder the man wanted to spend more than five minutes in her company. She'd done nothing but snap at him since she'd laid eyes on him. Well, some of it was warranted, she shot back, wondering who in the hell she was arguing with. Great, she thought as she grimly surveyed the desk and its scattered contents, by the time she left this place she'd be certifiable.

Her fingers moved in useless circles around the desk. She couldn't help Colin. Her father was a stranger to her. She didn't even know what he did for money these days. When she was a kid he used to haul lumber, then when the lumber mill went out of business he delivered wood during the winter months and did odd jobs during the summer. But surely, he was too old to be doing that now?

Erin turned the small desk lamp on, bathing the surface in a weak glow, and sat down. A calendar, some receipts and a few pencils were all that she could see. Pulling the calendar toward her, she read the few appointments he'd marked down. Aside from a star on each Tuesday of the week, the calendar was bare. Except, she noted, the week of her father's accident, there was a star on the day previous. Monday. Why? Her inability to come up with an answer made her toss the calendar back to its place. "You find anything?" she asked, turning away from the desk.

Colin emerged from the kitchen area, looking equally frustrated. "No. How about you?"

She shook her head.

"Well, how about the drawers? Did you check those, too?"

"Um, no." She risked an embarrassed laugh. "Guess I won't be quitting my day job anytime soon."

He flashed an unexpected grin, and she found herself smiling back, surprised by the appearance of a dimple in his left cheek. *Sweet...*

An odd pang of longing caused her to turn abruptly and jerk the first drawer open. Pencils, pens and a box of matches slid to the front with the force of her action. Annoyed at herself for acting like an idiot, she gently closed the drawer and proceeded to the second. Unlike the first, this one didn't open so easily. It felt weighted down. Gripping the handle with both hands, she pulled the drawer open with a mighty heave. The contents spilled out as she dropped the drawer to the ground and stared.

Magazines.

"You find something?" she heard Colin say over her shoulder but she couldn't find her voice to answer. Dozens of *American Photographic* stared back at her. Ripping her gloves from her hands so she could get a better grasp, she flipped through the magazines, searching for the publication dates. Her eyes widened. They were numbered sequentially from the first to the last of the year. Confusion and an inability to accept what she was seeing gripped her mind and the one in her hand slipped from her fingers. *American Photographic* wasn't available in Granite Hills, which meant he would've had to drive to Ontonagon, the largest city in the county, to get them. A picture of Charlie's beat-up truck rumbling toward civilization floored her.

Impossible. As much as her father loved to drink, he'd still hated the twenty minutes it had taken to drive to the pub. And she was supposed to believe that her father drove an hour to buy magazines she knew he'd never read? It was possible—though not probable—that he ordered a subscription. But as far as she knew, her father had never in his life opened a checking account. He preferred the security of cold, hard cash. It was easy to spend and easier to hide.

"You got something?"

She risked a look at Colin, hoping he couldn't sense the thundering in her heart from the confusion she was sure was in her eyes. "My magazines," she answered, hating the soft, vulnerable quality to her voice. She cleared her throat. "I'm sure it doesn't mean anything. It was just unexpected."

"How many?" he asked, ignoring her attempt to brush him off.

"Twelve," she said, amazed the words didn't get stuck in her throat. If she and her father had shared a normal relationship, the discovery of the magazines wouldn't have been out of place in the least. But their relationship was anything but normal. Didn't they hate each other?

"Well, if he has every single issue for the past year, he probably has more hidden somewhere. Any idea where he might stash them?"

His logic was in direct opposition to what she thought she knew of her father. But she couldn't deny the proof staring back at her.

"Erin?"

His gentle prodding drew her gaze. She licked lips that felt cold and dry, and focused on the question. "The hall closet, maybe…" she answered, slowly rising. "That's the only place I can think of. None of the bedrooms have closets."

Closing the distance between the desk and the hall, she opened the narrow door and flipped the light. There, stacked neat as a pin, were three piles of magazines, all bearing the *American Photographic* label. Confusion and something less easily defined sapped the strength from her legs. Dropping to her knees, she ignored the sudden pain ricocheting up her leg, and thumbed through the stack closest to her.

Another year. Every single issue accounted for.

Rocking back on her heels, she barely noticed when Colin dropped down to crouch beside her.

"*One* I might understand. That's easily enough explained…but all of them?" She turned to him. "From the looks of these stacks, he's kept every single issue since I came aboard *American Photographic*. That was five years ago. Why? Why would he do that?"

"He's your father," he answered, as if that were all the explanation needed. When she continued to stare at him as if he'd just spoken in a different language, he continued, "My parents have a garage full of my high school sport trophies and even old homework assignments. Hell, I've kept nearly everything Danni's ever made. It's just what parents do."

That's what *normal* parents do. Not hers. Her father hadn't even attended her high school graduation, or any other milestone in her life for that matter. Why would he start now? It was on the tip of her tongue to say just that, but she couldn't bear to see pity reflecting from Colin's eyes. Or anyone's, for that matter.

"Right." Rising, she pushed away from the closet and closed the door. "I was just surprised, is all. I never knew my father was much for magazine reading. I didn't even think he knew where I worked," she murmured, despite her decision to keep quiet. Colin looked ready to comment but Erin changed the subject. "So, did you find anything of value to your investigation?"

His mouth twisted and she knew he didn't want to let the subject go, but he did. Immensely grateful, she swallowed hard and gave him her full attention.

"Unfortunately, no," he said, his hands coming to rest on his hips, one poised right above his holstered Glock 40. "Seems your dad didn't leave much of a bread-crumb trail for me to follow."

She smiled in spite of the lingering shock. "You don't know how pleased he'd be to hear that. He values his privacy."

Like father, like daughter, Colin added silently. Moving away from the closet, he surveyed the rest of the small room. Talk about spartan living. There wasn't much to look at. A ratty old sofa, the desk and a scarred, wooden end table with thick legs were all that he could see. There wasn't even a television. Or a phone, he realized with a start. Who didn't have phones nowadays? He sighed. "Well, seems we've hit a big zero with this part of the house. Mind if we check the bedrooms?"

Erin paused and Colin could swear she was mentally preparing herself for the answer. The porcelain cast of her skin took on a deathly pallor but she nodded. "Go ahead," she said, striving for a nonchalance he didn't buy for a minute.

The false bravery tugged at his heart and reminded him of Danni. The urge to pull her to his chest and shelter her against whatever bad memories this place held for her was stronger than it should have been. Somehow the urge felt more primal than just the basic need to protect every cop feels for victims or, in this case, the victim's family. Frustration at the inexplicable feelings she evoked in him roughened his voice. "You can wait out here."

He didn't wait for her reply, and instead headed straight for the first bedroom, which, judging by the look, must've been Charlie's. Again, it was as bare as the living room but there were some personal items, such as a vintage shaving set and an odd assortment of fishing lures. Going to the dresser, he made quick work of opening each drawer, searching for something that might help him understand why a man would choose to plow headlong into a tree.

"Anything?" he heard her say from the doorway. He turned slowly, surprised by the tentative tone of her voice.

"No, not yet," he said, noting the subtle shiver that

rocked her body as she huddled into her coat for warmth. He wanted to ask what demons had chased her from this house—this town, even—but he held his tongue.

Turning from the dresser he ducked his head to check under the bed. Nothing.

"Are you sure your father actually lived here?" he said as he straightened, frustration lacing his tone. "I've seen prison cells with more personality. Was it like this when you lived here?"

"If by that question you mean was it this dreary, cold and devoid of life, then, yes." She thrust her chin out, as if daring him to murmur his apologies for such a dismal childhood. When he failed to offer anything of the sort, she softened. "Well, it does seem a little more empty than it did before."

He lifted an eyebrow for elaboration. "Such as?"

She slid into the room, pointing to the wall above the dresser. "There used to be an old oil painting that hung right there."

"Who painted it?"

She shrugged. "I don't know. Maybe my mother."

"She was an artist?" he asked, his interest piqued. Learning more about Erin's mother felt faintly taboo.

"I guess."

"You don't know for sure?"

"No," she said defensively. "She died when I was young. I don't remember much about her and Charlie wasn't one to share stories around the fire-place, if you know what I mean."

"Mind if I ask how she died?"

Erin compressed her lips. "She killed herself."

Her flat statement nearly sucked all the air out of his lungs as he stared at her in surprise. "I'm sorry."

"It was a long time ago."

A secret pain pierced his chest as he wondered if this was how Danni would react when people asked about her mother. That is, if he ever got up the nerve to actually tell her what had really happened to Danielle. He jerked his thoughts away from that particular quagmire, returning to Erin's situation. "Still, it must've been hard on you, growing up with that kind of knowledge."

"Well, that's where my Aunt Caroline comes in…she was always there for me," she revealed, the sudden shine in her eyes telling him he'd hit a sensitive spot. He started to offer some appropriate words of understanding but, true to her word, she wasn't interested in the pity of others. "What does my mother have to do with all of this? She's been dead for nearly thirty years."

"Well, maybe nothing," he admitted. "But then again, you never know. Maybe someone from your parents' past is trying to get back at Charlie for something."

"I can't imagine what that could be," she answered as another shiver rocked her body. "Or who, for that matter. Like you said, Charlie isn't the most social of creatures. Sometimes, I'm not even sure if the stories my aunt used to tell about Charlie and my mom were even true."

"What kind of stories?"

She shrugged. "Happy ones."

"Your parents weren't happy?"

"Were yours?"

"Actually, yes…and to my knowledge, they still are," he answered evenly. "At least judging by the latest e-mail I received showing my parents decked out in snorkel gear. Something that they can't exactly do here but my mom has always wanted to try."

"Oh. Sorry for that…comment," she mumbled, her troubled gaze making him want to smooth the worry lines from her forehead. "Is there anything else we need to do here?"

"No, we can go," he said, gesturing for the front door. "But, there is something else I need to tell you."

She stopped and turned, the look in her eyes wary. "What is it?" When he didn't answer right away, a bitter smile twisted her lips. "I'm not made of china, Colin. I promise I won't break, if that's what you're worried about."

Not china, porcelain, he countered silently, recalling his first impression of her at the station. And something told him she was wrong. His guess was that there were pieces of something precious lying shattered deep within her chest and she was fighting tooth and nail to keep it a secret. He rubbed at the back of his neck and wondered when he'd become such a sap. Her problems were her own but he was having a hard time remembering that.

"I ordered a mechanic's report on your dad's truck."

"Why?" Her question held a wealth of confusion and a trace of fear.

"It goes back to the no skid mark thing," he explained. "I want to find out if anyone tampered with the brakes."

"Why would someone tamper with the brakes?"

"Well," he began, wondering why he was even voicing his suspicion with so little to go on, "the easiest way to ensure an accident without needing to be around to cause it is to cut the brake line on a car—a few good pumps will bleed the line dry and then the icy roads will do the rest."

She nodded but the color had leached from her complexion. Still, she managed to ask the one question that was still tripping him up. "Let's say the mechanic's report comes back and it says the brakes were tampered with—what's the motive?"

"I don't know," he admitted, wishing he had more to offer. "But I'll be honest…I have a better chance of figuring that out with your help than without it." When she didn't flat-out laugh in his face or, worse, turn on her heel with a suggestion of where to stick it, hope flared in his chest. There was something lurking behind her troubled stare. Worry, concern, fear—he wasn't sure but it was something strong enough to root her to the spot considering his dilemma. His gaze found hers and held it for a heartbeat, daring to push a little harder. "So, what's it going to be? Can I count on you?"

"What do you mean?"

"I mean, are you going to stay and help me find

whoever did this to your dad or are you going to leave?"

He held his breath as he awaited her answer. Her hesitation made him wonder if someone was waiting for her at home. Did she have a husband or a boyfriend? As the question formed in his mind he realized he didn't like the thought of either one. It was none of his business but that didn't seem to matter. Lots of things didn't seem to matter when it came to Erin. He shifted on the balls of his feet, deciding to try a different tactic. "I'm sure you have questions, too," he pointed out gently. She gave a subtle nod and Colin moved closer. "What if this is your one and only chance to find out what happened to your family?"

Erin exhaled deeply and Colin knew he'd struck a nerve. For a split second he caught a glimpse of a softer person. He knew he was standing closer than was prudent, but his feet didn't seem to want to cooperate with the reasoning part of his brain. He was so close, her unique scent filled his senses. It was a heady combination of crisp outdoors and the faint, lingering fragrance of something exotic and spicy. In a word: intoxicating. This is lunacy, a voice whispered in his brain even as his fingers itched to touch the silken black hair that made the alabaster of her skin look unreal. *You don't even know this woman.* Step back, the voice warned. But he remained, demanding an answer with his eyes and wondering why he was taking such a chance.

"Will you stay?"

CHAPTER EIGHT

ERIN STARED UP AT COLIN and her breath felt ridiculously short. They were so close she could feel the heat radiating from his body and it took an act of sheer will not to close the distance.

"Erin?"

The low timbre of his voice curled around her senses and filled her stomach with languid warmth until she had to fight to remember why this was a bad idea.

"What's it going to be?"

Rousing herself from the safety of the moment she realized if one of them didn't take hold of the situation, they'd both end up doing something they regretted. Clearing her throat, she slid away. The movement was subtle but strong enough to put some space between them.

"You don't know what you're asking," she managed to answer. "I came here to settle my family's affairs, not chase after theoretical bad guys. And—" she held up her hand when he started to protest "—this trip…well, I have a life to return to…one that demands my attention."

"I understand that," he acknowledged. "But don't you think the circumstances have changed a bit?"

"Yes," she agreed with a slow nod. "But they really don't have anything to do with me. While you have your suspicions, I still think it was just a tragic accident and I'd rather put it behind me."

He took a step toward her. "I understand your grief and your need to move on and if there were any indication this was just an unfortunate tragedy, I'd be behind you one hundred percent. But, if I'm right everything changes. It goes from accident to murder."

She nodded but the knowledge didn't make it any easier to stay when every instinct urged her to go. "When will you get the mechanic's report back?"

"A few days, a week, tops."

A week. She drew a deep breath. "Fine. I'll stay until you receive the report. After that…I'm gone."

Colin nodded, something akin to respect lighting his eyes, sending her the silent message he understood and somehow knew how much such a concession had cost her. She averted her gaze, hating the sudden flutter in her stomach. When he spoke again, his voice was full of concern.

"Erin, I can't begin to pretend to know what your relationship was like with your dad. I was lucky enough to have two great parents whom I love and respect, but I also can't imagine you don't care at all." Her mouth opened but Colin wasn't finished. "Somewhere deep down, possibly buried under years of anger and sadness, is a kernel of concern for

Charlie. You're fighting it, I'll give you that, but it's there. And you don't have to be ashamed. Nobody said by admitting you care, you compromise your issues with him."

She bit down on her lip to keep it from trembling. He was wrong—she didn't care. She lifted her chin and deliberately hardened her voice. "Charlie can go to hell."

He drew back, stunned by her vehemence, and tears sprang to her eyes, betraying her words with their appearance. There may have been a time when she'd wished for a father who tucked her in at night and kissed away her fears, but that childish desire had been suffocated under the weight of reality. She blinked back the moisture in her eyes until she could safely meet Colin's gaze again. Silence hung between them like a heavy curtain, and Erin was tempted to walk away until Colin's voice stopped her.

"What happened here? What forced you from this place?"

None of your business. It was her standard answer but her mouth tightened, as if it were trying to protect her from herself, and she had to close her eyes against the memory of bitter cold, aching loneliness and bruises that filled the landscape of her childhood within these four walls.

"Erin, you can trust me. I promise."

She opened her eyes and wondered if there were ever anyone she'd ever trusted more than herself. When he didn't waver under the weight of her assessing stare, she shook her head in a wry manner. "What do you think happened? I was abused."

Inside, she braced herself for the sight of pity creeping into his eyes but they remained clear and for that she was grateful. Softening a little, she added, "It was a long time ago. I'd thought I was over it but being here…well, it seems as vivid as it ever was."

"It must've been pretty bad."

She nodded. "It was."

"Was there sexual abuse, too?"

Erin sighed and shook her head. "I guess I should be thankful for small favors, right?"

Although the last comment was flavored with the bitterness of sarcasm, he didn't seem to take note or offense. Instead he closed the gap between them to gently take her chin in his hand, lifting her face to his intent stare. "No one deserves abuse," he said, his voice firm but kind. "No one."

She risked meeting his eyes. It seemed a small thing to accept the truth of his words but a part of her didn't believe it. A part of her wondered if somehow she was to blame for her mother's suicide and her father's abuse. Somewhere inside of her there resided a bewildered child who didn't understand why fate had been so cruel. And it was the urge to protect her inner child that made her defensive and prickly to anyone who came close enough to catch a glimpse. "I don't need your pity," she managed to say as her throat thickened with unshed tears and choked the words out of her mouth.

"Whatever I'm feeling...it isn't pity," he admitted, almost sounding guilty. Her heart stuttered a little as he pulled her closer. "I see a woman who's facing down an army of demons alone. Most people would run as fast as their legs could carry them but you're still here."

Robbed of speech, Erin could only stare and wish she could see what he saw. He pulled her tighter and their chests felt as one. His strength was solid and comforting, and she allowed her senses to soak up the drugging warmth between them. "You're wrong," she protested weakly, wishing this moment, as absurd as it was, would never end. "I'm a coward."

"No, you're not." His gentle statement was without hesitation and it made her feel good.

"You don't know me," she countered.

"I know," he chuckled softly as if that little fact had him scratching his head, too. "But I want to." Then he dipped his head slowly and he pressed his lips against hers in a move that shook her with its power.

Curling her arm around his neck, she opened her mouth to deepen the kiss and he obliged willingly. The pleasure of it blotted out the ugliness surrounding her and for a second the memories faded. But the urge to remain in his arms forever was a stark reminder of how wrong it was.

Despite the comfort of his embrace, she reluctantly pulled away, severing their connection. Erin caught Colin's expression and winced. Apparently, she wasn't the only one questioning their good judgment. His distress only added to her embarrassment.

"Oh, God...I'm sorr—"

"Don't worry about it," she interrupted, just wanting to get past the awkwardness stretching between them. "You were just doing your job. You know, that damsel-in-distress thing," she added with false nonchalance, as if a kiss were nothing more than an elaborate handshake. "It's no big deal."

Please, let it go, she prayed.

"Yeah," he said, his mouth tightening. Another tense and uncomfortable moment passed and she sensed he was struggling with what he considered a breach of propriety. "So, just so I'm clear, you're staying right?"

Exhaling with a silent thank-you sent to whomever might be listening, she sealed her fate with a nod. "I'll stay and help you with what I can— but I'm not doing it for Charlie. He made his bed, he can lie in it for all I care."

It sounded convincing. Too bad it wasn't entirely true. Foreign feelings assaulted her when she thought of Charlie and his condition, confusing and frustrating her. But what bothered her more was that somehow Colin had seen through the layers she piled around herself to the bare truth underneath. His keen sense made him both dangerous and alluring.

"Who else are you doing this for?"

"Caroline, of course," she answered. "If this was deliberate, I want that person to pay for what he or she did. Caroline was the best person, and she didn't deserve to die. When it was her time to go, it should've been peaceful and preferably in her bed."

Something parallel to admiration lit up his face and Erin had to bite back a smile. "Stop that."

"Stop what?"

"Stop looking at me like I'm something special."

His grin widened and he almost looked boyish. "Sorry, no can do. When my gut talks, I listen."

Heat flared in her cheeks and the corners of her mouth twitched as she shook her head. "Careful, your gut could get you into more than you can handle."

"Hasn't happened yet."

Erin chuckled at his confidence. "There's a first time for everything, officer."

He grudgingly agreed and Erin returned the focus to the investigation. "So, what do you need from me?"

Straightening, he drew a deep breath as if he needed the break to cleanse his mind and get back on track. "Start with Caroline's place." Reacting to her sudden look of alarm, he apologized. "Trust me, I know what I'm asking. I'm sure the memories are tough to take right now. If you'd like I can meet you—"

"No," she blurted to stop him. "I'm fine. What should I look for?"

"Same as we did here. Anything that might seem out of place. Did your aunt keep a diary or journal?"

"I'm not sure," she answered. "But I can look. Although, to be honest, I really don't want to invade my aunt's privacy by reading her private thoughts."

"I understand, but if there is one, it could hold valuable information."

"Right." She shoved her frozen fingers into the deep recesses of her pockets, seeking warmth. Without the heat of their bodies between them, Erin felt every draft slicing through the poorly insulated shack and her teeth began to chatter. "How much longer do you want to hang out in this icebox? Pretty soon I'll turn into a popsicle and I won't be much help to anyone."

He glanced out the frosted window and agreed it was getting late. "I guess we've done all we can for now."

Once outside he flipped the collar on his coat to ward off the bracing winter wind that had kicked up while they were sheltered within the cabin walls and Erin headed for her Tahoe.

As if she were hungering for a double shot of the lunacy they'd shared only moments ago, a wistful sigh escaped from her parted lips and she was rewarded with a huge dose of reality. What was she thinking? She pulled out of the driveway without risking another glance at Colin. It was simple. Obviously, her head hadn't been calling the shots. She caught her expression in the rearview mirror. Her cheeks were flushed with color and her eyes were a deep blue. She scowled at the woman staring back at her. "Colin is not a part of your future. Remember that and you won't get hurt."

ERIN HEADED INTO TOWN, still troubled by what had happened at the cabin. They had kissed. And she had welcomed it. What did that say about her?

It said she was confused. What if there were more to the kiss than simple comfort?

She put the Tahoe in Park and grabbed her camera bag. It was nothing. Let it go, McNulty, she told herself fiercely as she shouldered her bag and headed for the ice rink in the town square.

Normally, it wasn't an ice rink. During the summer months it was a very pretty fountain but in the winter it froze solid, creating the perfect surface for taking a few turns around the ice. And, she thought as she narrowed her gaze at the people taking advantage of the rink, it made for great pictures.

She checked the built-in light meter on her camera against the milky light filtering down from the overcast skies and adjusted her f-stop. Then she watched and waited until a small voice at her shoulder made her turn.

"Erin?"

A surprised but genuine smile curved her lips. "Danni? What are you doing here?"

The girl shrugged, looking every bit the disenchanted teen. "My friends were supposed to meet me here," she answered, her eyes roaming the ice rink. "I guess they're late." She turned. "What are you doing? Getting some shots for your assignment?"

"Yep." Erin lifted the camera to her eye, wondering if Colin knew where Danni was. She snapped a shot of a couple skating hand in hand. "Want to help?" She paused a moment to gauge Danni's reaction.

"Sure," Danni agreed, then shrugged again. "Well, at least until my friends show up."

"Of course."

"So, what should I look for?"

Erin paused, then as an idea struck her, slowly lowered the camera. "Want to try?"

Danni's eyes widened in surprise. "Me?"

"Sure." She started to hand over the camera but Danni's sudden protests stopped her. "What's the matter?"

"I don't know anything about photography. What if I break the camera or something?"

Erin almost chuckled but when she realized Danni was dead serious, she sobered and slipped the camera strap over Danni's head. "This will keep the camera from dropping, so don't worry about that. Now, look through the eyepiece and see what you can see out there."

"What am I looking for?" Danni's tone was hushed as she adjusted her hold on the camera for a better fit. "Just cute stuff?"

"Anything that catches your eye." Erin bent down to watch the scene at Danni's level. "Whatever your gut tells you to shoot."

Danni bit her lip and scanned the rink, pausing every now and again as she watched the scene through the lens of Erin's camera. Another moment went by and then Danni hesitantly depressed the shutter button with a soft *snick*. She quickly lowered the camera and looked up at Erin. "How'd I do?"

"Let's see," she said, accepting the camera from

Danni as she removed it from her neck. Switching from the camera viewfinder to the LCD screen, Danni's picture of a small girl wearing brand-new white skates moving gingerly on the ice, arms outstretched, appeared. When Danni didn't seem impressed with her own work, Erin offered her genuine opinion. "Wow. Not bad for a beginner. Not bad at all."

Danni gave her a hesitant, yet hopeful smile and Erin knew the girl was hooked. Sensing that piling on the praise would only make Danni uncomfortable, she lifted the camera to her eye as she started talking.

"The secret to capturing a great photo is patience," she explained, scanning the area, knowing without having to see it that Danni was listening with rapt attention. She resisted another smile and continued. "The best picture is the one that makes you work for it. Sometimes it happens when you least expect it, which is why you should always be ready to shoot. It's the first snowflake landing on a child's tongue, the single tear of a stoic mother as she says goodbye to her only child as he or she goes off to war, or perhaps it's the mist as it creeps off the shore of a still lake. And sometimes it's just an old building no one else will remember after they tear it down unless you immortalize it with pixels or celluloid. It's all those things and more but you won't catch the essence of a single one if you don't open your eyes and wait." She lowered the camera and turned to Danni. "And that's exactly what you did to catch your shot. You waited for the right moment. I think you may be a natural, kid."

"Really?" Danni's tone was dubious but Erin caught the faint trace of interest hidden behind it. "You think so?"

She met Danni's gaze. "How easily you forget…I don't do or say anything out of courtesy, remember?"

Danni cracked another smile. "It's one of your most enduring character flaws, right?"

Erin laughed. "That's right."

They talked a few minutes more about cameras until Danni spotted a group of kids lounging at the far end of the fountain. Erin followed her gaze. "Those your friends?"

Danni nodded and glanced down at her boots as she dug the toe into the packed snow. "My dad hates them."

Erin lifted her camera and zoomed in. Not exactly the Brady Bunch. She lowered the camera. "Yeah? Why?"

Danni raised her head, snorting. "Because he's a jerk, that's why."

"C'mon, give me more credit than that," Erin said. "There's got to be a better reason."

"Well, I guess he doesn't like them because I've gotten in trouble a few times since I started hanging out with them."

"Sounds like a pretty good reason," Erin acknowledged, pausing to put away her camera. She met Danni's sudden defensive stare. "Don't you think?"

Danni's chin went up a notch. "They're my friends."

"What happened to your old friends? The ones you used to hang out with?"

"They're around."

"And why don't you want to hang out with them anymore?"

The baby brown of Danni's eyes darkened and her mouth turned down. "I just don't, okay? What's the big deal?"

Erin sighed. Whatever was eating up this kid was big enough to send her running from her old friends so they didn't see her pain. The reaction was something Erin could relate to. She could remember keeping to herself throughout high school if only to avoid the inevitable questions about her mom. For some reason having a mother who killed herself and the town drunk as a father made great conversation fodder in the opinion of other people. "Just don't do anything you can't take back when it's all said and done," Erin cautioned, catching the fleeting appearance of sadness in Danni's expression before it changed to defiance.

"I was arrested the other day," she said, her tone almost daring Erin to pass judgment.

"How was it?"

Danni blinked. "What do you mean?"

"Did you enjoy the experience?"

"Not really," Danni admitted, sounding oddly disappointed. Then, she brightened. "But it really freaked my dad out. He was so mad I thought his head was going to explode."

He was probably worried, too, Erin added silently. "So, you want to fill me in as to why you're trying to make your dad's life miserable?"

It was a bold question, one she wouldn't have been surprised if Danni completely ignored, but the hesitation Danni offered instead gave Erin hope that perhaps she was ready to share. Erin knew how it felt to keep something bottled up inside, needing someone to talk to yet fearing the vulnerability that followed and she hated to see a kid as young as Danni carrying such a heavy load alone. The pause lengthened and Erin tried not to let her disappointment show.

"He lied...about my mom," Danni began, then looked up quickly to gauge Erin's reaction, as if waiting to see if she believed her. When Erin didn't say anything she continued. "He told me she died in a car accident when I was a baby...but she really died of a drug overdose five years ago."

The open misery reflecting in Danni's face accentuated just how young she was despite the fact she was blossoming into a young woman. Erin bit her lip and frowned, wondering what to say. She didn't want to offer something like "Your dad must've had a good reason" because, frankly, she didn't know if he did. She really didn't know him at all. He seemed like a good guy but what did she know? "How'd you find out?"

"I was cleaning my dad's office for him." She lifted her shoulder in a flip motion. "I was going to surprise him. And I found the death certificate."

Yikes. "That's rough, kid," Erin murmured in commiseration and Danni nodded in agreement. "What'd he say when you found it?"

"He got mad." She looked away but not before Erin caught the sudden sparkle of tears in her eyes. When she started talking again Erin could see the effort it took to keep her bottom lip from trembling. "He yelled at me."

Erin wanted to draw her into her arms like Caroline used to when she was hurting, but she wasn't sure how such an act would be received. "I'll bet your dad feels real bad about yelling at you," she offered, to which Danni gave a valiant attempt to appear as if she didn't care. "Has he told you why he chose to lie to you about your mom?"

Danni swallowed and shook her head. "He doesn't want to talk about it. He just keeps saying it was for my own good." Anger crept into her voice. "What's that supposed to mean?"

Erin didn't know. She had a feeling Caroline had kept things from her for the very same reasons and she couldn't exactly say it had done her a whole helluva lot of good. If that was the reason Colin was keeping the truth from his daughter she had to disagree with his motives. "So, is this—" she pointed toward the motley group of kids across the square "—your plan to get back at him?"

"What if it is?" Danni shot back.

Erin sighed, recognizing the bravado for the pain of a broken heart. Hadn't she refused all contact with her father as punishment for what he'd done?

Except the situations were completely different, a voice in her head growled at her attempt to draw parallels. She shifted uncomfortably. "Danni, I understand how you feel. My mom died when I was a baby and I still don't know why. I think my family was trying to protect me, too, but that doesn't make you feel any better when you have questions no one can answer. But don't let it make you do something you'll regret later. Hanging out with kids like that could get you into more trouble than you bargained for."

"I know what I'm doing," Danni countered, though her tone wasn't as confident as the words.

"I hope so," Erin said, knowing already the girl was in over her head with those kids, but what could she do?

Shouldering her bag, she started walking toward the Tahoe, hoping Danni would follow. She wasn't disappointed. Erin opened the hatch and slid her camera bag inside. "I'm planning to take some more pictures tomorrow. You're welcome to tag along if you want. I might even have a camera you can borrow."

"Really?" Danni answered, her tone instantly excited until she must have realized how eager she sounded. "I mean, I'll think about it."

Offering Danni a small grin, she scribbled her cell phone number on a piece of scratch paper she found in her camera bag, handed it to her and said, "You let me know." Climbing into her vehicle, she hoped Danni would take the bait. A moment later,

Erin had to bite back her smile when Danni waved to catch her attention.

The kid looked younger than her thirteen years as she stood on the side of the road, shifting from foot to foot. Erin didn't blame Colin for not wanting his pretty, fair-haired daughter around that bunch. "Yeah?" she asked.

"Um…could you maybe drive me home?"

"Sure." Erin shrugged, the movement carefully orchestrated to hide the immense relief she was feeling at the request. She knew it wouldn't fix the problem but at least for tonight, Danni would be right where she belonged—at home with her dad.

CHAPTER NINE

ERIN STOOD BEFORE GRANITE HILLS Medical and wondered if the frigid air had short-circuited her brain. Spending time with Danni yesterday had pricked her conscience in ways she didn't even realize were sensitive, and this morning, shortly after gulping down a cup of instant coffee, she found herself heading into town with one destination in mind.

It was what Caroline would've wanted her to do, she muttered when her feet refused to take her into the building. As if she were standing right beside her, Erin heard Caroline's voice plead Charlie's case.

He's still your father.

Genetically—yes. Emotionally? Never.

A sliver of their last telephone conversation came back to Erin.

"People make mistakes," Caroline had said. "But your daddy's not as bad as you think he is. Sometimes people do things they regret. And, sometimes the things they are most ashamed of are the things that were done out of survival."

Erin knew all about survival. Dragging her beaten

body down the road to Caroline's house in the middle of the night had been an act of survival, she'd wanted to retort with all the bitterness in her heart.

In her whole life Erin had never been rude to her Aunt Caroline but that comment, delivered with such soft conviction, had nearly caused Erin to slam the phone down. Didn't she remember what had happened that night?

Erin shuddered, pushed both memories from her mind and stared up at the building, wondering why nothing ever changed in this place.

She sighed and let her gaze rove the area. The hospital was located at the edge of town, but even if it'd been plopped right smack in the center the place wouldn't have changed. There was an unhurried quality here that Erin had forgotten.

The sun was rapidly disappearing behind a new storm front, taking any semblance of heat with it, and Erin knew she'd freeze if she stayed outside much longer.

Drawing a deep breath as she approached the receptionist, Erin prepared to utter words that were foreign to her mouth.

"I'm here to see Charlie McNulty," she said, as she rubbed warmth back into her frozen appendages. "I believe he's in ICU?"

"Are you family?" The blue-haired volunteer peered from beneath her bifocals.

"Y-yes." Erin swallowed, then forced a brittle smile. "May I see him? I've come a long way."

"Sign your name here." She pointed to a clipboard, which held a sign-in sheet. After giving Erin's signature a quick once-over, the receptionist revealed the room number. "Only two at a time. Hospital rules."

Erin rounded the corner and found the double doors leading to the ICU. Placing her hand against the smooth metal, she hesitated for the barest of seconds before giving the door a gentle push. In her mind she was prepared for what she'd see. In reality, it was another story.

She'd known it was going to be uncomfortable facing the man she'd happily left behind, but the feelings ricocheting through her were stronger than discomfort and shockingly more disconcerting.

Tubes and wires wound their way from his body like something out of an H.R. Giger drawing. His face was nearly unrecognizable in its swollen, bruised and scratched state. Erin's heart did a strange stuttering beat and her feet felt rooted to the spot. The last time she'd seen her father he'd been robust, drunk, and pissed off. The man before her was a stranger.

Where was the guy who'd thrown his bottle of Jose Cuervo at the cops when they'd come to remove her from the home? The man who'd only been subdued after four officers practically dog-piled him?

It was surreal to be standing there. Her gaze traveled over his still form. The anger that had been vivid only yesterday was inexplicably absent, leaving a hollow void in its place.

"D-Dad?" What was she supposed to say? Everything that came to mind sounded trite at best and insincere at worst. But anything was probably better than just standing there. She cleared her voice and tried again. "Can you hear me? It's Erin."

His eyelids twitched and Erin held her breath. It was an odd thing to be torn between hoping he'd awaken and praying he wouldn't. Whether her heart's desire had been answered or ignored was anyone's guess, but Charlie didn't stir.

Erin closed her eyes against the memory of their last encounter, still fresh in her mind despite the years that'd passed.

The Charlie she'd known had been indomitable, fearsome and damn near incorrigible. A disquieting sense of vertigo stole her equilibrium and she clutched at the handrail for balance.

Everything was wrong with this scenario. She didn't know how to feel or even how to act faced with her father's mortality.

An ugly gurgling sound interrupted her private crisis and she looked around in alarm, searching for help. Surely a noise like that wasn't a good sign. He couldn't just die right there in front of her. Something mean clamped down on her heart and made her suck for air.

To her immediate relief, a nurse quickly entered just as an alarm sounded and she made adjustments to the machine monitoring his vitals. She offered Erin a brief smile. "Sorry," she said. "It does that when the IV fluids are low. I hope it didn't startle you too much."

Erin swallowed and shook her head, though her heart was beating like it was trying to escape her chest. Giving herself a mental shake to get a grip, she backed away from the bedside.

What was she doing here? This was insane. It wasn't like a happy reunion was in their future. They didn't have a future at all.

DANNI FIDGETED WITH THE strap on her father's digital camera and waited anxiously for Erin to arrive. They were going to shoot more pictures today after school. She wasn't sure where they were going, but she was up for anything that kept her from spending time with her dad.

Who was she kidding? She missed her dad. They used to do all sorts of things together. Tobogganing down Sanguigan Hill was her favorite. They'd stay out until their fingers were numb from the cold and their snow pants were nearly frozen stiff. Afterward, it was their tradition to share a heart attack special—double-decker cheeseburger with an order of chili cheese fries—at Sammi's. Sometimes, they'd even split a sundae. Up until this point, Danni had thought her life was pretty good; now, her life sucked.

Danni thought of Erin and wondered how much longer she was going to hang around Granite Hills. Probably not long, she realized with an unhappy frown. Once she finished her personal business and got enough pictures for her assignment Danni doubted it would take much longer after that for Erin to hop the next plane out of this place. She sighed. She didn't blame her. If she could leave, she would, too.

Danni glanced out the window, relieved to see Erin's SUV pull into the drive. Finally! As she grabbed her jacket, her cell phone rang and she paused long enough to see who it was.

Allen.

She bit her lip, wondering if she should answer. Erin's horn beeped and she made the decision to shut her phone off. He'd probably never call her again; he was always accusing her of being too young to hang out with him and his friends, but Danni had proven to him that she was no baby. The memory of that night came to her in uncomfortable detail and Danni grimaced as the feeling of being forever stained invaded her system.

Erin beeped again and Danni slid her arms into her jacket, almost glad that she wasn't taking Allen's call. There was no telling what he'd want her to do this time.

IT WAS EARLY EVENING BEFORE Colin got home. The sight of the darkened house caused alarm to ring his senses. Danni was supposed to be home by now but he knew just by looking that the house was empty.

Maybe she went to the library, he reasoned as his stomach muscles started to spasm with worry.

Or maybe she's out with that hoodlum Allen Johnson again. The kid had a rap sheet longer than most adults and Colin didn't want him anywhere near his baby girl. Yet, Danni had taken a shine to the bad boy; no doubt, to piss him off.

Opening the door, he called her name, hoping for once she was hiding in her bedroom.

No answer.

He went through the house, calling her name, only to receive silence in return.

Damn it!

Grabbing the cordless, he quickly called both his sisters to find if Danni had stopped by. The surprised tone of their voices when he asked told him all he needed to know. Danni hadn't been there, either.

Dialing the station, he quickly apprised Joe of the situation, asking if the night patrol could keep an eye out for her.

"I know it's a lot to ask," he said, grimacing at the bitter taste in his mouth as the acid in his gut started to eat away at the lining of his stomach.

"No problem, Col," assured the dispatcher. "If she's out there, we'll bring her home. Don't worry."

Right.

"Thanks, Joe," he muttered, knowing worry was all he could do these days when it came to his daughter. "I owe you one, buddy."

Joe laughed. "We've all had teenagers, Col. It's part and parcel of those so-called growing pains."

If only.

Colin accepted Joe's sentiment and hung up. Suddenly, the light of headlamps flashed through his living room as someone pulled into the driveway and Colin was up and out the front door two seconds later.

"Where have you been?" he nearly shouted, as

Danni emerged from the passenger side of what he realized was Erin's SUV. "I've been worried sick."

The driver-side door opened before Danni could answer and Erin intercepted, her expression instantly apologetic. "I'm so sorry, we lost track of time. I'd thought we'd be back before sunset but this happens a lot when I get into a groove. Time ceases to exist." She flashed Danni a proud smile, faltering only a little when she noted the mutinous expression Danni was sending his way. "You have quite the budding photographer here. Um…am I missing something?"

"She was with you?" Colin asked, his pulse slowly returning to normal.

"Didn't you get the note?" Erin asked, shooting Danni a confused look. "You did write one, right?"

Danni shrugged. "I guess I forgot."

"To your room, missy," Colin instructed sternly. "We'll talk about this later."

Danni stalked past Colin without seeming the least bit apologetic and all the good feelings Erin had had that day quickly evaporated. "I don't know what to say," she admitted, feeling like a complete idiot for not asking Colin's permission to take Danni. "I should've checked first."

"Yes, you should have."

The stern rebuke, although warranted, made her bristle. "I said, I know that."

"You can't just take off with someone's kid and not let them know where they are. Do you realize if any of the patrol guys had caught you with Danni they might've hauled you in for kidnapping?"

"Why would they do that?"

"Because I'd just called and told them she was missing. How was I supposed to know she was with you?"

"Well, how was I supposed to know Danni hadn't left you a note?"

His expression faltered as he considered her point. "Well, you still should've called," he added.

"Point taken. It won't happen again."

"Thank you," he said, blowing a short breath as if he'd been holding it, the action only making Erin feel worse.

"I should go." *Before I can do any more damage to this family.* Colin started to say something but Erin wasn't in the mood to listen. She climbed into the Tahoe even as Colin approached.

"Erin, wait...."

She paused before closing the door. "What?"

Although the lines of frustration were still bracketing his eyes, there was something else there as well. A long moment went by as he struggled to put into words what was showing in his expression. "This is the second time you've kept my daughter safe. I'm sorry I snapped," he admitted, his mouth drawing to a tight line. "At first I thought she was hanging out with that kid, Allen, and I went out of my mind with worry. I'm sorry."

Erin felt herself softening, wishing Danni knew what a good father she had. "I don't blame you for worrying." When Colin raised an eyebrow in question, she explained. "Generally, I'm not one to judge by appearances but if Allen is a kid who looks about sixteen and hangs out with a posse that would do Snoop Dogg proud, I'd worry, too."

His expression disintegrated and Erin could almost feel the weight dragging on his shoulders. "You need to tell her the truth," she murmured without thinking.

"What?" Colin looked at her sharply and Erin cursed her inability to keep her mouth shut when it really mattered. "What did you say?"

Now you've done it. Well, since she'd already put her foot into it, she thought with a resigned sigh… She met Colin's inquiring stare. "Tell her the truth. That's what she needs from you."

Colin stiffened. "You don't know what my daughter needs."

"Yeah? Well, apparently, neither do you," Erin shot back, bristling all over again at his tone.

"I think I know how to raise my daughter," he said, pulling away, his tone so defensive she almost felt sorry for him. *Almost.*

"Yeah, I can tell you're really doing a bang-up job of reaching her when she needs you the most. Interesting technique."

Colin glowered at her but Erin held her ground. She knew how it felt to be the last to know what was going on when it was nobody else's business. She really didn't care what Colin's reasons were for keeping the truth from Danni. If the kid wanted to know, she had a right to. Plain and simple.

A tense silence followed and Erin wondered how

long she should wait for him to say something. She wasn't quite sure what she expected him to say, but she didn't feel right leaving it like this. "Colin—"

"I appreciate you bringing her home," he interrupted stiffly, obviously still smarting from her blunt observation. He turned to go back inside, leaving Erin to stare after him. The door closed behind him and Erin shook her head. *Men.* She was half-tempted to follow and demand an apology for his attitude, when she was only trying to help him reach his daughter.

Don't get involved, McNulty, she warned herself. *You've got your own problems.* If he didn't want her help, she shouldn't force it on him.

The last thing Colin needed was for her to start meddling in something she had absolutely no experience in fixing. And if she started to forget that small fact, all she had to do was bring up the image of Charlie, lying broken and defeated, to remind her.

Her breath hitched in her throat and something too close to regret threatened to swamp her mind and drown out her good sense.

"Oh, Caroline," she murmured, wiping away a suspicious drop of moisture from her eyes. "A little advice wouldn't be uncalled for in this instance… because I don't know what the hell I'm doing anymore!"

THE FOLLOWING MORNING ERIN opened both eyes reluctantly. The distinctive chirping of chickadees preening for the attention of a new mate just outside

Erin's window was more effective than any alarm clock, but unfortunately lacked a snooze button. Throwing an arm over her eyes to blot out the bright sunlight that was attempting to thaw the frozen landscape, she knew the effort was useless. Within minutes she'd be fully awake.

Her thoughts still fuzzy from sleep, she offered little resistance when her mind returned to the events of last night.

Why'd she stick her nose into it? It wasn't as if she knew them very well, anyway.

Danni.

The kid was practically screaming for her dad to validate the pain she was suffering, yet he refused to start the healing process by telling her what she needed to know. Erin wondered if it would've made a difference in her life if Caroline had been forthright with her about whatever had happened in the past. Of course, it didn't matter now, but it could matter in Danni's case. She was poised at a precipice and Erin couldn't just watch her dangle on the edge without at least throwing her something to hold onto. Honestly, she thought irritably, why couldn't Colin see what was so obvious?

She groaned, pushing a vision of Colin's wounded expression from her memory and choosing to remember a less complicated time.

He wasn't hard on the eyes but he was almost as stubborn as she was. Before she realized it was even there, a tiny smile played on her lips.

Snuggling deeper into the blankets, she pushed

away those types of thoughts and drifted into a hazy dream state.

A small fragile dragonfly carved from a hunk of white wood materialized in her mind, perched on the surface of a dresser that looked familiar. Larger than actual size but detailed to the point of delicacy, it looked as if it waited for a stiff breeze to put it to flight.

Erin slowly opened her eyes, still wrapped in the warmth of the dream. Had it been real? Erin couldn't remember owning a whittled dragonfly but the vision in her mind didn't recede like most dream imagery, it remained vivid, almost as if she had seen it just yesterday. An inexplicable sense of loss filled her. Where was the dragonfly now? After another long moment spent searching her memories and finding nothing that matched, she gave up and grudgingly dismissed the vision as nothing more than mental garbage, meant to be forgotten in the light of day.

She heard Butterscotch walk into the room and whine softly, reminding her of her new responsibilities as a pet owner. "Hold your horses," she grumbled as the dog licked her chops and whined again. "I know, I know, you're hungry and you probably need to go to the bathroom. Well, join the club."

Rubbing the sleep from her eyes and shivering as she pushed the thick blankets from her body, she donned her robe and slippers and left the cold room and its unsettling images behind.

After letting Butterscotch out the front door, she wandered into the kitchen with a yawn. As she skirted the large antique table that was one of Caroline's most prized possessions, she tried not to think of what she was going to do with it. Her apartment was entirely too small for a table that seated six, without the leaf, but she couldn't just sell it. Caroline used to tell her the story of how her great grandmother, Mum-Mum, had brought it over from Europe by boat in the early 1900s.

Opening the refrigerator, she pulled out a carton of orange juice and gave it a sniff before pouring herself a glass. As she sipped the juice, all the while wishing it was a hot cup of coffee, her mind returned to the dragonfly of her dreams. She frowned as she knew without a doubt she'd seen it before. Where, she wasn't sure.

Setting down her half-empty glass, she walked to the pantry, ostensibly to find something to eat that didn't require firing up the stove, but when her search found a photo box perched upon the top shelf, her hunger disappeared as she removed the box and sat down at the table to survey the contents.

Erin lifted the lid. She sucked in a surprised breath as she saw pictures of her mother. Lifting one, then another, she realized she'd never seen them before.

"Oh, Caroline—" She released the breath she'd been holding to sift through the pile, torn between wanting to examine each one for minute details and desperately tearing through them like a starving woman who'd just caught a whiff of New York steak on the grill. "What is this?" she whispered.

She examined the one in her hand, two girls linked arm in arm, smiling for the camera. They could almost pass as twins. Both shared jet-black hair secured by thick white swaths of ribbon, short white, sleeveless dresses and matching patent-leather sling-backs.

She flipped the picture and read the back, the words written in the playful penmanship of a young girl.

Me and Rosie. Sept. '64.

It was surreal staring at her mother, a woman she'd never been given the chance to know, yet Erin was transfixed by the cache of pictures in her hands. More of the same greeted her as she quickly went through the box.

Sudden tears crowded her sinuses but Erin held them back as she returned to the first photo. The girl in the picture had been happy. What caused a girl who looked like that to kill herself? What kind of woman robbed her daughter of knowing her? Had being a mother been so horrible?

Replacing the picture, she carefully shut the box and clamped hard on the urge to succumb to the awful rending in her heart. Why hadn't Caroline showed her these pictures? Why had she kept them from her? Erin stared at the box, the questions it raised pushing away her grief and replacing it with a potent mixture of anger and frustration. She needed answers.

At one time her mother had posed for the camera, mindless of her slightly crooked front tooth and lopsided grin. Laughter had erupted from her lips and happiness had shone in her eyes.

What had sucked the joy out of her smile? What had changed her from the girl who'd loved life to the woman who'd discarded it?

The common denominator was obvious. Charlie. It would seem hers was not the only life he'd ruined with his selfish disregard for others. Yet, she thought with a troubled frown, Caroline would never abandon him—no matter what he'd done to Rose. A flutter of trepidation grew in her stomach until she could no longer ignore it. Perhaps Colin was right about the past having something to do with the accident. She couldn't imagine how but she knew something wasn't right. Forgetting about breakfast, she left the box on the table and hurried upstairs to get dressed. She needed to talk to Colin right now.

CHAPTER TEN

AS SHE DROVE INTO TOWN, the questions that had started with the discovery of the box continued to play through her mind. Apparently, there was much her beloved Aunt Caroline had kept close to her breast, only Erin had been too self-absorbed to notice or care. Snippets of a past phone conversation with Caroline rang in her mind.

"You know, I'm not the only one who finds the single life rewarding," she'd retorted after Caroline had brought up the subject of her single status yet again. "Why didn't *you* remarry after your husband died?"

Caroline, startled by the unexpected topic, sounded flustered. "Oh, goodness," she exclaimed. "It's been so long I hardly remember my reasons by now." She chuckled, but the effort was forced. "What an odd question. What made you ask that?"

"I was just curious. I don't remember much about him and I just wondered what kind of man had captured my favorite aunt's heart, I suppose."

Another nervous chuckle and Erin's smile had faded, wondering what Caroline wasn't saying.

"Hank was a one of a kind, that's for sure. Lord, that was a long time ago."

"Hard act to follow?" supplied Erin, hoping her aunt must have found all other men lacking after her husband died. It was exactly the type of romanticism she'd expect of Caroline.

"You could say that," she answered, making Erin wonder at her evasiveness.

She hadn't grasped the significance of their conversation at the time, but suddenly Erin realized how little she knew about her aunt's past. Hank had died around the same time as her mother and she'd been too young to remember either with any clarity. There weren't any pictures of him in the box, or out of the box for that matter, and she was ashamed to admit she'd never asked why. That ominous feeling returned for no good reason other than she felt something bad was coming her way and she could do nothing to stop it.

WITH HIS THOUGHTS STILL CENTERING on Erin and the unexpected effect she was having on his life, Colin walked straight to his desk, almost missing the cordial hellos from passing colleagues.

"How's the home life treating you?" Leslie asked, coming to lean against the partition, the rookie Missy Reznick right behind her. "Things getting better between you and the Rugrat?"

Colin looked up from his paperwork long enough to smile but didn't elaborate. He didn't much feel like sharing right at the moment, especially in front of Missy. "What's up, O'Bannon?" he asked, cutting the invitation for chitchat.

"That good, huh?" Leslie grinned, seeing right through him. Colin allowed a smile and she handed him a slip of paper. "I figured you might want to see this right away. It's the mechanic's report on the McNulty investigation. The plot thickens. Seems someone tried to off old Charlie just like you thought."

Missy leaned forward, eager as most rookies were to be a part of the action, until a look from Leslie sent her back to her place. Leslie as a training officer, Colin chuckled silently, was a rough gig for a newbie.

Quickly scanning to see for himself, Colin felt a grim satisfaction in knowing that his gut instinct had been on target. "'Partial cut through the brake line,'" he read.

"Yep." Leslie shook her head. "Boy, that family has tragedy written all over them."

"So I hear."

"What'd you find out?"

Colin paused and Leslie sensed the reason for his hesitation. She turned to Missy, who was once again crowding her. "You know that stack of old case files I showed you earlier?"

"Yeah," Missy replied, her expression wary as Leslie smiled.

"It's got your name all over it. Remember," she added as Missy turned to leave, clearly unhappy with her task, "file by case number, not date."

"Right," Missy grumbled, sending one last look Colin's way as if asking for his intervention, but when he only offered a smile and a short wave she had no choice but to follow orders.

"Thanks," he said, knowing Leslie would understand the sensitive nature of his investigation.

"No problem. She was invading my space anyway. So, whatcha got?"

"Well, just that Erin's mom killed herself when Erin was barely out of diapers and a week before that Caroline's husband, Hank, died in a bad car accident near to the same place Charlie wrecked his truck. Did I miss anything?"

"Sounds about right." Leslie sighed. "You know, I feel bad for Erin. It's not like you can pick your family."

"Was there ever any question as to whether the accident was truly an accident?"

"Hank Walker's?" Leslie asked, her forehead furrowing. He nodded and she pursed her lips as if unsure whether or not to share. Finally, she relented. "Well, there was some scuttlebutt about the crash but I was just a kid. I don't remember the details. Why do you ask?"

"Just something the bartender down at the Lucky Coin said."

"Yeah? What'd he say?"

"Said the last time he saw Charlie was a few months ago. He ordered his usual, but didn't touch a drop…just stared at it all night. Then he mumbled something about 'making right with the past' and left."

He looked at Leslie. "Does that make any sense to you?"

Leslie shrugged. "Well, rumor has it that Hank's accident and Charlie's wife's suicide were linked. Maybe Charlie was aiming to come clean about what he knows."

"How were the two incidents connected?"

She shrugged. "Not sure. But you'd be surprised how easy it is to cover something up in a small town. I'm sure there's a report buried in the archive somewhere and even some newspaper articles. But you aren't going to find anything of value. The trail's been covered for years and the only person left on the force from those days is the chief."

He looked up quickly. "The chief?"

"Yeah, he was a young officer then. Almost fresh out of the academy. His daddy was the chief before him. It was a shoe-in that he'd get on the department. Back then, the rules against nepotism weren't as strict."

"So, he should know something about the case, then...."

She stopped him. "I don't think that's such a good idea."

"Why?"

"It's just not."

"No reason?"

The jocularity had long faded from her voice, leaving unease in its wake. "It's old country gossip but I'd heard rumors here and there that the chief was once in love with Erin's mom, before she married

Charlie. Who knows if it's true. I think it caused a huge rift between him and Charlie. They were supposed to be best friends at one time."

"You're sure about this?"

Leslie shook her head. "Of course I'm not sure. Like I said, a lot of it is pure gossip, but it was big enough to keep this town whispering about it for years. Hell, I'll bet if you go down to Barclay's barber shop, you'll still find some old-timers who'd love to tell you about the Granite Hills scandal."

His heart sank at the image of a young Erin left to stand alone against the rumors.

"Listen, that stuff's old news, best left alone. You know? I'm sure whoever had a beef big enough with Charlie to mess with his brakes had nothing to do with the accident that happened on Old Copper. It's probably just a weird coincidence."

"Probably..." he acknowledged. "Thanks, O'Bannon."

"Sure." She turned to leave, then paused, giving Colin a wry look. "Just do me a favor...don't go and get yourself into trouble. I'd hate to have to come and rescue you."

Colin chuckled and returned to his desk to begin compiling dates. He needed to know which files to pull and figure out where they might be in the archives. Otherwise, he'd be up to his eyeballs in dusty boxes looking for what could turn out to be a needle in a haystack.

CHAPTER ELEVEN

ON THE WAY TO THE STATION Erin detoured to Granite Hills Medical. She wasn't sure why she was making the effort but she felt compelled to check on Charlie's status. As she made her way to his room, she ignored the waves of anxiety that made her feel like retching and pushed forward with single-minded determination. Whether she liked it or not, she was his only living family.

Charlie's doctor was at his bedside, noting his condition and reading his vitals from the chart as she entered.

"You must be Char— I mean, my dad's doctor." She extended a hand for a brief shake, keeping her gaze steady but away from the vision of helplessness her father presented. "Has there been any progress or…" She swallowed. "Or decline in his condition?"

The doctor—identified as Samuel Rivera— pocketed the pen he was using and addressed Erin with a frankness that she could appreciate.

"Your father has suffered a major trauma. While we were able to patch the damage to his liver, the years of alcohol abuse have taken their toll. To be honest, it's just a waiting game. The next few days are crucial to his recovery. Unfortunately, the longer he stays like this—" his gesture forced her gaze to the hospital bed "—the less chance he has of pulling through. I'm sorry."

Erin nodded, thanking him for his honesty. "Is there anything I can do for him?" she asked, not quite sure why the question even popped from her mouth. It wasn't as if she had much experience with offering comfort to her father.

"Studies show talking to a patient can help speed recovery, interacting with them as if they were coherent and participating in the conversation, engaging in some kind of normalcy." When she didn't seem comfortable with that idea, he added, "Or even just holding their hand. Letting them know they're not alone works wonders."

She nodded and the doctor graced her with a short and efficient smile before leaving to check on another patient.

Hold his hand? That technique might work for normal families but the McNulty clan had never subscribed to the average definition of *normal.* Somehow she doubted the hospital staff would appreciate their brand of reaching out. If she'd ever held a semidecent conversation with her father where he wasn't slobbering drunk or she wasn't locking her door and covering her ears against his bellowing, she sure as hell couldn't remember it. The steady hiss of the respirator and bleep of the machine monitoring his vitals drew her attention. A subtle frown formed as she faced her father. There were so many questions yet the answers were locked in his head. If he died, the truth would die with him. Something too close to grief at the thought of losing him roughened her voice as she gave his blanketed foot a subtle shake. "You'd better wake up, you old fart," she muttered. "You're not getting out of your penance this easy. If you think I won't chase you into the hereafter you've got another thing coming. So you can just forget about dying."

"Interesting bedside manner."

Startled, she turned and saw Colin smiling at her. A secret thrill unsettled her stomach but she was relieved to see he wasn't holding their last encounter against her. "You should see our Christmas dinners," she quipped.

He chuckled and removed his hat, taking time to ruffle his hair free of the flattened look before coming to stand beside her. He gestured toward Charlie. "Thought I'd come and check up on him. How's he doing?"

Erin shook her head. "No change, really. The doctor said the longer he stays this way, the less chance he has of pulling through."

"That's rough," he said, genuine sorrow reflecting in his eyes. "This has got to be hell for you."

Erin gave a short nod but didn't elaborate. Instead, she concentrated on quelling the disquieting flutters in her belly. "You know, you didn't have to come all the way down here…you could've placed a phone call," she said, sensing there was more to his visit and conflicted by the hope that his motive was more personal than business.

"You got me," he admitted. "I called the house but you weren't there so I was hoping to find you here."

"Well, you found me. What's going on?" As if reading his mind, she felt the color drain from her cheeks. "Your instincts were right, weren't they? Someone tampered with Charlie's brakes."

His sigh was answer enough. "Whoever did this could get charged with murder."

Someone tried to kill her father and, in doing so, killed Caroline. The realization stole the strength from her legs.

She tried making it to the chair against the window, but Colin caught her just as her knees buckled and she sagged against him for strength.

With one arm slung around his shoulder, he placed her carefully in the chair she'd been aiming for. She murmured an embarrassed apology but Colin waved it away.

"That's a natural reaction, don't beat yourself up over it," he answered, a bit gruffly. "I've seen bigger men faint at less upsetting news. You've got nothing to be ashamed of."

That was easy for him to say. He wasn't the one who'd just crumpled like a Victorian lady with the vapors. She shook her head to clear it but a surreal sense of "I can't believe this is happening" remained.

"Listen," he began, kneeling beside her. "We need to talk. I know you agreed to help but I feel I should be honest with you. I've got a feeling that finding the

answers we both seek might turn up some unpleasant truths about your family."

A familiar chill settled in her body. The whispers,
the looks, the rumors… She met Colin's gaze. "What
kind of unpleasant truths?"

"Not sure," he admitted. "But it has something to
do with your mom's suicide and your Uncle Hank's
death." He raked a hand through his hair in an
agitated manner. "Unfortunately, all I have to go on
are thirty-year-old rumors. The trail is colder than a
Michigan winter and there's no one who wants to
dredge up the past. I think your dad may know the
whole story…and for some reason decided to break
his silence. That's what put him in danger."

"So what do we do?"

"We need to get back to your dad's place, see if
we missed something the first time." He paused, his
facial expression softening. "I know it's not your
favorite place. I promise we'll only stay as long as we
need."

She swallowed and nodded, thankful he understood her reluctance. Drawing a deep breath, she
readied herself for another trip down Memory Lane.
"When do you want to leave?"

ARRIVING AT THE CABIN TWENTY minutes later, Colin
put the SUV in Park and glanced over at Erin. Her
face looked as if it had been chipped from marble
and anxiety radiated from her body. Regret at having
to put her through this again made him reach across
and caress her cheek. Leaning into his touch in a

subtle, almost subconscious gesture, she closed her eyes against the feel of his fingers against her skin. Colin's heart rate quickened and he was overcome with the protective feelings that flooded his chest for a woman he hardly knew but ached to know better. Seconds later, she pulled away and Colin felt her withdrawal as if it were a physical thing.

"Let's get this over with," she said, avoiding eye contact as she exited the vehicle and immediately heading for the cabin.

He waited a moment to reorient himself to the task at hand, then followed.

If he were smart, he'd follow her lead and back off, no matter how deep the attraction went, but he was dangerously drawn to her unique personality and it was almost useless to fight it. His head was still a little muddled when he walked into the cabin.

"Tell me again what we're looking for?" she asked, frustration lacing her tone even as she shivered.

Instead of answering right away, he walked to the woodstove and gave it a cursory inspection. It seemed sound and there was a box of old papers in a wooden crate beside it. "First, we're going to build a fire in this icebox. We can't focus on anything if we're too busy listening to the chatter of our teeth. Does your dad have a woodshed out back?"

She nodded.

"Good. Give me a few minutes and I'll have this place warmed up."

Colin glanced out the window. Dark, ominous

clouds gathered on the horizon, promising another snowstorm before long. He figured they had a few hours before they'd have to get out of there. Otherwise, they'd end up spending the night in this rickety shack.

Within minutes he'd built a serviceable fire in the ancient woodstove and heat was already pouring into the room as the flames devoured the seasoned wood. Erin ceased to shiver and her body began to lose the obvious tension bunching her shoulders.

"What a Boy Scout you are," she murmured with the hint of a smile.

He acknowledged her comment with a grin but it soon faded. It was time to level with her.

"What's wrong?" she asked.

"I don't think we'll find much more than we did the first time we came here," he admitted. "But I figured this was the one place we could talk without fear of being interrupted or being heard."

"You brought me here to talk?" She scowled. "This isn't really a place that encourages me to open up. If anything it makes me want to forget."

"I know," he answered gravely, knowing he had a small window to work with and one wrong move could slam it shut. "And if things weren't as serious as they are, I wouldn't dream of bringing you here. But, as much as you hate this place, it might trigger a memory that could help."

"Colin, you're talking about memories I'd rather leave alone. It's taken me a long time to put the past where it belongs. I know I said I'd help in any way but I'm not sure if I can do what you're asking." Her voice dropped an octave and Colin's heart nearly broke. "I'm afraid I'll never be the same if I go back down that road."

Her lip trembled and the subtle motion tore down his last defense. Without waiting to second-guess how appropriate it was, he closed the distance between them and gathered her in his arms. When she sank against him, burying her nose into his shoulder, he inhaled the subtle scent of her midnight hair that followed her like a gentle breeze. He stroked her back, his fingers lightly dancing up and down her spine, reminding him she was still too thin for her height. He pressed a kiss to her crown and she seemed to move closer, as if craving more, yet unable to ask for it.

"You can trust me," he whispered. "You're not alone this time. I'll be with you every step of the way. And I swear to you, I won't let anything or anyone hurt you."

And that was the bare truth, he realized with a start. She slowly drew away and met his gaze. He could tell she was weighing his words, fighting her instinct to close herself off. Hope blossomed in his chest. He pressed a little harder. "Erin, together we can find the answers that will break this nightmare apart. You've avoided Granite Hills for fourteen years…how long are you willing to give the past that much power over you?"

Her face flushed and Colin thought she was about to cry but no tears appeared. "I don't even know where to start," she said in a husky whisper.

"I'll help you," he answered softly. She was close enough that he could almost reach out and caress the soft spot on her neck where her heartbeat pulsed with a steady rhythm. Fighting the desire to nuzzle the sensitive area, he cleared his throat and headed for the door. "First, I'm going to get a blanket out of the SUV. Be right back."

There was something dangerous happening between them and there was no sense in denying it any longer. Despite the heat filtering through the small room, Erin hugged herself. Colin was a good man and certainly didn't need the trouble that came with her. But not even her conscience could keep her body from craving his touch or her heart from wishing for more than she deserved. When he reappeared with a soft, thick blanket, she couldn't stop the smile from curving her mouth. Grateful he was too busy setting the blanket by the fire to notice the way her eyes lingered on the muscular swell of his biceps, she allowed her gaze to roam. Shaking her head, she wondered if she truly were a glutton for punishment.

"There." Colin dusted his hands on his backside and looked to Erin. "That ought to keep our rears from going numb at least for a while."

Sensing he was waiting for her to make the first move, she nodded her agreement and sank down on the blanket. It was wonderfully soft and fleecy and as her fingers lightly skimmed the material her mind taunted her with images that were neither appropriate nor warranted under the situation. She ducked her head before Colin could see the burn in her cheeks.

"You okay?" he asked, misinterpreting her reaction. "If this is really too hard…"

She waved away his offer, anxious to focus on the reason they were here. "No, you're right. I have to stop letting the past rule my life. Let's begin."

Although concern and a touch of uncertainty remained in his eyes, he pulled a small notebook and pen from his chest pocket. "First, tell me what you were told about the day your mom died."

Erin closed her eyes against the emptiness that always seemed to swallow her soul each time she thought of her mother and pushed forward. "Caroline told me my dad came home to find my mother in the bathtub. She'd slit her wrists sometime earlier and bled to death. By the time my dad arrived, there was no saving her." Although Caroline had never provided the gory details, Erin had a mental snapshot of her mother lying in a tub filled with blood. Bile rose in her throat and she fought the urge to gag. When she opened her eyes again, Colin was watching her tenderly. His presence bolstered her courage and she continued. "I don't really know why she did it. Caroline said something about being depressed but I'm not so sure."

"What do you mean?"

Erin frowned. "Well, I don't have memories per se of her, but more of what you would call fleeting residual feelings. And what I remember is an overall sense of happiness. Plus, this morning I found some pictures of my mother when she was young and she looked far from the kind of person who was depressed."

"Sometimes a depressed person can hide their true emotions so well not even their own mother would know," he answered quietly, his face drawn. "Maybe she just hid it well."

Erin shook her head. "No… I can't explain it— it's a feeling. I think she was really happy."

Colin roused himself from his own thoughts and noted Erin's comments. "Where were you when this happened?"

"With Caroline."

"Caroline?" He flipped through the notebook. Suddenly, he stopped and stared at a page. "But hadn't Caroline lost her husband only a week prior?" At Erin's nod, he shook his head at the information. "Don't you find it odd, that one week after losing her husband she's babysitting for her sister-in-law? Wasn't she grieving?"

Erin shrugged. "I guess… I mean, I don't know I never really asked. But now that you mention it, it does seem a little odd. But, then again, everything about my Uncle Hank is weird."

"How so?"

"As far back as I can remember, there's never been any pictures of him, and Caroline never shared details. It's almost as if he was erased from our family history." *Just like my mother.* A chill shook her as an abhorrent thought came to mind. What if the rumors were true and her mother and Hank were having an affair at the time of their deaths? "In fact, it was only recently I learned my mother and Caroline had been best friends at one time."

Colin's brown eyes lit with a dawning light. "I heard the police chief and your dad were once real tight. Do you know anything about their friendship?"

Erin thought hard. She barely knew Roger Hampton but she did recall times when Roger had brought Charlie home instead of putting him in the drunk tank to sleep off a bender. She'd always just chalked it up to small-town generosity but suddenly it seemed like something more. "Actually, it's nothing specific but when I was a kid he used to come over…before Charlie was drunk all the time." She faltered as memories, long forgotten, flashed in rapid succession. Her dad, cracking a smile at something she'd said or done. Eating cold pork and beans straight from the can and loving it. Sitting at Charlie's feet watching as wood shavings floated to the cracked wooden porch.

"Erin?" Colin's voice broke into her jumbled thoughts and she was overwhelmed by the sheer confusion clouding her brain. "What's wrong? Tell me."

Erin threaded her fingers through her hair, agitated. Wrong? Everything. What were these memories? It was as if someone had suddenly implanted another person's life in her head. Her father laughing? She couldn't remember a time when her father wasn't yelling or at the very least growling. She shook her head, not knowing exactly what to say, how to communicate that her whole world had just been challenged. In the end, she said nothing, forcing her mind to return to Colin's original question. "Roger Hampton stopped coming around when I was about six, I think. I remember a lot of arguing and then he never came back on social calls. If he came at all, it was to drop Charlie off after he was so far gone he wouldn't have known if Santa Claus had given him a ride home on his sleigh. So to answer your question, I guess they were friends at one time but I don't know what happened between them."

"Is it possible the falling-out was about your mother?" he ventured carefully. When she didn't immediately answer, he added, "The other thing I heard was that at one time the chief and your dad were in love with the same woman."

Erin's mind wandered to the vibrant, smiling girl immortalized in the picture sitting in Caroline's box in the pantry, and a sharp pain pierced her chest. "I suppose that's possible. She was very beautiful."

"If she looked anything like her daughter I can understand how two friends might have gone their separate ways," he murmured.

Erin looked away, shamed by the hot tears immediately flooding her eyes. Caroline had often told her she was a carbon copy of her mother. It was a compliment that never failed to raise conflicting feelings. She ached to know her mother yet somehow looking similar was a pain that rivaled the emptiness in her life. "Colin..." she managed to croak, and in seconds she was cradled in his arms.

He held her until her silent tears stopped coursing down her cheeks. He seemed to sense she needed his physical comfort more than reassuring words. His solid strength was a balm against the torn edges of her exposed heart and it felt good. What was happening between them? And why wasn't she fighting it? As if in answer, he leaned slowly to meet her lips in a soft kiss.

Melting inside, she opened her mouth to his and her fingers were soon traveling up his neck to twine in his thick hair. Their tongues touched, sparking an ember-hot heat and before Erin knew or cared how it had happened, she was lying in the soft cushion of the blanket, pressed beneath the welcome weight of Colin's body. He made love to her with his mouth until she was tearing at his clothes, eager to feel his skin against her own.

His hands, rough and masculine, were a tantalizing torture as they roamed her skin, making her forget the anguish of her past if only for a few precious moments. Wrapped in his arms, crushed under his weight, she was far from her memories. She groaned as his mouth closed on her nipple and she embraced the oblivion that followed. The freedom was intoxicating. Her last coherent thought left as Colin took possession of her body, his expression, both fervent and intent, beautifully captured in her mind's eye, forever replacing what she considered breathtaking.

Later, as she drowsed in his arms, warmed by the glow of the fire and the reassuring presence of Colin's body, she knew it couldn't happen again, but she was content to enjoy the moment while it lasted.

CHAPTER TWELVE

COLIN WAS UNSURE HOW it happened but he wasn't sorry it had. His only fear, as he glanced down at Erin snuggled at his side, was that she would come to regret their interlude and pull away. As if trying to stop that from happening, he pulled her closer against him. She seemed to mold perfectly to his body, almost as though she'd been made for him. He smirked at his own thoughts. Most cops didn't believe in fate. They believed in the here and now because circumstance could change your life in the blink of an eye. Yet, here he was wondering if he'd just managed to find his soul mate in a woman who was as skittish as a feral cat. He wasn't a fool. Just because they'd made love didn't mean she meant to stay. He couldn't think of that right now. First, he had a job to do. Then, he'd deal with his feelings.

She shifted against him and he knew she was awake. He met her clear-eyed gaze, hoping he didn't see regret creeping into her eyes. When she stretched against him with a satisfied smile, he relaxed.

"Do you always conclude your interviews like this?" she asked, playfully.

He chuckled. "This isn't something they taught at the academy."

"I should hope not." Erin snuggled against him and his arm closed around her. She sighed and he knew how she felt. They remained in each other's arms for another long moment until finally she moved away. He tried not to let his disappointment show but he wasn't ready for this to end.

She dressed quickly and he reluctantly followed her lead.

"You know, I can't remember ever being warm in this place," she remarked softly, staring into the flames. "Once I tried building a fire but it was green and all it did was smoke. I was so cold my teeth had stopped chattering. I think I was close to hypothermia. If Caroline hadn't shown up…" She looked to Colin, then shrugged. "But she did and I spent the entire winter with her that year."

"How old were you?" he asked.

"Nine or ten. I don't even remember Charlie coming around to see if I was all right."

"You spent a lot of time with Caroline growing up, didn't you?"

She nodded. "She was like the mom I never had. And I guess, I was like the daughter she never had. It worked both ways I suppose."

A minute passed, the silence a comfortable thing between them, until he felt Erin become restless. When he found her gaze, it was troubled. "What is it?"

He could tell she was weighing her answer, won-

dering if she should share what was on her mind, and
Colin gently pushed a stray strand of hair from her
face. She stared at him intently and he almost felt as
if he were being measured against an invisible yard-
stick. "Why won't you tell Danni what happened to
her mother?"

Colin drew away, feeling the intimacy of the
moment fade. Why couldn't she just let him handle
it his way? "I don't think that's what's best for her
right now."

"I disagree." She paused then plunged forward
despite what he knew wasn't an inviting expression
on his face. "All my life I sensed something terrible
had happened in my family, something no one would
talk about, except behind my back. Please don't do
that to Danni. Don't let her go her entire life wondering what had been so awful that you had to lie to
her. If she asked, she's ready to know."

He snorted and moved away, the distance
between them growing by the minute, but she
wouldn't back down.

"She's a smart kid. Give her some credit. I think
she can handle whatever you've been hiding from
her." When he didn't offer more resistance, she
pressed a little harder, this time he sensed from
personal curiosity. "Why did you lie to Danni about
her mom?"

Colin ran a hand through his hair, hating how the
story sounded to his own ears, but it started to come
out anyway. "I did what I thought was best at the
time but I never thought when the time came to tell

her the truth it would go this badly. As she got older, I realized I never wanted her to know the truth."

"And what is this horrible secret that's worth destroying your relationship?"

He expelled a short breath, hoping the action would dispel the ache in his chest, but all he needed to do was glance over at Erin to have it blossom behind his sternum again. He felt sick about the situation with Danni and Erin was right. It wasn't getting better. He shook his head, defeated. "Danielle was sick. Not with cancer or anything like that—" Hell, he would've welcomed cancer at one point, he thought selfishly. "She was diagnosed manic-depressive with psychotic tendencies when Danni was a baby. In fact, if I hadn't come home unexpectantly I wouldn't have Danni at all." At Erin's puzzled expression, he decided to stop beating around the bush and just tell her, like ripping a Band-Aid off in one fell swoop. "I walked in on Danielle smothering Danni in her crib."

Erin gasped but he continued, intent on getting this over with. "Danielle had been hallucinating for weeks, seeing things that weren't there, bugs mostly, but she refused to take the medication the doctor said would help. She claimed she didn't need it and I was too busy, fresh out of the academy, trying to make a name for myself on the force to insist she take it. We were both young and I figured she'd get better. Plus, I never really thought Danni was in danger." His throat closed and he needed a moment before he could speak again. "The thing is, I realized Danni would never be safe with Danielle because she didn't believe she was sick. I tried sticking it out but I was too young to handle a sick wife and a child and I took the coward's way out. I filed for divorce," he said, hanging his head in shame at his selfishness. "Getting sole custody was relatively easy. Danielle defaulted when she never showed up for court. Danni and I moved to Granite Hills not long after."

"What happened to Danielle?" Erin asked.

"She was in and out of hospitals for a few years. She'd get better when she was on her meds and I'd receive a letter from my attorney stating she was suing for joint custody, but she'd go off her meds again and she'd disappear. It went on like that for years, until one day I received a letter stating she'd overdosed on prescription-grade morphine. A death certificate followed."

"How did someone with Danielle's medical history get a hold of morphine?" Erin asked, voicing one of Colin's first questions to the investigating officer. "I mean, it's not like you can get it off the streets like crack or heroine."

"I know. But before Danielle got sick, she'd just finished her nursing degree. According to the report, she faked credentials and managed to walk into a small community hospital, procure what she was looking for and walk out."

"So, she killed herself." It was a statement, not a question.

He nodded. "She didn't leave a note but it seems fairly obvious. Danielle knew how much to give herself to do the job. I'd like to think that Danielle is in a better place now. Before she got sick she was a wonderful person. Caring, sweet, yet independent and strong."

"So you told Danni her mother died in a car accident to protect her."

"I'd like to say it was that simple. But I think I did it for myself, too. Unfortunately, when the time came to come clean, I bungled the situation and now Danni hates me."

"She doesn't hate you," Erin said. "She's hurt and doesn't understand. Talk to her, explain just like you did with me and she'll come around."

He shook his head. "You don't see how much she's changed."

"She misses you. But she needs to know the truth—no matter how hard it may be to hear."

"She's too young. It'll scar her for life."

"C'mon, Colin, give the kid some credit. She's tougher than you think."

"And what if she's not?" he asked, fear roughening his voice. "What if I lose her even more when I tell her the truth? What then? I won't be able to take it back. At least now, I can protect her."

"That plan will backfire," she answered, frustration lacing her tone.

"How do you know? I hate to keep pointing out the obvious but you aren't a parent."

Erin lifted her chin and her eyes glittered with the anger he could feel building between them. "No, but I was Danni twenty years ago and I know what

I went through because no one would explain to me what the hell was going on. Trust me, you don't want that for your daughter."

No, he didn't, but neither did he want to see his daughter's horrified expression when she found out what her mother had tried to do. The corners of his mouth turned down and Erin obviously mistook his expression as one directed toward her. "Erin—" he said grabbing her hand when she looked ready to leave his sour attitude behind. She watched him warily but stayed where she was. "I'm sorry. I appreciate you're trying to help. I'm just…" Dare he admit it? What the hell, it probably wasn't a revelation. She already seemed to know more about his situation and how to handle it than he did. "Scared."

"I know you are." She gave him a small smile. "But so is she."

Colin inhaled deeply, struck by how beautiful she looked at that moment. The depth of her understanding made him feel as if he'd been splashing around the kiddie pool with floaters on. "Erin—"

She put a finger to his lips, telling him with her expression she wasn't ready for what he'd been about to say. Disappointment almost made him say it anyway, but she had circumvented the opportunity by changing the subject.

"Since we're here, I'm going to take another look around," she said, heading toward the short hallway.

What could he say? Nothing and she knew it. They were here for a purpose, to find answers—not delve into matters of the heart. He agreed with his silence to let the subject go—for now—but he wasn't about to let it go completely. When the timing was right, he'd revisit the issue.

Erin turned into what used to be her bedroom. There was only the slightest hesitation at the door, then she disappeared inside. He had to give her credit. Whether she liked it or not, she was conquering her demons, one memory at a time.

ERIN STOOD IN THE MIDDLE of the tiny, square room and let out a discreet breath. Too many things were going on in her head at once to try and sort them all out. A part of her was still reeling that she and Colin had just made love and the other part of her was balking at the foreign memories that had come out of nowhere.

Being with Colin had been explosively primal, yet somehow his touch had soothed her ragged nerves. Running a shaky hand through her hair she almost laughed at her own behavior. When it came to sex, she was extremely cautious, downright conservative, and never had she considered making love on the dirty floor of an old shack romantic in any sense of the word. Yet with Colin, none of those old issues had reared their ugly heads. It had been so natural to be in his arms. And now she had the aftermath to deal with. They weren't a normal couple, free to explore where this might lead. He was trying to uncover a big, nasty secret hiding in her family closet, and she would soon be leaving.

Not to mention, they hadn't exactly been responsible sexually. She sent a look to the ceiling, wondering if she'd left her brain back at her apartment in San Francisco. Ever since she came back to Granite Hills she'd been doing all sorts of things that in another lifetime she would've considered absolutely *nuts.*

Way to complicate things, she mused darkly.

Still, she didn't regret it. She smiled as the reminiscence washed over her. A floorboard creaked beneath her as she started toward the bed and she stopped. Something about the sound triggered a hazy image. Bending down, she ran her fingers along the roughened plank and pressed. It creaked in response. Drawing her eyebrows together, she gave the wood a solid knock, then tapped the floorboard beside it. Hollow. Pulling at the plank with her fingers and ignoring the shot of pain that followed, she grunted with the effort it took to pry the board loose. It opened with a cloud of dust and Erin had to clear the air with her hand before she could peer into the small hole.

Thoughts of spiders and rats made her hesitate to stick her hand into the darkened space, but curiosity overrode her fear and she reached in slowly.

At first she felt nothing but cold dirt, then her grasping fingers closed on something oddly shaped. It was hard and smooth and when she brought it out of the hole she nearly dropped it.

It was the dragonfly of her dream.

Colin appeared in the doorway. "I thought I heard something…." He spied the wooden piece in her hand. "Where'd you find that?"

"In the floor," she said, still staring at the delicately carved, incredibly detailed insect.

Carved from American basswood, nearly white despite its age, it was finely shaped and nearly perfect. Colin knelt beside her. "It almost looks real," he said, echoing Erin's own thoughts. "Whoever did this is a true artist. How'd you know it was in the floor?"

"I think I put it there," she answered slowly, turning to catch Colin's surprise. "I mean, I don't remember exactly, but I remember the creaking floorboard and that made me take a look. The question is why would I put something this beautiful in the floor?"

She searched her memory for the answer to her own question but nothing revealed itself. A growl of frustration escaped. "Ever since coming back here, it seems I've been discovering holes in my memory. Why can't I remember anything? I mean, I thought I was pretty good in the memory department, but there are things I can't explain and it's driving me crazy."

Replacing the floorboard, Colin helped her to her feet. "Listen, it's fairly common for people who've lived through traumatic events to have 'holes' in their memory. It'll come back to you but it might come in fragments."

Seems like fragments were all she had these days. Sighing, she took a final look around the room yet knew somehow there was little else to find. Her fingers closed around the dragonfly in some desperate hope her memory would come flooding back, filling the holes. When nothing happened, she exhaled and looked to Colin, who was watching her carefully. She met his gaze, grim determination ringing in her voice. "There's only one person who can tell me about this." Her fingers closed around the dragonfly. "And that's Charlie."

CHAPTER THIRTEEN

THE STORM THAT HOVERED above the cabin had finally been unleashed as it lashed the roadways with sleeting rain, making visibility minimal at best. Erin was grateful when she finally pulled into Caroline's driveway, safe and in one piece.

It'd been a long time since she felt like a teenager with a secret crush and she wasn't quite sure how to deal with it. It wasn't as if she made a habit of making love to men she hardly knew. A self-conscious chuckle escaped and she could only shake her head at the whole experience. If only things were different....

Would it matter? The thought came back to her quickly, just as it had the first time she'd felt herself slipping into dangerous territory, but this time she actually found herself hesitating. There was something about Colin, something that dared to make her wonder *what if?* when she'd spent years training herself to ignore such questions.

There's no time to wonder about a future that had no chance of becoming a reality, she realized with a shake of her head. Her life wasn't here and she wouldn't dream of asking Colin to uproot Danni at such a critical juncture in her life.

So, that's that.

Putting the vehicle in Park, she placed the dragonfly carefully in her jacket pocket and slipped and slid her way to the front porch as fresh snow started to drift lazily to the ground, promising at least a foot by night's end.

Butterscotch padded to the foyer and whined just as Erin unwound her scarf from her neck. "Oh, crud…" She bit her lip, feeling like a heel for leaving the dog for so long. "I bet you have to go, don't you, girl?"

Butterscotch gave another whine, this time a bit more urgent, and scratched at the door. Erin obliged and opened it a crack as Butterscotch made her way gingerly out into the cold. The old girl's gait pinched her conscience and she realized she was running out of time to find a home for her. Erin waited a few minutes and soon Butterscotch was eagerly returning to the warm house. In spite of herself, she reached down and gave the dog a friendly rub on the nose. "You're kind of cute, you know? For an old girl, that is…" she added, almost playfully.

Shaking her head, she latched the front door and made her way to the living room, where a fire burned low in the woodstove. She'd forgotten how long a good piece of seasoned oak could keep a house toasty. Tossing another piece on the embers, she sank onto the sofa opposite Caroline's favorite wing-backed chair and wondered what had become of her life.

What life?

As Caroline had been fond of reminding her, what she had been doing could not be considered truly living.

"When was the last time you ate a good meal?" Caroline had inquired sharply during one telephone conversation. When Erin had hesitated she pounced. "Aha! See? I knew you haven't been eating. I could tell from the last picture you sent, you know the one with all your office buddies? And by the way, who was that delightful young man in the background? He seemed quite nice! You looked entirely too thin, love. You're practically wasting away!"

Erin chuckled at the memory even as it pained her to think of Caroline. She smoothed a hand down her belly, trying to forget the shivers of anticipation that had sent her stomach quivering as Colin's tongue had traced a hot trail from her navel down to her… The breath hitched in her throat and she pressed a knuckle to her heated cheek. "Totally inappropriate," she muttered, jumping to her feet in an agitated movement. As she did so, Colin's scent, mingled with her own, caused her to inhale deeply. Eyes widening, she gave her head a quick shake and bounded up the stairs.

A quick shower later, she pulled a sweater over her head and grabbed her cell phone from the bottom of her bag. She glanced down at the window and grimaced. Four missed calls. She didn't even need to look to know who had kept ringing her. Harvey. Under the circumstances, she was half tempted to pull out of the assignment, but a deeply ingrained sense of professionalism kept her from calling him. She could download her photos later tonight and e-mail Harvey a few to shut him up. She wasn't really worried about the deadline. Erin had long since learned Harvey enjoyed moving deadlines to see how quickly his employees could finish a project and how high they'd jump to do it. Well, this time, Harvey was just going to have to wait. She had more pressing issues to deal with.

Pocketing her cell phone, she headed back downstairs. As she descended the last stair, her gaze fell upon the box of pictures lying on the table where she'd left it earlier that morning.

Sitting down, she pulled the box to her and lifted the lid, grabbing a handful of photos and spreading them out on the table.

There were so many. She had never seen so many pictures of her mother in one place. Rose was a subject rarely brought up. As a young girl, Erin had tried, but Caroline had always found a way to turn the conversation in another direction. All she'd ever had was one faded picture of her mother, and even that had mysteriously disappeared one night. Erin had her suspicions but Caroline wouldn't hear of it.

"You probably just misplaced it, love," had been her answer when Erin had approached her, distraught over its missing status.

"I wouldn't misplace the *only* picture I have of my mother," Erin had returned angrily. "Did he take it?"

Caroline looked distracted as she pulled croissants from the oven. "Who, dear?"

Erin snorted in exasperation. "You know who. Charlie."

"Erin Mallory, have some respect. He's your father, not the mailman," Caroline had gently admonished without answering Erin's question. Instead, she'd smiled and handed Erin a piping hot croissant with fresh butter dripping from the sides. When Erin wouldn't budge, she waved away her concerns. "Honestly, Erin, it'll turn up. I'm sure of it. Now eat your croissant before it gets cold."

But it hadn't shown up and to this day Erin still thought Charlie had taken it. Why, she couldn't hope to guess, but losing the only picture she'd thought existed of her mother had been like a sword to the heart. Now, standing before a veritable treasure trove of lost memories, she couldn't help but feel betrayed by Caroline.

"Seems Charlie's not the only one with secrets," she murmured, idly sifting through the pictures, wishing she knew the histories behind each and every smile, goofy expression and laugh.

Butterscotch wandered in and settled with a grunt at her feet. Erin leaned down to pat her head. "And what am I going to do with you?" An ear twitched but otherwise the dog was silent. "Yeah, I don't know, either. But if I don't figure it out…" Thinking better of her next statement, she just gave a short smile and returned to the photos. Gathering the ones she'd placed on the table into the box, she replaced the lid and contemplated her next move.

She looked back down at the dog. "Want to go for a ride?"

As if understanding, Butterscotch lumbered to her feet and went to the door and sat down. Impressed, Erin secured the woodstove, and after scooping up the box along with her coat and keys she met Butterscotch at the door. "Let's go, then."

Butterscotch barked and Erin found herself grinning. "All right, smarty-pants, but you're not riding in the front seat. Dog hair makes me sneeze."

Making their way carefully to the Tahoe, they got in and Erin backed slowly out of the snowy driveway, realizing she was taking a big chance at just showing up at Colin's door—with a dog, no less. But somehow she knew if there were a clue to be found in the box, Colin would find it. And at this point, wasn't that what was most important in the big scheme of things?

Right.

"Just drive, McNulty," she said, not really comfortable with what was staring her in the face. "Just drive, for crying out loud."

CHAPTER FOURTEEN

COLIN HAD JUST FINISHED putting the remains of dinner away in the fridge when a tentative knock sounded at the door. Wiping his hands, he hollered out that he would get it and opened the door to find Erin and her dog shivering on his doorstep.

"Hi. Can we come in?"

He recovered quickly to usher them in. "Is everything okay?" he asked, concern replacing his surprise.

"That depends on your definition of the word," she answered, pausing only long enough to watch as Butterscotch made herself at home in front of the fireplace. She arched an eyebrow and Colin could only shake his head. Shrugging, she fished a medium-sized photo box out from under her jacket. Before he could question her further, she thrust the box into his hands. "I think there's a clue to this damn mystery in here. It's a bunch of old pictures. I figure if anyone can help me, it's you," she concluded, looking up at him with clear expectation and a touch of desperate hope. She swallowed hard and the effort made her appear vulnerable. "I didn't know who else to turn to."

A surge of protective feelings washed over him and he moved to help her out of her jacket. "You came to the right place. Let's take a look at what you've got in this box."

A short smile of relief graced her lips and Colin had to pull himself back not to lean in and kiss her.

"Are you sure you're not too busy? I feel kind of bad for dropping in on you like this," she admitted, following him into the dining room. "With a dog no less. But, it seems Butterscotch has taken a shine to your hearth. I hope you don't mind."

"Not at all," he said, waving away her concern. "Danni's doing homework—" He paused to send a pained glance toward a closed door in the hallway that only partially muffled the sounds of hip-hop music beyond. "Or at least I hope she is, and I was going to spend the rest of the evening sorting through the old files. Actually, I'm glad you're here. It'll make the process a lot faster."

"I'm not sure about that," she said, her voice dropping with frustration. "Somehow it feels like I've caught a glimpse of someone I never knew."

"Your mother?"

"No," she answered. "Caroline."

"How so?"

Erin followed as he went into the dining room, setting down the box as she selected a chair. "I'm ashamed to admit, all my life I always considered Caroline easy to read. When she wasn't trying to play matchmaker she was trying to fatten me up. She volunteered, she was the co-chair on a dozen or so committees and everyone loved her. She was probably as sweet as they come."

"And what has changed?"

Erin tapped the box lightly with her index finger. "This. This box changes everything. Never in a million years would I have thought that hidden in her house was a box full of pictures of my mother. Why didn't she share them with me? She knew how distraught I was when I lost the only picture I had of her. Why didn't she offer up one of these? It's apparent she had a few to spare."

The last part was delivered with a hint of bitterness and Colin knew it was born out of pain she couldn't hide.

"I just wish I knew why she kept them from me," Erin said, sounding very much like a lost little girl. "I mean, she was my mother, for crying out loud."

"All I can say is I'll bet she had a pretty good reason," Colin offered softly, reaching up to brush away a tear she hadn't even realized had slid from the corner of her eye.

"Yeah? And what reason could that be?" she asked, the twist in his gut at the open anguish in her voice making him wish he had the answer. She shook her head. "Wasn't it bad enough my mother killed herself and my father was a worthless drunk? Did she have to take what little else I had away from me?"

Erin slid her gaze away from his until he cradled her jaw in his hand and gently turned her head. He tried not thinking of what had passed between them only a few short hours ago, but at the moment he wanted to pull her into his arms and brand her with a kiss so hot it might set their lips on fire. But this wasn't the time nor the place, he reminded himself sharply even as he found himself leaning toward her. Stopping mere inches from the sweet promise of her lips, he pulled up short and placed a soft but quick kiss on her forehead.

"Let's reserve judgment until we figure out what we can from this box," he said, smiling when she seemed disappointed in his sudden change in direction.

"Right." She nodded, unable to argue with his logic. "No, you're right… I'm still just a little thrown over this whole situation. It's a lot to take in on one visit."

He chuckled at her ability to look at things with her signature dry humor during such an emotional time and lifted the lid to the box. Reaching in, he pulled out a handful of photos and placed them carefully on the table.

It didn't take long for him to identify those which featured Erin's mother. It was like looking at the twin of the woman beside him, except for one small difference. Rose, for all her flashing smiles and playful winks at the camera, seemed strangely fragile. It reminded him of Danielle. The correlation tugged at his heart. He risked a glance at Erin. The sadness she was trying to hide was obvious. He could only imagine how this case was tearing her up inside. "She was beautiful," he said softly.

"Thanks," she answered, taking a halting breath as if drawing on a near empty well of strength. Straightening, she gestured at the pile. "Where do we start?"

"Let's try making two separate piles," he suggested, shuffling through the pictures. "Ones with Rose and ones without."

They settled into their own rhythm until each was absorbed with the task. Erin had separated the pictures with her mother, while Colin took the others. He was looking for anyone who might trigger a memory, perhaps someone with a record, but the faces were as unknown to him as they were to Erin. Suddenly, Erin paused and he leaned over to see what she was holding.

"Is this your chief?" she asked.

Colin studied the picture for a moment and then nodded before returning to his own pile.

Erin sighed. "It's kind of sad my dad and Roger Hampton parted ways. Maybe if they'd remained friends longer he could have straightened Charlie out."

"Maybe," Colin said, though his mind was elsewhere. "How does your Uncle Hank fall into all this? Did they know each other from school?"

Erin shook her head in dismay. "I really don't know. But, if I were to hazard a guess I'd say they went to school together. This is a pretty small town. It's not like there's much opportunity to meet anyone new."

"Is that why someone never snatched you up?" he

asked before he could stop himself. When she looked at him sharply, he could feel his ears reddening. He waved away his comment with a chagrined smile. "Sorry, I think I just picked up a signal from the Cheesy Pick-up Line Channel. Won't happen again. Promise."

A half smile formed on her lips and for the first time since she walked through the door she seemed to relax a little. "Well, as long as you promise…"

"Scout's honor," he murmured, enjoying the sultry tone of her voice.

"When were you a Boy Scout?" She cocked her head, sending him a look that nearly took his breath away but most certainly made his pants a little tighter.

"A long time ago," he growled, eager to finally close the distance between them to claim her lips with a possessive kiss. She was like a drug, spiraling through his veins, sparking heat with each connection throughout his body. And he wanted more. So much more.

The door to Danni's room opened and they both jumped apart, probably looking as guilty as two teenagers caught making out in the back seat of a car at Lover's Lane. Danni stopped short at the sight of Erin sitting beside him and there was no mistaking the questioning look in her eyes.

"Erin? What are you doing here?" she asked, moving into the dining room, her hair springing in unruly wisps from the messy ponytail atop her head. Immediately, she corrected herself. "I mean, it's cool to see you again but…"

Colin put some additional distance between him and Erin, then gestured to the photos spread on the table. "Erin brought some old pictures that might help with her father's case. Did you get your homework finished?"

Guest forgotten, she fixed him a caustic stare. "Of course, Dad," she answered, moving past him to the kitchen.

He started to say something in reference to Danni's tone but the soft feel of Erin's hand on his stilled his tongue. He turned to catch a soft shake of her head and he nodded in understanding. *Pick your battles.* He drew a deep breath and focused on the pictures in front of him. Erin removed her hand just as Danni returned with a bowl of chocolate ice cream. Completely ignoring Colin, she directed her attention to Erin, who had also returned to perusing the pictures.

"Did you get those pictures from the festival developed?" Danni asked, her speech only slightly slurred from the giant spoonful of ice cream in her mouth.

"Actually," Erin said, looking up from her pile, "I shot them digitally so I just have to download them. I was going to e-mail a few to my editor later tonight. Any suggestions?"

Danni smiled, instantly warming to the subject. "I really liked the one with Old Henry. I think the colors were cool with the bonfire in the background."

"Me, too," Erin said. "You've got a good eye, kid. Keep it up and it might take you somewhere someday."

."Like all the places you've been?" she asked, her eyes lighting.

"And then some." Erin winked.

"Cool!" Danni sent one final grin Erin's way before placing another spoonful of ice cream in her mouth. Her gaze slid to Butterscotch snoozing at the hearth and for a split second Colin thought she was going to call to her, but the moment passed and Danni disappeared into her room.

Erin's gaze collided with Colin's. "She's a great kid," she offered, dropping her eyes to the pile of forgotten pictures. Although she was fighting hard to hide it, he sensed a deep sadness pulling at her. When she realized he was still watching her, she looked up. "What?"

"You're good with kids," he said with a smile.

"No, I'm really not," Erin murmured almost apologetically. "Ordinarily, kids and me are like oil and water. I don't understand them and they don't understand me. But Danni's different. Like I said, she's a good kid."

"You never wanted a few of your own?"

She paused, as if her mind were more on the picture in her hand than his question, but somehow Colin knew she was struggling with her answer. Finally, she forced a bright smile and shook her head. "Never really thought about it."

She was lying but his gut said to let it go. He sensed the shadow of the past had a lot to do with her reluctance to start a family and it only made him more determined to find the answers she needed.

ERIN'S HEART THUDDED PAINFULLY in the aftermath of Colin's unexpected personal question. Kids. How would she tell him she never felt worthy of children in light of her past? The thought of drawing an innocent child into the morass of bad memories that comprised her childhood made her shudder. She refused to be that selfish. Besides, her career wasn't exactly conducive to setting up a home. One minute she was in the office, but in the next she could be flying over Hawaii.

Thus far, sticking to her guns hadn't been overly difficult, but then again, she'd never come across a man like Colin. Somehow his presence had tripped her biological clock and it was ticking as if the world were coming to an end tomorrow. Long-buried maternal instincts were flickering to life as she allowed her imagination to run wild. She wanted to teach Danni what she knew about photography and she wanted to be there when the kid developed her first roll of film. She wanted... Swallowing hard Erin blinked back the sudden tears. What she wanted didn't matter. It never did. Not when she was a kid and certainly not now.

"You okay?"

Colin's voice broke through her wall of self-pity and she brushed away any moisture that might have betrayed her. "I'm fine. Eyelash in my eye," she said, wiping at the imaginary complaint. Before Colin had the chance to call her bluff she gestured quickly at the picture in his hand. "What do you have there?"

He didn't buy it but he let it go. Relief made her

offer a brief smile in return. He tossed the picture to the pile. "Nothing. More of the same," he answered. "But it does raise an interesting question. Why aren't there any pictures of Caroline and Hank in any of these?"

She wished she knew. "I've wondered the same thing. I don't know why I never really noticed before but now it seems glaringly obvious...."

"What?"

"I think—" A shudder rippled down her spine and Colin placed his hand atop hers. She gave him a brief smile for his concern and decided to level with him. "As much as I hate, and I mean, hate, to even consider this possibility, I think my Uncle Hank and...my mom were having an affair when she died."

"What makes you think that?" he asked.

"I've got nothing concrete but why else would my Aunt Caroline remove all pictures of my uncle and my mother?"

Colin digested the information, then continued slowly with an idea. "Let's just say for the sake of argument that Hank and your mother were having an affair and somehow your dad caught the two together. Why were their deaths a week apart? And why would someone try to kill Charlie now? Doesn't make a lot of sense."

Erin agreed. The holes in the theory were big enough to trip up Bigfoot but she couldn't fathom anything more plausible. "Let's look at the police reports...maybe there's something in there we can pick up," she suggested.

"Good idea," he said, moving to drag one of several boxes over to the table where they were working. When he opened the lid, he gave her advance warning. "They're a mess. Apparently, logging evidence and keeping files in order weren't high on someone's priority list back in the day. It's amazing how computers have revolutionized the way we file reports. Here, you search these." He handed her a stack of papers. "I managed to narrow down the files to this pile but I hadn't actually located the reports on your family yet. Unfortunately, the boxes were only labeled by year."

She nodded and took the stack. Thumbing quickly, she scanned for the names McNulty and Walker. After a half hour, her eyes started to cross and she wondered how Colin had managed to get through two entire boxes. She looked up to check his progress. Head bent, Erin could just make out the determined set of his jaw as he concentrated on his task. She paused in her search to watch him. The intensity of his expression brought their earlier lovemaking to mind and her heart rate quickened. She could spend a lifetime basking in that particular heat. In all her life she'd never been as warm as she was while wrapped in his arms. Stop it, a voice in her head commanded, jerking her to the present. She dropped her eyes to the paperwork lying forgotten in her hands and she reluctantly returned to her task. Ten minutes later, every sense awoke screaming as she stared down at the report in her hand.

McNulty, Rose
Maiden: Rawlins, Rose

"Here it is," she announced, her voice sounding strangled and foreign. "I've found it."

Colin's head jerked up and he let the paper he was holding drop to the table. Watching her closely, he waited for her direction. When she didn't move, he placed a hand on her shoulder. "Do you want me to go over it first?"

The concern in his voice made her realize her hands were shaking. She sent him a grateful smile and passed him the report. She was ashamed of her weakness but knowing she was holding the gory details of her mother's suicide in her hands sent her bravado packing.

She held her breath as he quickly scanned the report. He finished and pursed his lips, as if dissatisfied with what he'd read. "Well?" she pushed, her nerves pulled taut. "What does it say?"

"Nothing." He sighed, dropping the report to the table. "It's a standard ten-forty-four report. Says that Rose Rawlins McNulty, twenty, was found in the bathtub, dead, after suffering lateral cuts on her right and left wrists. According to the coroner's report, the estimated time of death was between one to four hours of discovery."

"That's it?" Erin asked, unable to believe the end of her mother's life was only worth a few lines on a report. "Does it state who found her?"

Colin flipped the page and scanned for names. He nodded. "Charlie."

Erin swallowed, trying not to picture her father stumbling across his wife's lifeless body. "Only twenty years old," she whispered as the tears she'd so desperately tried to hide earlier came rushing back. Without bothering to wipe them from her eyes, she met Colin's gaze and demanded an answer from someone…anyone. "Why?"

Colin shook his head, worry and frustration drawing lines in his forehead. "I don't know," he admitted with a trace of bitterness in his voice. A tear snaked down her cheek and he gently brushed it away as he made a promise to her. "But I swear to you, we'll find out."

THE NEXT MORNING BROKE COLD and gray and only intensified the dread Colin felt as he climbed into his SUV. Glancing at the manila envelope lying on the passenger seat, he wondered if he were about to open Pandora's box.

An hour after Erin had left, he'd found the file he was most interested in: Hank Walker's accident report.

On the surface it was as bland and straightforward as Rose's suicide report had been. He glanced down at the signature line and read who had filed it: Roger Hampton.

A growing sense of unease refused to recede even as he thought about what the chief's signature was doing there.

Leslie had already told him the chief had been a deputy back in the day.

But given Roger's close friendship with the McNulty family, policy would've dictated someone else investigate the accident. "Conflict of interest," he muttered to himself.

So, the question rose again: Why was Roger Hampton chosen to file the report?

A queasy feeling returned to his gut as he considered the possibilities. No, there was a good reason. Maybe the department had been understaffed and Roger was the only available officer. The answer was probably just as benign, he reasoned, refusing to believe the chief, who was a mentor to every single young cop who came through the department doors, was involved with anything as sordid as a coverup.

Yet, there were questions....

After ensuring that Danni got to school on time, he pulled up to the station, and headed toward, what felt like career suicide.

Sliding his ID badge through the thin slot, he was greeted by Leslie, who was on her way out.

"Hey, stranger," she called out, the smile on her face mirroring the tone of her voice until she caught the grim set of his jaw. Without saying a word, she knew where he was going. "Something bad?" she asked.

"I'll let you know after I talk with the chief."

Leslie looked alarmed but Colin moved past her. She started to follow but he gave a resolute shake of his head. He didn't need an audience for what he was about to do.

ERIN HIT SEND ON HER LAPTOP and leaned back to watch as four-megapixel photos made the seconds long trip to Harvey's desk in San Francisco. She'd meant to forward them last night but fatigue had sent her straight to bed. And, honestly, her last thought before fading into oblivion had not been of a cantankerous egomaniac. She smiled at the absence of guilt and disconnected her Internet wire.

Closing her laptop, she half listened to the sounds of the expensive piece of machinery powering down and wondered if it were possible to reclaim the life she knew before touching down in Granite Hills.

Somehow she doubted it. When the dust settled and everyone returned to their individual routines, where would Erin be? For the first time, Granite Hills wasn't the demon in her nightmares and San Francisco no longer seemed like home.

At the naive age of eighteen she'd thought this place was the epitome of small-town hell. Now, she realized she may have painted the place with a pretty wide brush. She'd forgotten how much at one time she'd loved the melancholy of the fog rolling off the lake and settling on the sandy shore. But it'd been the aching beauty of her native soil that had sparked her desire to pick up a camera. Unfortunately, the urge to run far and fast had blotted out any of the good memories left from that time.

Hugging herself for warmth, or perhaps reassurance, she sighed and headed downstairs.

She entered the kitchen and pulled a mug from the cabinet and set the kettle on the stove. Five minutes later she was pouring hot water over the instant coffee packet, impatient for the caffeine it promised. Her mouth held a faint grimace as she lifted the mug to her lips, wishing she was holding a barista-prepared mocha latte instead, and took a bracing sip.

Butterscotch padded by and Erin wondered what the dog would say if she could talk.

"I'll bet you know what secrets this family's been hiding," she said wryly. But just like everyone else who had the answers, the dog wasn't doing any talking, either. "Caroline, I love you and miss you, but if you were here right now I'd wring your neck."

She placed her mug in the sink and paused to stare out the window. A sea of white met her eye as last night's storm had added almost a foot of new snow to the ground, making the landscape as stark as it was beautiful. Pushing away from the sink, she made her way into the living room to stoke the woodstove and wait for the hot water to heat up so she could take a shower.

On her way, she paused before Caroline's room, torn between the need to do a simple inventory of what should stay and what should go and her desire to shut the door and never open it again.

Not very practical.

She sighed. She might as well get it over with. And it wasn't like Caroline was going to need any of her stuff anyway.

"But I better not find anything weird that might

scar me forever," she grumbled to thin air until Butterscotch wandered around the corner with an ear cocked, making her feel that much more nuts for talking to herself. "Right. Just disregard that," she said, waving at Butterscotch before entering the room with a deep breath.

An hour later, Erin had decided which clothes would go to the local women's shelter and which items would stay, such as Caroline's crocheted shawl she wore at night to keep her arthritis at bay, and the hand-sewn lace doilies Caroline liked to make for friends that were unfinished in the closet.

Taking a break, Erin sat down on Caroline's bed, bunched the shawl under her nose and inhaled deeply. It smelled distinctly of Caroline, the soft mixture of lavender and rose bringing tears to her eyes. Wrapping the shawl around her and hugging it to herself, she could almost pretend Caroline was simply in the kitchen and Erin was home for a visit.

Except Erin had never come home to visit.

She dropped her head. "I wish I had, Caroline," she whispered. "I'd do anything to see you one more time. And that's the God's honest truth."

Erin wasn't sure how long she sat there wrapped in Caroline's shawl but she guessed it was probably longer than a few minutes. Rousing herself from her grief, she drew a deep breath and opened the bedside drawer to start the process of cleaning it out. An odd assortment of pens rolled to the front, hitting what appeared to be an address book. Picking it up, she started to thumb through it, only to realize it wasn't an address book at all.

A journal.

Erin let out the breath she was holding with a soft hiss as she considered what to do. Ethically, she felt, even in death, Caroline deserved her privacy. But what if Caroline knew who was behind the accident? What if she'd written down her suspicions before it happened? Or, Erin thought as a chill crept along her spine, what if she had revealed in its pages her private heartache, telling what had really happened the night Rose died?

The last thought prompted Erin to open the first page with trembling fingers as she pushed aside the screech of conscience and searched for passages that might be useful to either the investigation or the past.

As Erin made her way through the journal, she realized most of the passages contained some kind of sad, reflective prose revealing how Caroline wished Erin would meet someone nice. But as Erin read between the lines, she realized the real push had been for Erin to come home. Lifting her head from the book, she swallowed a lump that had risen with the last passage she'd read.

I'm afraid she's pulled herself into a cold, little knot, afraid to love because of the past. So much like me. I wish things were different. For both of us.

"So much like me?" Erin repeated, wondering what Caroline meant. She returned to the passage, hoping to find out.

Although I'd never want Erin to know what happened the night Rose died, in a way, I wish she did so she'd understand why things were so hard. Lord, how I miss that girl. Damn Hank Walker to hell for ruining my family.

Shocked, Erin pulled back. The confusion she felt outweighed the feeling of unease that hovered at the edge of her consciousness, as she considered the implications of Caroline's journal entries.

What had Caroline been hiding?

Erin scanned the pages, all semblance of propriety quickly disappearing as her hunger for knowledge grew with each flip of the page. The answers were close and nothing was going to keep Erin from finding them.

COLIN PAUSED BEFORE ENTERING the chief's office. A voice inside his head told him to stop and think before charging in with both barrels. He was letting emotion rule his actions and that's what got cops killed in the field. Taking a deep breath, he reminded himself of the oath he took to uphold the law and turned the corner.

The chief was bent over a report and didn't notice Colin. He gave a short rap on the doorframe to announce his presence and Roger looked up. He looked relieved as he gestured for Colin to enter. "Damn reports are making my eyes swim," he said, leaning back in his chair as Colin took a seat. "What can I do for you?"

Colin licked his lips, unsure how to proceed. A look of concern passed over the chief's face. "Danni okay?" he asked, suddenly at attention.

"Danni's fine," he assured him, realizing there was no point in beating around the bush and wasting time. "Actually, Chief, I need to talk to you about some things I've found during the course of my investigation into the McNulty accident."

"Oh?" The chief's eyebrows went up in wary interest. "What sort of things?"

"Just some questions...."

"Questions? About what?"

Colin drew a deep breath. "It seems someone cut the brake line on Charlie's truck."

Roger's gaze narrowed. "Go on."

"And, well, in digging a bit I found reason to look into the events that happened in Charlie's life thirty years ago...such as his wife's and Hank Walker's deaths."

"What reason would that be?" Roger's mouth tightened and all sense of good humor fled from his expression. "Rose's death was a suicide and Hank Walker's was an accident. Case closed. No mystery and no bearing on what happened to Charlie on Old Copper."

Colin tensed under the rebuke but didn't back down.

"You mentioned being friends with Charlie at one time."

"Yeah? So? That was ancient history."

"So, why were you chosen to file the report on Hank's accident? Seems there'd be a conflict of interest."

"There was no conflict," the chief said, his tone almost a bark. "Because I was never Hank Walker's friend."

"Yes, but—"

"But nothing. There was no conflict."

The chief sent a hard stare Colin's way, word-lessly telling him to drop it. "What if Hank's death wasn't an accident?" Colin blurted out, despite his good sense screaming for him to stop. "Maybe you missed something."

"What's to miss? There was ice on the roads, he took a bad spill and bam! He died. There was nothing anyone could've done to save the poor bastard. It was an open-and-shut case."

"Just like Charlie's?" he said softly, catching the chief's pointed stare. Colin took a step forward, placing both hands on the desk. "Did you run a mechanic's report on Hank's truck?"

Roger looked away. "I'm telling you, there was no need."

"Chief—"

The sound of Roger's heavy fist slamming down on the desk stunned Colin into silence. "Enough! Leave it be, *detective*."

The two men stared at each other until Roger

heaved a short breath, satisfied the conversation was over. Not quite sure what to make of the chief's oddly vehement refusal to talk about the old case, Colin turned to leave.

"Don't waste too much time on Hank Walker. He isn't worth the effort."

"And why's that?" Colin dared to ask.

"Because he liked to beat women." The chief looked away, then continued with a hint of disgust, "And he wasn't what you'd call faithful, either."

Caroline—a battered woman. Something told him Erin had no idea.

The chief shifted in his chair and his shoulders relaxed subtly. "Colin, you're a good cop. I'm sorry I lost my temper."

Colin read true regret in the older man's expression, adding a perplexing new layer to the situation. He nodded his acknowledgment of the apology, but the chief's reaction had left him restless and edgy.

As he walked back to his desk, he realized he'd come away with very little in the way of resolution. He'd hoped the chief would absolve himself with a few simple answers, but instead, Colin was left with the sinking feeling that the chief had something to hide.

Colin sank heavily into his desk chair and stared at the stack of reports waiting for him but he made no move to start. His mind was elsewhere and his stomach was twisted in knots. He didn't care what the chief said. Something awful happened thirty years ago, bad enough to create a secret between three people that was worth killing to keep quiet. But secrets, as Colin knew, had a way of coming to light sooner or later. He just had to ask the right questions. He closed his eyes for a second and concentrated on his options. Suddenly an echo of Leslie's advice came to him in a flash....

There should be a newspaper article or two somewhere.

His eyes snapped open and a grim smile followed. God bless the press. If anyone could sniff out a secret, it was a journalist with the scent of blood in his nostrils. There was bound to be something he could glean from the newspaper archives he could put to use. And then—his smile faded—he could take the next step. What that step was he didn't like to think about.

ERIN'S EYES WERE DRY AND GRITTY and her legs were cramped from sitting in one position for hours as she'd poured over more journals, though she'd been disappointed to discover nothing new in Caroline's later ones. It was nearly noon and her stomach was loudly reminding her that it was getting accustomed to the idea of food on a regular basis.

Walking stiffly into the kitchen she grabbed a banana and had just snapped the tip to peel it when a knock at the front door stopped her. Her first thought was of Colin and she had to admit it wasn't an unpleasant one. A rush of tangled feelings overwhelmed her ability to think clearly.

Opening the door, she was surprised to see not

Colin, but a burly man wearing a stern expression to go with his shiny badge. Although it'd been a while since she'd seen him, she recognized the man instantly. "Mr. Hampton?"

His skin paled as he stared, his expression changing from businesslike to something else, and Erin felt distinctly vulnerable without anything heavier than a knickknack to serve as a weapon. Her heart rate accelerated and her hands became clammy. *Calm down.* "What are you doing here?" she asked.

"You've grown up to be the spitting image of Rose," he said in a choked whisper. "God help me…the spitting image."

"I'll take your word for it, I don't remember her," she said, feeling awkward. "What can I do for you?"

As if awakening, the tips of his ears reddened, and he dropped his gaze to the ground before bringing his hands to rest on his generous hips. "May I come in?"

Erin's hesitation must have been obvious, for he begrudged her a smile. "I'm sorry. You caught me off guard. If I didn't know better I'd swear I was looking at Rose. I just came by to offer my condolences in person. Caroline was a good woman."

At the mention of Caroline, Erin softened and waved him in. "Sorry, I didn't mean to be so rude. It was a rough morning," she said, leading him to the living room, where they took seats opposite each other.

"No need to apologize. I'm the one who's

bargin' in on you, coming unannounced. I know the reason you've come home isn't social. At one time Caroline was a good friend. She'll certainly be missed in this town."

"Thank you," she murmured, pushing down the familiar lump in her throat.

Roger fidgeted a little, seeming a bit lost, and Erin's feeling of unease returned.

"Were you and your aunt close?"

"I'd thought so," she said, her mind returning to the journals she'd found and the cryptic bombshells of information they had revealed. When Roger looked at her sharply, she found herself reluctantly explaining. "I found some journals...." she said, shrugging. "And, I've realized my aunt had many secrets."

"Secrets?"

Erin chuckled, missing the subtle change in his voice. "Yeah...just some things about my family that weren't too savory."

"Such as?"

"Well, I think my mother and my Uncle Hank were having an affair...."

At this admission, Erin was surprised when Roger actually looked relieved as he shook his head. "No. Never in a million years. Trust me on that."

Erin cocked her head. "How do you know?"

"Well, we were once really good friends and I knew your mother quite well. She hated Hank Walker. Almost tore the friendship between her and Caroline right in two when they started dating. I'm not one to speak ill of the dead but Hank Walker was no peach of a man."

Erin frowned, more than a bit confused by this new tidbit of information. "How do you know all this?"

Roger shifted and pressed his lips together as if he were regretting having said too much already. "It's all water under the bridge now. I didn't mean to stir things up." Erin started to protest, hoping to get him to share more but he was already standing and getting ready to leave. "I just wanted to drop by, let you know if there's anything you need, you can give me a ring. It's the least I can do for Caroline."

Hungry for more information, Erin wanted to ask him to stay, but he was in a hurry to go. In two quick strides he was at the door and after a polite goodbye and another condolence, he was gone.

As the door closed behind him, Erin frowned at the odd exchange. Instinct told her she ought to call Colin and tell him of Roger's visit, but first she wanted to check something. Caroline had once mentioned that she had a special keepsake chest she kept in the attic. Erin had never had cause to think about it before, but after Roger's revelation about her Uncle Hank, she wanted to see if Caroline had hidden Hank's photos in the chest.

Taking the stairs two at a time, she pulled the trap door on the ceiling that led to the attic and started climbing.

It didn't take long to find. Within minutes, Erin had pulled open the chest with her heart in her mouth.

Just as she'd hoped, it was full of treasures from the past. Baby booties she assumed were hers, a lace garter and other odds and ends she regarded for a moment before setting them aside, searching for something that might help.

Her questing fingers found a bundled bunch of photos, which she snatched up eagerly.

Hank Walker.

Finally! In her hands she held photos of the man Caroline had grown to hate, yet at one time had loved enough to jeopardize one of her most beloved friendships. Erin studied the black-and-white photo as if it might offer an answer to the questions in her mind. Hank Walker had a bright smile but there was a mean glint to his eyes that almost made them flinty. A lot of people said photography lied but Erin disagreed. Most people just didn't know what to look for. The eyes were the window to the soul and it didn't take more than two seconds for Erin to see that Hank Walker's soul was dead.

An awful feeling settled in the pit of her stomach at the thought of Caroline married to such a man. Returning the photos to the bottom of the chest, she shut the lid quickly and wiped her hands free of the fine layer of dust clinging to everything in the attic. At least she had a face to the name, she thought, eager to leave the cold confines of the attic.

She couldn't wait to tell Colin what she'd found.

COLIN FLIPPED THROUGH THE microfiche scanning for newspaper articles on Hank Walker's accident.

At the time there were two publications, the *Granite Hills Tribune* and the *Poison Ivy*. While he struck out with the *Tribune* he managed to pull two substantial articles from the *Ivy* that warranted attention.

The writer, Emmett Jones, wasn't a name Colin recognized but since the *Ivy* went out of business years before he even came to Granite Hills, he supposed Jones moved on to a different paper. The article was full of veiled accusations, that skirted the line of good journalism, but raised interesting questions.

Accident or Foul Play?
By Emmett Jones
Staff writer
Hank Edward Walker, a local man known for his charm and wit, died of head injuries after his Ford pick-up truck crashed head-on into a full-grown birch tree on Old Copper Road. Although the police report states Walker died from wounds sustained from the accident, a source within the county coroner's office refutes that conclusion, stating, "Walker's wounds are not consistent with trauma associated with a vehicle accident." Questions have been raised as to the possibility of foul play, but the local police refute that theory.

"Our investigation has concluded that Hank Walker died as a result of injuries sustained in a head-on vehicle collision," said Granite Hills

Police Chief Ronald Hampton. "It's unfortunate and certainly tragic but we've found nothing to support the theory that anything criminal may have occurred."

Colin scanned a little further.

Inquiries have also been raised as to whether Roger Hampton, the young officer who filed the report, was seasoned enough to take on such a complicated case. Hampton, the only son of police chief Ronald Hampton, had been on the job for three months before the crash and some feel a more experienced officer should have handled the incident. Despite a cloud of suspicion, the case remains closed.

Pulling away from the view screen, he rubbed his hand over his eyes to alleviate some of the strain caused by the microfiche machine and jotted down some notes. He needed the autopsy report from Hank's accident. Somehow he had a feeling it was long gone. A quick call to the coroner's office would solve that mystery. His cell phone rang, interrupting his thought process. The name *Erin McNulty* registered on his caller ID. He picked it up before it rang a second time.

"I need to talk to you," she said, her voice strangely subdued.

"What's wrong?" he asked, instantly on alert.

"Can we meet somewhere private?"

"Of course," he answered readily, suggesting his place. "Danni's at school until three p.m."

"Thanks, Colin. I'll see you in about twenty minutes."

She clicked off and Colin returned the phone to his belt loop. Printing double copies of the two articles, he paid for his prints and headed for home. On impulse he dialed the coroner's office as he drove the short distance.

"County coroner," a congenial voice sounded on the other end.

"This is Detective Colin Barrett with the Granite Hills Police Department. I'm looking for an old autopsy report on a Hank Edward Walker, DOB, 7/26/47."

"One moment, please."

Colin pulled into his driveway and shut the truck off to wait. After about three minutes she came back on the line and apologized.

"I'm sorry but we don't seem to have that report. Are you sure it was filed in this county?"

"Pretty sure," he answered, not quite surprised. "Don't worry about it. Thanks for your time."

He hung up and headed for the house. The report, if it corroborated what Emmett Jones wrote in his article, would've given him the authority he needed to reopen the case. But, someone had known that and effectively took care of the possibility.

He went inside and sat down to wait for Erin to show up. Her tone had him on edge and the information he'd found in the archived newsprint had his mind moving in sickening circles.

If it turned out that the chief had a hand in Charlie's accident, could he really arrest the man who was more of a mentor than a boss to every single cop in the department? Was he willing to make that sacrifice?

A rap on the door alerted him to Erin's arrival. He quickly let her in and to his surprise she went straight into his arms and buried her face against his chest while Butterscotch pushed past to commandeer her spot by the fireplace.

He wasn't about to complain but he knew something had spooked her. "What's wrong?"

For a long moment Erin just remained pressed against his chest, as if trying to hide from something and, although curiosity was eating him up, he didn't want to sever the connection he felt between them. He wanted to savor it.

"I think my Uncle Hank was a bad man," she finally said, pulling away to stare up at Colin with pain in her eyes. "That's why there are no pictures of him anywhere. Caroline hated him…and so did my mother."

"I think you're right," Colin agreed, remembering the small bit of information the chief had let slip about Hank Walker. "He used to beat Caroline."

Erin inhaled sharply, her eyes glittering. "If he were alive, I'd kill him," she said vehemently.

He chuckled. "I believe you. But then, I'd have to arrest you."

Erin cracked a smile. "Dudley Do-Right."

"That's me," he said, tightening his arms around her, loving the feel of her, the smell of her sweet hair against his nose. "Defender of helpless women—"

"Helpless?" Erin pulled away with an arched eyebrow. "Who are you calling helpless?"

Colin laughed and pressed a kiss at her crown. "Certainly not you. You are probably the most independent, completely self-sufficient woman I've ever run across, but I like it."

"Oh?" The laughter faded from her eyes and she seemed to hold her breath, as if not quite sure what to think of such a statement. Colin held her gaze, wishing he could explain the feelings she created. She started to pull away but he wouldn't let her. "What are we doing?" she asked, the halting tone of her voice giving it a husky sound that drew his entire body taut with desire.

"I don't know," he admitted. "But at the moment I don't care. Whatever it is…I like it and I don't want it to stop."

"I'm not staying," she said with a sad shake of her head. "You know that, right?"

Yeah, I know. "Why not?" he asked, the question popping out without his permission but he realized he wanted to know the answer. "Do you hate it here so much?"

Erin pulled out of his arms, avoiding his stare as she put distance between them. "It's complicated," she answered, her eyebrows knitting together in a frown. "But, even if it weren't, I have a life to get back to, which includes a career I love."

Colin nodded, pretending to understand, but he didn't. No, that wasn't entirely true. His head understood; his heart did not. Exhaling deeply, he tried not to let the bitterness he felt creeping into his chest color his words. He still had a job to do. "Fair enough," he said, his mouth drawing into a grim line despite his best efforts. "I won't badger you about it anymore."

"Thank you," Erin murmured, yet her expression didn't support relief. There was a sadness pulling at the corners of her mouth that he didn't miss and it gave him hope.

Closing the distance between them, Colin pulled her back into his arms with little resistance on her part. "I promise not to bug you about leaving if you promise to allow us to enjoy whatever this is between us for as long as you're here."

Erin looked bewildered and a little concerned. "But what about Danni? I'm not sure that's the best example for her...."

"Danni likes you more than me right about now," he said wryly. "I think she'll be fine with you coming around for dinner now and then."

Erin broke out in a hesitant smile as she slowly nodded. "All right, as long as it's okay with Danni...." She paused. Then smiled tentatively as she continued, "I wouldn't mind spending more time with you, too."

Sensing the admission caused conflicting feelings, Colin reined in his urge to shout at the top of his lungs and instead celebrated his triumph with a firm kiss that clearly communicated how he felt about her with the press of his lips and the thrust of his tongue. He agreed not to badger her but he didn't say anything about not trying to use other means of persuasion.

"Now," he said, once their breathing had slowed and their respective hands had stopped exploring, "tell me how you came to this new information and I'll share what I've found as well."

As Erin related the information Roger Hampton had imparted with his odd impromptu visit, as well as the pictures she'd found in the attic, she watched as Colin's expression changed from interested to wary. "What's wrong?"

"It could be nothing." His expression told her he didn't like what was forming in his mind. When she pressed him for details, he bit off a muttered curse and pulled a photocopy of a microfiche newspaper article. "Read this."

Erin took the paper and scanned it quickly. Her brow furrowed as shock registered with the implications. "A police coverup?"

"It would seem," he answered grimly.

"But why?" The question came out sounding like a plaintive wail, but Erin didn't care. She was tired of all the secrets that kept creeping up to ambush her every time she turned. "What the hell is going on around here?"

"I wish I knew." He grasped her hand, eyeing her intently. "But I promise you, we'll find out."

"So where do we go from here?" Erin asked, pulling away.

"We need to backtrack Charlie's schedule the week before he was in the accident. We might find some answers there that were overlooked," he said, reluctantly letting her go.

"What about the stuff about the department?"

The grim look on Colin's face intensified. "Leave that to me."

IT WAS NEAR TO FIVE O'CLOCK when Colin returned to the station, his heart leaden but his step determined. There was no turning back now.

He caught the chief just as he was readying to leave. Colin walked in and immediately shut the door.

"Problem?" Roger asked, slowly sliding his arm into his wool overcoat, his expression dull.

"I'm afraid there is." Colin nodded gravely, pausing long enough to remind himself that he was obligated as an officer to follow the evidence. "You might want to sit down for this."

"I prefer to stand if that's all right with you. What is it?"

"It's about the Walker case," he began.

"I told you to drop it." The chief's mouth was drawn but the resigned look in his eyes sapped some of the fire from his statement. Sighing heavily, Roger took his seat. "Go on."

"I found an old newspaper article on the case. Apparently, there was evidence suggesting Hank Walker didn't die in that car accident but rather…somewhere else. According to this article, a source revealed Hank's injuries weren't consistent with a car accident. Since you were the investigating officer, something tells me you knew that."

When the chief didn't balk at the accusation Colin grimaced as the polished image of his mentor cracked in two. His voice broke as he demanded an answer. "What happened that night, Chief? Tell me why the coroner's report didn't match what you put in your report. God, Roger, tell me something I'll understand!"

Roger closed his eyes and the corners of his mouth turned down. "I can't."

"Did you kill Hank Walker?" Colin asked in a choked whisper.

"With my bare hands," Roger answered dully, staring down at his clenched fists as if he could still see the bloodstains.

"Oh, God!" Colin moaned, his voice rising. "How could—"

"The son of a bitch had raped her!" Roger snapped, his lip trembling with the force of the memory. "By the time we got to the cabin, it was too late. Our beautiful Rose was lying bleeding and broken, never to be the same…because of him." When Roger met Colin's stare, it was hard. "We gave what he had coming…and then some."

"You and Charlie?" Colin guessed, filling in the holes. "How'd you know what Hank had done?"

Roger pursed his lips as he took a moment to compose himself. "Me and Charlie were cutting trees on a private piece of property near Porcupine

Mountains when Caroline radioed on the CB sounding frantic. She said they'd had a bad fight and Hank was in a temper, heading for Rose's place. She was afraid he was going to do something terrible. Well, she was right." He sighed, continuing. "Hank always had a thing for Rose but she wouldn't give him the time of day. Guess he and Caroline had words about it and it pushed the crazy son of a bitch over the edge."

"And the coroner's report?"

Roger smiled thinly. "My daddy made it disappear." When Colin swore under his breath, Roger shook his head. "What else was he supposed to do? We were just a couple of young kids and we made a mistake, but going to prison for that worthless piece of trash just didn't seem right."

Colin was torn by his need to see justice served and the heartache that was piercing his chest at the chief's revelation. "It was not your right to be his judge, jury and executioner. Vigilante justice has no place in today's world. What you did was wrong."

Roger looked away as if unable to meet Colin's condemnation, but he didn't deny the accusation. How could he? When he spoke again his voice was weary. "Have you ever loved someone so much it hurt just to look at her?" Roger slowly turned to regard Colin sadly. When Colin didn't offer an answer, he shrugged and continued. "Well, I have. It just so happened the woman I loved was in love with my best friend. I had to make peace with that. And I made myself content to be her friend. Things were getting better…and then we got that call." He closed his eyes in remembered anguish. "To be honest, I can't even remember who took the first punch."

"What about Rose? She must've been hurt pretty bad. Why wasn't she treated at the hospital?"

"We tried but she wouldn't let us. The only person she'd let near her was Caroline. Then a week later, she was gone."

Silence hung between them. Colin felt sick inside. "Is that why you tried to kill Charlie? To protect this awful secret?"

Roger looked up sharply, surprise in his eyes. "I didn't try to kill Charlie. Not even for that. Even though we've drifted apart, I could never hurt the man. At one time he was like a brother."

"But you were the only one who knew about that night…."

"I won't lie…when Charlie came to me and told me of his plans to come clean, for a panicked second I considered stupid stuff but then I came to my senses. I'm not that hotheaded kid I once was. And Charlie, for all his faults, was once my best friend. Sometimes the ties that bind never truly lose their ability to hold us—no matter how we'd like to let them go."

Stunned, Colin stared at the chief. "Who was it then?"

At the resolute shake of the chief's head, Colin felt the bottom of his world drop out. Someone else knew about that night and he had a feeling he was dealing with a person who had a thirst for revenge that might involve Erin's whole family.

"I need to find Erin, right now!"

CHAPTER FIFTEEN

ERIN RETURNED TO THE HOUSE, her mind and body still spinning from the overload of information. Was it possible to just enjoy the time she had with Colin instead of trying to figure out where their future may lead? They were both consenting adults, not two lovesick teens. She grinned wryly at the comparison as she rubbed her tingling palms together, loving the warmth flooding her cheeks at the memory of their time together.

And then there was Danni. She was one cool kid. Erin couldn't wait to see Danni's reaction when she revealed she'd submitted the ice-rink photo. It was amateur but full of classic hometown coziness and Erin figured if Harv had a problem with it, she'd just suggest they tack a Junior Achiever stamp on it and sell it as a promo for another assignment.

Yet, even as she enjoyed considering the possibilities with Colin and Danni, hovering at the edge of her mind was the knowledge her aunt had endured an abusive marriage.

"Oh, Caroline," she whispered, troubled. It hurt to realize how little she'd actually known her aunt.

Was it possible Charlie or Caroline had something to do with Hank's accident? Had her own mother? Had guilt driven her mother to kill herself? Had remorse driven Charlie to the bottle?

A chill shook her body and she moved into the foyer to grab her coat where it was hanging against the wall. Slipping her hands into the pockets she was startled when her fingers grazed an oddly shaped object. "What the…?" she asked, pulling out the dragonfly she'd found days earlier at the cabin.

She'd forgotten it was in there. Turning the lovely piece of wood that had been carved with such attention to detail, she traced a finger along the grain, wondering at the artisan's skill.

Your father's an artist!

Bits and pieces of old arguments floated to the top of her consciousness and Erin frowned. "No…"she breathed, resisting the memory.

"C'mon, love, he wanted you to have it," Caroline had said, attempting to put the dragonfly in Erin's resistant hands.

"If that's the case then why didn't he give it to me himself?" Erin shot back with all the teenage rancor she could muster. "You're just saying that. Face it, Aunt Caroline, he doesn't care and he never did. It's probably his fault my mother killed herself."

That last part she'd tried half-heartedly to say under her breath, but Caroline, who had the ears of a bat, caught it and her face paled. "Don't you ever say that again, Erin Mallory McNulty or so help me, I'll never forgive you. And that's the God's honest truth. That's pure nastiness coming out of your mouth and I won't hear it."

Erin had bit her lip to keep the tears from spilling but she gave a glum nod to indicate she'd heard her. "Well, I don't want it. If you make me take it, I'll just throw it away."

Caroline had given Erin a long look filled with disappointment yet had pressed the piece into her palm anyway, saying, "If you do, that's your business and your cross to bear. But you ought to know…it belonged to your mother. Charlie gave it to her the day you were born as a gift. Do with it what you feel fit."

Caroline had walked away and Erin stood paralyzed, holding the wooden piece. She couldn't bring herself to throw it away as she'd claimed, but neither could she look at it without bursting into tears. So, she'd pried the floorboard open in her room and placed it inside, safe but hidden, until the other day.

Stunned at the memory, which now seemed crystal clear and cuttingly brutal, Erin could only stare at the beautiful piece and wonder why their family had been chosen by fate to bear such horrible burdens.

All these years Erin nursed a pain deep inside with the conviction that her father was a deadbeat loser who had driven his wife to kill herself with his hard-drinking ways. Now, she had to wonder if there had been more to his alcohol abuse than she'd known.

Did the reasons matter?

She stiffened slightly. No, she answered, soothing the inner child that immediately took issue with her defense. It didn't excuse his behavior but the possibility gave her insight. For the first time, Erin felt the stirrings of compassion toward her father. It was altogether foreign and frightening but she didn't shy away from it.

A knock at the door brought her back to the present, and after carefully setting the dragonfly on the kitchen table, she went to answer the door.

"Erin McNulty?" A uniformed female officer asked, her gaze darting past to Butterscotch, who had suddenly appeared and was standing beside Erin watching the woman intently.

"Yes?" she answered, thinking today must be her lucky day for receiving uniformed officers. She didn't think people committing a crime saw this many cops in one day. "What can I do for you?"

Butterscotch growled, startling Erin, but before she could react, she was looking down the barrel of the woman's gun.

"Holy sh—"

"Get inside! Now!" She pushed at Erin with the gun, nearly causing her to stumble over Butterscotch, who kept trying to put herself between the woman and Erin.

"What are you doing?" Erin asked, stunned.

"Is this a robbery? Because, frankly, if it is, you picked the wrong house. The only thing of value here is the kitchen table and you'd need a forklift to get that thing out of there."

"I'm not here to rob you."

"Then, why are you here?"

"How nice of you to ask." The woman smiled. "I'm here to kill you."

"Oh." The breath slipped from Erin's lips as her mouth formed the single word. *Sorry I asked.* And all this time she'd been under the assumption nothing exciting ever happened in Granite Hills. She took it back. God in heaven—did she take it back.

COLIN MADE THE TURN TO Caroline's driveway and spotted a cruiser parked out front. Puzzled, he killed the engine out of sight of the house and radioed the chief.

"Do you have someone with Erin?"

"Negative. Why?"

"There's a cruiser parked out front. I can't quite make out whose car though. Something's not right. I can feel it."

"I hear you, Colin, but I want you to wait for backup before you go charging in there."

Colin squinted, scanning the property for signs of anyone else. "I'm just going to peek around and see if anything's about. It's probably nothing but with everything that's been going on…"

Colin let his statement trail but Roger understood. "I'm sending backup right now," he said, adding gruffly, "Be careful, Col."

"Ten-four, Chief."

Colin grabbed his coat and made his way silently toward the house. The crunching of snow beneath his boots was the only sound in the air until the sharp crack of a gunshot sent his adrenaline racing, heightening his senses and putting his entire body on alert. "We have gunshots! I repeat, we have gunshots!" he exclaimed into his shoulder radio. He broke into a run, a cold sweat plastering his hair to his head and Butterscotch's frantic bark ringing in the frigid air.

Staying clear of any line of sight, he made his way carefully to the front porch, wincing as the old floorboards creaked in protest, sounding louder than any alarm Colin could've designed to warn the gunman of his presence. He froze, waiting to see if he'd given away his position. When nothing happened, he crept around to the back door and slowly let himself in through a room that served as a laundry porch. Voices caught his ear.

"A hair to the left and I could've taken your head off," a voice commented in amusement, then hardened. "Don't try that again. I'm not quite ready to kill you yet. And for God's sake shut that friggin' dog up before I put a bullet between its eyes!"

Colin drew back as Erin tried soothing the frightened dog. He knew that voice. Somehow Erin managed to get Butterscotch to stop howling, but the dog continued to emit an intermittent nervous whine. The woman continued, and Colin bit back an oath. Missy Reznick. The newest cop to join the department. And either crooked or crazy. How in the hell did she slip past the background check?

"Why are you doing this?" The faint tremor in Erin's voice betrayed her fear, causing Colin to grit his teeth and wish he could just charge in guns blazing like they do in the movies. Instead he had to wait for his opportunity and each passing second made his palms sweat as panic threatened to override his training.

"Payback," came Missy's answer.

"For what?" Erin asked incredulously.

"For screwing up my retribution."

"I don't kn—"

"Hank Walker was my daddy."

Both Erin and Colin sucked in a surprised breath as Missy went on. "Yeah, that's right. Shocked? Good. But I never got the chance to know him—thanks to your family." Erin started to protest, or perhaps offer some kind of apology, but Missy cut her off. "More specifically—your Aunt Caroline."

"What are you talking about?" Erin's voice lost its tremble as she openly bristled under Missy's attack. "My aunt didn't even know you existed."

"Are you sure about that?" Missy taunted, seeming to enjoy Erin's defensive tone. A tense silence followed until she continued with a chuckle. "Did I hit a nerve? Well, let me tell you a little more. Caroline knew but she refused to grant my daddy a divorce so he could come home to his real family."

Erin made a sound of disgust. "What a crock of sh—"

"Watch it," she growled. "I'm the one with the gun, remember?"

Colin didn't need the reminder. Where the hell

was that backup? Sliding against the wall he froze as the worn floorboard groaned in protest, but Missy was too wrapped up in her conversation with Erin to notice. He breathed a sigh of relief and strained to listen.

"When he died, my momma blamed Caroline, said if it weren't for that bitch he'd still be around. All my life I listened to my momma pine for the man that was taken from her and when she died I promised payback."

"You weren't trying to kill Charlie that night?" Erin's voice was so faint Colin almost didn't catch it. Missy's laughter was her answer.

"That old drunk?" Missy snorted. "No, but I knew they'd be together on account of his AA meetings. Caroline always rode with him into town. All it took was a slice to the brake line and the icy roads did the rest. Fitting, don't you think? My daddy died on the same stretch of road almost thirty years ago. It's almost damned poetic, if you ask me."

Clearly Missy didn't know the whole story or else Caroline wouldn't have been the target.

"Great story. What does this have to do with me?" Erin asked.

"Isn't it obvious? If you hadn't gotten involved with Colin, things would've blown over and no one would've looked twice at the accident. Case closed."

"That's not true," Erin countered. "Colin was already suspicious. He's a good cop. He would've pieced it together eventually whether I was here or not. What then? Were you going to kill him, too?"

"Who knows? Accidents happen in the field all the time. Now, shut up. I'm through talking to you."

Colin tensed, sensing things were about to get ugly.

"You should've stayed in San Francisco," Missy said, the cocking of her gun rivaling the loud rush of blood in Colin's ears. "Look on the bright side. Now you can finally meet your mother."

Colin couldn't wait for backup. The moment was now. If he didn't do something Erin was going to die.

"Reznick!" Colin roared.

"Barrett, is that you?" Missy called out. "C'mon, now. Don't be unsociable. It doesn't have to be this way. You're a good cop. Come out now and I won't blow your girlfriend's head off."

"Colin, watch out, she's nuts!" Erin shouted.

Colin tightened his grip on his gun and inched forward along the wall. "You don't want to do this, Reznick. Think about it."

"Shut up, Barrett. You don't know jack about what I want."

"This isn't her fight!" he shouted, sweat beading his forehead. "Let her go!"

"Sorry. No can do."

He peered around the corner cautiously, ducking behind the wall before Missy spotted him. Erin was standing stock-still, her face pale but anger radiating from her normally cool eyes.

"If it weren't for McNulty trash I might have grown up with a father. Maybe I might have turned out better."

The last part was dropped as a joke, but Colin wasn't laughing. She had nothing to lose at this point. Her career was ruined and she knew it.

"You ought to thank your lucky stars Hank Walker was never in your life," Colin said, hoping to either pique her interest or incense her enough to make a mistake. Backup would be arriving any second. Perhaps he could keep her talking long enough to stall for their arrival. He wasn't disappointed.

"What's that supposed to mean?" she asked sharply.

"From what I gather he was a mean S.O.B. He used to beat Caroline and the night he died—" he closed his eyes, wishing there was a different way to tell Erin of the events leading up to her mother's death "—he brutally raped Rose McNulty."

Colin peeked around the corner just in time to catch Erin's horrified expression. He closed his eyes but the image remained. Swearing under his breath, he focused on holding Missy's attention.

"You're lying. My father was a good man."

Colin managed to snort despite the tight feeling in his throat. "Really? Cuz he doesn't sound like a man up for Father of the Year to me."

Silence bounced back at him and he sensed he'd hit a sensitive spot. He pressed a little harder. "It's just a guess but I'd say growing up without Hank Walker was a blessing. If you don't believe me, just ask the chief. There's no telling what the man was capable of."

"He was a rotten son of a bitch."

Startled, Colin peered around the corner and saw Roger with his gun drawn and three officers flanking him similarly armed. Never in his life had he been so happy to see another man in uniform. Colin came out from his hiding spot, sending a wordless communication to Erin that it was going to be okay.

"Now, drop that gun!"

For a tense, horrified moment Colin worried that, knowing she was busted, Missy would try to go out in a hail of gunfire. But just as Colin's teeth threatened to shatter from the pressure he was exerting from his clenched jaw, she dropped the gun and raised her hands in surrender.

As the other officers swarmed around Missy, clapping her in handcuffs, Erin seemed to lose the strength in her legs and sank to the chair behind her.

Sparing a brief second to send an appreciative nod the chief's way, he immediately went to Erin. Her eyes were wide and glazed, and Colin worried she was going into shock.

"I'm so sorry," he said, feeling helpless. "I didn't want you to find out that way but I needed to distract her." He searched her face. His voice broke as a fierce desire to protect her rolled through him. "She was going to kill you. I had to do something."

Without a word, she allowed him to gather her in his arms and Colin inhaled deeply as if he couldn't get enough of the feel or smell of her. Seeing Erin with a gun to her chest, knowing she was seconds away from death, had rattled him, causing him to take a hard look at what he was feeling for her. It was scary but it frightened him more to think of watching her walk out of his life.

Roger appeared beside Colin and cleared his throat. He laid a hand on Colin's shoulder. "We'll talk later," he said, swiveling on his heel to leave. Suddenly pausing, Roger turned to give Colin a look full of respect. "No matter what, you're a good cop, Colin Barrett."

Colin acknowledged the compliment with mixed emotions. They both knew sooner or later they'd have to deal with the issue of Hank Walker's death. But for now, he wanted to focus on Erin.

"On second thought, why don't you take the day off," Roger suggested, giving Colin a pointed look. "The rest can wait until tomorrow."

He wished it could wait a lifetime but Colin accepted the offer with a nod and pressed a kiss to Erin's forehead. He didn't think another day was going to make him feel better about what he had to do but he was willing to take it. Returning to Erin, he noticed she was trembling. "Are you all right?" he asked. She gave him a cynical look and he almost chuckled. Stupid question. "Let me rephrase that…are you going to be all right?"

Erin pulled away. She stared out the window and watched as the marked units navigated the slushy driveway toward the highway until they disappeared. "Is it true? What you said to Missy?"

Colin nodded grimly.

An aggrieved frown creased her forehead as she

looked at him with questions in her eyes. Colin grasped her hand tenderly, wishing he could soften the telling somehow.

"I found a newspaper article in the archives at the library. It suggested Hank Walker didn't die in a car accident as the police report said." He drew a deep breath. "I confronted the chief about it and he told me what really happened that night."

Erin listened intently as Colin related what Roger had shared, including his and Charlie's involvement with Hank's death, and he held his breath as he awaited her reaction.

"So, Missy doesn't know what really happened to her father?"

"No," he answered, wishing he knew how to proceed. If he brought Roger and Charlie up on charges for Hank's murder, everyone would know.

"Good."

Colin refrained from offering an opinion but his silence prompted another comment from Erin.

"Whatever Hank Walker got, he deserved."

Erin's expression gave him the chills. It was almost…vicious. The tug of war he was feeling inside must have shown on his face, for her tone became incredulous.

"You don't agree?"

Now wasn't the time to get into this particular discussion. He didn't know where he stood with his feelings. A part of him understood the rage that had prompted two men to commit murder, but the other part was appalled justice had been sacrificed in the name of personal vengeance. The fact that he couldn't come to a clear position on what to do about the chief made him bite back a frustrated oath. "Listen, it's been a helluva day. Let's just leave it be for now. Okay? We have plenty of time to pick apart the *whys* and *hows* later."

"That's easy for you to say," she returned, surprising him with the cool quality to her voice. "It wasn't your family he destroyed."

"I know how it feels to lose everything precious to you," he countered. Erin conceded his point by offering a barely perceptible nod but the look in her eyes remained resolute. He tried not to pass judgment but he was having a hard enough time reconciling the fact that his own boss was guilty of covering up a crime, much less accepting that given the choice Erin would've probably helped kick the shit out of Hank Walker right along with them. Hell, in her current state of mind she probably would've thrown the first punch.

Silence stretched between them until Butterscotch ambled over to Erin and nudged her with her nose, leaving a slightly wet spot against her jeans. Cracking a reluctant smile, Erin reached down and scratched between the dog's ears. "So much for that killer instinct, huh?" she asked with a wry twist of her lips. "Guess I won't be playing up your watchdog skills."

She met Colin's gaze and the small smile she wore slowly faded. There was still a lot left unsaid between them. "Can we leave?"

He nodded. "Just say the word."

Somehow her frozen lips formed a smile, and after calling Butterscotch to her side, walked out the door still unable to believe what had just happened both now and in the past.

THE RIDE TO HIS HOUSE HAD BEEN silent but he could almost feel the turmoil that was surely knotting Erin's insides. Her expression was that of a traveler lost in a foreign country with no passport or friends to call, and Colin desperately wanted to reach out, to let her know she wasn't alone.

He'd called ahead to ask his sister if Danni could stay the night so Erin could have a measure of privacy and Sara willingly agreed, despite the fact that the last time Danni was supposed to hang around she'd happily ditched Sara to hang out with her loser friends.

Erin followed behind him and he quickly unlocked and opened the door for her.

Once inside, he turned up the heat and headed toward the kitchen. "Erin, can I get you something to eat? You've got to be hungry by now."

Erin shook her head but Colin brought her a glass of orange juice just the same. "Here, drink this. It's full of vitamins."

He was rewarded with a small smile but she took it. She headed for the sofa and sat down, the glass still in her hand, untouched. As if remembering, she slowly lifted it and took a sip. She nodded then put the glass down on the end table. "Where's Danni?" she asked, her voice scratchy.

"At my sister Sara's house," he answered, wishing she'd drink some more but knowing not to push it. "Her husband is stationed in Iraq, so she's always happy for a little help with the baby."

Erin gave a slight nod then looked up at him. "I'm sorry for disrupting your life," she said, her voice catching. "I never meant…"

Unable to take another minute, Colin shushed her gently and pulled her into his arms. Somehow he knew she was talking about more than just what had happened with Caroline and it worried him. She hadn't disrupted his life, she had enriched it. His mouth burned to tell her that somewhere along the way, he'd fallen in love with her but the knowledge she'd probably bolt made him keep his confession to himself. Instead he pressed an urgent kiss to the top of her head and held her tight.

"It's not fair," Erin said, shaking her head. "My mom, Caroline…Charlie…such tragedy."

A shudder went through her body and Colin held her tighter. When Colin felt the shivers stop, he loosened his hold but didn't let go. A few moments went by before she lifted her head to meet his stare. The loss reflecting back at him was more than he could stand. Tenderly, he cupped her chin and brought her lips to his for a soft kiss. Resting her head against his chest, she went on, "To think I've lived my entire life in the dark about what happened to my own family. Why didn't Caroline tell me?"

"I'm sure she was trying to protect you," he answered, hearing the echo of the excuse he'd given to her about Danni. He pushed the uncomfortable comparison aside. "Caroline was that type of person, always thinking of others before herself."

Erin sniffed back impending tears. "She was, wasn't she?" She laughed softly, though the moment was fleeting. "Damn it, Caroline. Why couldn't you have been just a little less selfless? If I'd known…"

"Nothing would've changed," Colin countered quietly. When she pulled away and gave him a look of protest, he continued, "You needed to go. Even though I don't believe in stuff like destiny, I have to believe you were meant to find your place somewhere else. To find yourself. You have an amazing talent, one you wouldn't have fostered if you'd stayed here." *A talent that was bigger than this town could contain.*

The rest he left unsaid. It was selfish of him to want her to stay but he did. He wanted much more than she was offering. But at the very least he had this moment and he was going to take it. Pulling her to him, he took her mouth with all the fierce emotion twisting his insides and confusing his brain.

He groaned as her tongue slipped into his mouth to twine with his own and he was lost to all reason. Cradling her bottom with his hands, he picked her up without breaking the kiss and strode into his bedroom.

They fell onto the bed, their hands touching and stroking, while their mouths tasted and devoured, and soon both were burning to feel skin on skin. Their clothes were left in a discarded pile at the foot of the bed and Colin reveled in the perfect texture of her skin, the unique, intoxicating scent of her body.

The urge to possess her was nearly equal to the ferocity of her passion to receive him. Pausing only long enough to grab a condom from his nightstand drawer, Colin delighted in her excited moan as he slipped inside, burying himself within her hot folds. Her breathing became shallow and her body stiffened, arching, and his release followed seconds later. His body exploding into a million pieces.

Pulling from his last reserve of strength, he reluctantly rolled from Erin's body to lie beside her with one arm thrown across her naked belly. His eyelids drooped and a fatigue unlike any he'd ever known dragged on his body. His last thought before dropping off to sleep was inadvertently mumbled against her shoulder. *I love you.*

CHAPTER SIXTEEN

ERIN AWOKE EARLY TO find herself curled around Colin's body, momentarily content with the delicious and comforting feel of his solid warmth. The sound of his deep, rhythmic breathing told her he was still fast asleep. Closing her eyes briefly, she savored the stolen moment for as long as she dared before carefully sliding from the bed and quietly gathering her discarded clothing.

Making love had been a temporary balm to the bone-wrenching pain spreading like a cancer through her body, but she knew reality would eventually awaken the beast curled inside, waiting to devour her soul. She gulped down a sob and jerked her clothes on. If she stayed another minute in Granite Hills, she'd lose her mind to the grief that at this very moment threatened to snap her in half. She had no choice but to return to San Francisco. She'd bury herself in work, she reasoned, when something deep inside broke and wept at the thought of leaving Colin. "He's better off without me," she whispered to herself. But even as the words left her mouth she felt a part of her growing cold and brittle inside.

Shaking her head, she mercilessly turned her mind to the issue of leaving and blocked all feelings that protested in response. There was much to do before she could leave this nightmare behind. First, she needed to make some phone calls.

When Colin awoke an hour later, Erin had already given instructions to the hospital for Charlie's care, and called Granite Hills's only taxi service to pick her up.

"Morning," he said, his voice still husky from sleep. The sound threatened to coax a smile from her lips until she reminded herself of what was to come. "Want some coffee?" he asked.

She checked her watch. The taxi should be here in about fifteen minutes. She probably had time for one cup. "That would be great," she said politely.

At her tone, Colin's vision seemed to clear and all remnants of sleep disappeared. "You're leaving, aren't you?"

His grim tone told her an answer wasn't needed but she nodded anyway. She swallowed and waited for his response but he gave her none. Instead, he walked to the kitchen and began to prepare the coffee. The sound of fresh coffee beans grinding sounded altogether too comforting, almost homey, and Erin had to blink back the tears springing to her eyes. This was what she wanted. This felt like home.

He took a seat opposite her. "Do you need a ride?" he asked, drawing her eyes to the bitter set of his jaw.

She gave a small shake of her head, almost not trusting her voice not to waver when she replied. "I called a taxi."

He snorted and looked away. "I'd hardly call an old beat-up Buick a taxi. Why don't you let me take you?"

Because if I spend too much more time with you I won't leave.

Her heart contracted and she forced herself to say the exact opposite of what she felt. "Because I don't want you to." At the sudden hurt shining in his eyes, she quickly amended. "It's not personal.... I just think it's time for me to go."

The soft beep of the coffeemaker distracted him and she was glad. There was no sense in dragging out the inevitable. She'd known this time would come, though she had no idea that when it did she'd feel as if someone were tearing out her heart with the dull edge of a butter knife.

He returned with two cups of steaming coffee, one of which she accepted with genuine gratitude. The first tentative sip sent heat and blessed energy spiraling into her veins. It didn't erase the pain but it gave her the strength to do what was needed. A horn, which sounded more like a whoopee cushion being sat on, was followed by a loud backfire outside and Erin nearly dropped her cup. "I guess that's my ride."

Colin stood grim-faced as Erin shouldered her purse and prepared for an awkward goodbye. She avoided his eyes, knowing that if she caught the depth of his feelings, it would take very little to override her good sense and fall back into his arms. "Thank you for everything," she said, tentatively offering her hand.

His gaze narrowed but he took it just the same. The familiar feel of his strong hand enveloping hers awoke heated memories and desire weakened her knees. As she tried to snatch her hand away, Colin pulled her to him. Tears sprang to her eyes and she tried to shake her head, to communicate how if they kissed she'd lose herself but her mouth wouldn't form the words. Instead, she felt herself, pressed against him with the warmth of his mouth nuzzling her neck, inhaling his unique scent as if committing it to memory.

"Colin," she cried softly against his mouth as a single tear slid down her face. How was she to survive leaving him when she'd already lost so much? The pain came back in a wave, slapping her hard enough to make her gasp for air. Pushing away, she moved quickly to the door, snapping her fingers for Butterscotch to follow.

"Erin!"

The anguished sound of her name stilled her hand on the doorknob but she refused to look at him.

"Please don't go."

She knew in her heart Colin wasn't the kind of man to beg and it bowed her that she had caused this strong man to bend so unnaturally.

"Erin. I love you," he said, his voice breaking. The very sound dragging on her heart and pulling her gaze despite her attempts to fight it.

Ignoring the keening of her soul and the strong desire to run to him, Erin purposefully hardened her voice to deliver what she knew would be a crushing blow. "Don't. I've got nothing for you. I can't stay here. Even if it weren't for the memories of the past tripping me up, there'd be these *wonderful* new ones of a homicidal nut job holding me at gun point to deal with. I'm sorry."

She turned but not quickly enough. She jerked the door open and ran to the vehicle that was idling in the driveway but she knew no matter how fast she ran, she'd never escape Colin's crestfallen expression. Not even if she lived to be a hundred.

As the plane taxied down the runway, Erin kept her mind carefully blank.

Things will settle down once I get back into a routine, she promised herself, yet a golf-ball-sized lump made her words feel hollow.

She worried about Butterscotch, riding in the cargo bay with the rest of the animals, and hoped the poor girl didn't suffer a heart attack from the ordeal.

Harvey already had another assignment waiting for her, which suited her just fine. Work kept her mind from straying into territory that was off-limits or giving in to the urge to hide in a darkened corner and weep for days.

There had only been time to make a few calls to a local service to close up Caroline's house before she had to get to the airport. The need to get the hell out of Dodge had been her driving force, but in hindsight she hoped the mother-daughter team was trustworthy. All she'd asked them to do was box everything up and haul it to the attic.

The cold, analytical side of her said the smart thing to do would be to give it all to Goodwill, but despite her intentions to do just that, at the last second she changed her mind. She could always have it done at a later date if it came down to it and she hadn't wanted to deal with the emotional repercussions.

Closing herself off to the feelings threatening to swamp her, she purposefully shut her eyes and drifted into a black, dreamless sleep.

CHAPTER SEVENTEEN

ERIN WAS GONE. Cursing himself for being ten times the fool for falling for a woman who had been up front from the beginning that she had no intentions of staying, he tried pushing the memories of their short time together as far away from his conscious mind as possible.

Now two weeks later, he realized that he couldn't keep Danni in the dark any longer. He didn't want their secrets to destroy his daughter as they had Erin's family.

Going into his office, he pulled a box from his safe that contained the mementos of his life with Danielle before she became sick, and called Danni into the living room.

"What?" Danni's tone was impatient. He gestured for her to take a seat and her gaze zeroed in on the box. "What's that?"

"This," he said, removing the lid and pulling out a framed wedding photo, "is your mother as I like to remember her."

Danni's expression changed from wary to one of wonder as she took the simply framed photo from his hand. Although Colin had kept a few pictures of Danielle around for Danni, this was one she'd never seen. Danni traced her finger down Danielle's shining yellow hair, caught forever on film, and looked at him with sad tears in her eyes. "She was so pretty... Do you think I look like her?"

Colin's voice caught in his throat. "Almost right down to the stubborn tilt of her jaw whenever she thought I was being an ass."

Danni smiled shyly and returned her gaze to the photo. "Can I have this?"

He nodded. "Of course, you can. I'd always meant to give it to you but..."

As if remembering she was still angry with him, her expression darkened and she clutched the photo to her thin chest. "But what? You were too busy making up lies to tell me about her?"

He chose to ignore her dig but when she jumped to her feet to leave, he gently pulled her back down. "I'm not finished," he said, his tone firm. Once he was certain she understood he was serious, he continued, "I was wrong to lie to you about your mother. I suppose it doesn't matter but my intentions were good. In the end, it caused more hurt than it prevented. You're old enough now to hear the truth."

Danni's expression lost some of its glare and suddenly she looked a lot younger than her thirteen years. "I'm listening," she said in a small voice that was surely meant to sound more mature than it came out.

"Danielle was sick." Colin reached into the box

to pull assorted medical records from a manila envelope. "Bipolar with psychotic tendencies. I know you don't understand what that means but if you ever want to know more about your mother's illness, here are the records. You're welcome to read them."

Danni eyed the stack of paperwork and seemed overwhelmed by it. "I don't understand. Is it like a cancer?"

His daughter's innocence made his heart contract painfully with the memory of Danielle's illness. "No," he answered, his mouth drawn as if he were sucking on something bitter. "It's worse. Sometimes cancer can be cured. Being bipolar is a life sentence for most people. For those who recognize that they truly have a disease, it means a lifetime of medication and therapy to help ease the symptoms. But for those who don't believe they have a problem, it eventually destroys their lives. That's what happened to your mom."

"Is that why I never got to see her?"

Colin drew a deep breath, dreading this moment. He held his daughter's questioning gaze and hoped what he was about to say didn't scar her for life. "Throughout her sickness, your mother loved you very much but sometimes she didn't realize what she was doing could hurt you." Drawing on inner strength he didn't know existed until this moment, he went on. "One day I came home to find her trying to smother you with a pillow."

Shocked tears sprang to Danni's eyes and she shook her head. "My mom...tried to kill me?"

"Honey, she didn't know what she was doing. She'd stopped taking her medication and she was hallucinating. Once she realized what she'd done she was sick with remorse and made a solemn promise to stay on her meds, but she couldn't stick to it and I knew you'd never truly be safe. It broke my heart but I had to do what was necessary to protect you." He smoothed her hair and swallowed hard. "When Danielle gave herself a lethal dose of morphine I think it was because she didn't have the strength to keep fighting—and in the end, perhaps she didn't want you to see her that way."

They sat in silence and Colin rocked her like he used to when she was small. The ache in his heart at their rift slowly started to diminish as he realized coming clean was its own type of therapy for them both.

"Dad?" she asked, pulling away to meet his gaze. "What was she like before she got…sick?"

A genuinely warm smile formed on his lips as he looked down at Danni. "She was beautiful inside and out. Just like you."

She risked a tentative smile and Colin knew they were going to be all right. Even though it hurt just to think of her, Colin silently thanked Erin for her part in bringing his daughter back to him.

ERIN HANDED HARVEY THE FINISHED proofs that she'd e-mailed prior but, unlike before when she would've waited anxiously for his approval, she walked away before he'd even opened the folder, Butterscotch trailing at her feet.

"McNulty," he barked, causing her to pause in the doorway. When she turned and gave him her attention, he gestured to the proofs. "Don't you want to hear what I think of these? What if I don't think they're up to standard? And what's that dog doing here again!"

At his ludicrous and ultimately insulting questions, Erin almost laughed out loud and a moment of perfect clarity made her realize what her future with *American Photographic* would be if she took the position he had grudgingly offered upon her return. She graced him with a smile that had nothing in common with laughter and said, "Mr. Wallace, I don't give a damn what you think anymore. The pictures are good and you know it. If they're not up to your 'standard' then find someone else to provide you with ones that are. And the dog goes where I go. Get used to it." As if to illustrate that point, she reached down and gave Butterscotch an affectionate rub behind the ears.

Erin was vaguely aware that motion and chatter had ceased in the newsroom and she turned to see everyone staring and waiting fearfully for the explosion that would surely follow, but she didn't care. If she were honest with herself, there wasn't much she truly cared about these days. Not even the fervor in which she threw herself into her work managed to blot out the pain that seemed to linger like a malignancy in her system.

At this point, Harvey Wallace could kiss her ass. Judging by Harvey's shocked expression, that exact sentiment was written all over her face. Sensing for once Harvey had nothing to say, she turned on her heel and disappeared into her office.

Logging on to her computer, she purposefully avoided the file marked Hometown America, and tried focusing on her newest assignment—a *Vanity Fair*-type spread on an upcoming action hero—but it really couldn't hold her interest for long. Butterscotch whined at her feet and Erin sighed. "You're right. I'm tired of this place, too. Want to go home?"

Butterscotch licked her chops, rose as quickly as her stiff hip would allow and padded to the door expectantly. Erin chuckled. "Sometimes I think you're the smartest dog I've ever met. All right. You win. Home it is."

Except, she noted silently, her apartment no longer felt like home. "Details," she grumbled to the voice in her head only to feel completely stupid for talking to herself again. Eventually, the ache carving a hole in her chest would fade and she'd return to the life she left behind.

Right. And Butterscotch will start spouting proprietary information about baked beans, too.

Shouldering her camera bag, coat and gloves, she clicked Butterscotch's leash in place and headed for her apartment.

Later that night, a forgotten glass of wine in her hand as she stared out her window to the lit-up sky of her adopted city, she wondered what Colin was doing and how Danni was faring with the small camera she'd left behind for her. It was an innocent musing but the moment she pictured their faces a well of sadness threatened to drown her. Grimacing, she drained the glass and deliberately turned out the light, forgoing brushing her teeth or washing her face in the hopes sleep would come quickly. Although she knew even as she tossed, her dreams would provide no relief as Colin was there, too. Except in her dreams, when he asked her to stay...she did.

TWO WEEKS LATER, COLIN WAS called into Roger's office. He knew what the chief wanted to talk about and it didn't make his step any lighter.

"Go ahead and close the door, would you?"

Colin nodded, doing as he was asked, then took the chair opposite the chief. They sat evaluating each other until the chief broke the silence.

"I know what you're thinking. I helped kill a man and there's no statute of limitations on murder." When Colin didn't contradict him, he added, "I live with that every single moment of my life. I know you have to do what you feel is best. But I wanted you to be the first to know I've decided to retire."

Colin was shocked by the chief's announcement but he nodded in understanding.

"Here's another thing I'd like to present to you, perhaps something you haven't thought of." At Colin's puzzled expression, Roger leaned back in his chair, his face solemn. "As you've already found out, the trail is cold on Hank Walker's case. The records are gone and the only witnesses to it are dead and in a coma. Opening up this case would drag a good woman's name through the mud, ruin my career and send a man who's struggling to make a new life straight back to the bottle once the whispers and rumors start all over. I'm not saying what we did was right, but you're wrong if you think any one of us got off scot-free. We lost our innocence…and we lost Rose. It might be presumptuous of me to believe this, but we paid our dues to Hank Walker."

Colin's first impulse was to counter the chief's explanation with a stubborn adherence to the law. It was up to the courts to decide the measure of a man's guilt and penance, but as he thought of the destruction that had already touched the McNulty family and the knowledge that reopening the case would only cause further pain and suffering to everyone involved—including Erin—he couldn't bring himself to say the words.

"So you plan to retire, then?" he said, eyeing the chief.

Roger sighed. "Yeah, my health isn't what it used to be and truth be told, I'm tired. Vera's been after me to retire for some time but let's just say recent events have convinced me that it's best to enjoy the time we have left on this planet with our loved ones."

Caroline's face popped into his mind and Colin felt a wave of sorrow wash over him. He knew without having to be told Erin was suffering from an acute case of regret. If he hadn't been mired in his own pain at the realization he was losing her, he might've seen past the façade to the turmoil hidden inside. He had her cell phone number but each time he picked up the phone to call, his fingers refused to dial the number. The sound of the chief's voice jerked him to the present, forcing him to push thoughts of Erin away so he could function.

"No matter what your decision, I've decided to recommend you as my replacement."

Colin was unsure he'd heard the chief correctly. "Replacement…as chief?" Roger nodded and Colin's vision began to swim. "I'm hardly qualified—"

"Let me be the judge of that," he said gruffly. "Colin, to tell you the truth, before any of this happened, I was eyeing you as my replacement. You're a man of solid character, a good cop and an excellent role model for this department. As far as the other stuff…well, therein lies the advantage of small town politics. Leave that to me. Basically, if you want it, the job is yours."

Colin could only stare but Roger seemed to understand and didn't hold his silence against him. "I'll give you a few days to think about it," he said.

Chief of police. His heart rate accelerated. Becoming the chief had always been his ambition someday. "Chief… I don't know what to say…."

"Say you'll do it. Granite Hills would be lucky to have you at the helm." A playfully wry smile lifted the corners of the chief's mouth as he added, "And I'm not just saying that because I'm trying to stay out of prison."

He chuckled softly in spite of the topic, still overwhelmed. "When do you need an answer?"

"As soon as possible…on both accounts."

Colin left the office, his head crammed with possibilities. He couldn't help but wish Erin were there to help him with the decision. When was he going to get over her? The pain of her leaving seemed to get worse, not better, as each day passed and he wondered if she ever thought of him the way his mind seemed to never let her go.

DANNI HEARD HER DAD COME in and go through the motions of unloading his gun from the holster and securing it in the locked safe in his office. She was doing homework, or at least trying to focus on the reading materials assigned, but her mind kept wandering. Her gaze strayed to the camera Erin had left for her and her forehead furrowed. She wished Erin had stayed. She wasn't like most grown-ups, who ignored kids or treated them like they had nothing interesting to say. Although she wouldn't admit it at the time, she had sort of hoped Erin might like her dad. Now, in hindsight, she realized with a proverbial smack to the head her dad might actually be in love with Erin.

She'd been too busy to notice the signs before but now, as she searched her memory, she realized what had been staring her in the face the whole time.

She dropped her pencil into her book to mark her place and padded over to her camera. Her enthusiasm had been slightly dampened by the realization that Erin wouldn't be around to teach her to use it properly, but she loved snapping pictures of whatever caught her eye, waiting for the right moment, as Erin had taught her.

Wandering back to her bed, she let herself fall, not even caring when the row of stuffed animals bounced to the floor. Stuffed animals were for babies anyway. At least that's what Allen said. She scrunched up her face at the thought of him and wondered if she even cared what he had to say. Since making up with her dad, she realized she had nothing in common with the kids she was hanging around with. All they wanted to do was play mailbox baseball or sit around and smoke cigarettes—or worse. Her cheeks flamed in embarrassment at being caught with marijuana. She didn't even like the smell of the stuff. It stunk like dirty socks left in a wet hamper too long but at the time it'd been worth it just to catch her dad's expression. Now, she just felt ashamed for worrying him. What the heck was she doing with those wastoids, besides ruining her life? After her court appearance next week, she was never going near Allen and his crew ever again. Besides, she missed her old friends. A shadow passed over her thoughts. What if they didn't take her back? Then, she'd make new ones, she countered. But something told her, she wouldn't need to go down that road. Her real friends were there for her. No matter how much she's screwed up.

Her gaze roamed to the framed picture of her parents that now sat on her dresser. She wanted to make it up to her dad somehow. Lately, he seemed…sad. He tried to hide it but she knew him too well.

Peeking around the corner she saw her dad busy trying to throw something together for dinner. Tip-toeing to his cell phone she snagged it and quickly returned to her bedroom. She had a feeling he kept Erin's number in the memory. Scrolling, she smiled when she found it.

Wasting no time, she quickly dialed. It rang twice before Erin picked up, her voice hesitant.

"Hello?"

"Erin? This is Danni."

Was that a breath of relief or disappointment…? Danni couldn't tell.

"Hey kid, how's the camera treating you?"

"Good! I love it. I want to show you some of the pictures I took and see what you think. Do you have an e-mail address I can send them to?"

Erin did and gave her the address without hesita-tion. The subject of photography was an easy ice-breaker to what Danni was really interested in talking about. After a few questions were answered regarding lighting and some confusion over the f-stops was cleared up, Danni bit her lip and plunged forward.

"Erin…I think my dad misses you a lot," Danni said, holding her breath a second before adding truthfully, "and I do, too. When are you coming back for a visit?"

On the other end, Erin's heart raced and she would've laughed at Danni's childish straight-forward manner if she hadn't felt as if someone had put their fist through her chest. He missed her. Tears sprang to her eyes but she tried to keep the watery sound from her voice. "It's hard to say, Danni. I'm up against some pretty tight deadlines...."

Suddenly an echo of Caroline's voice stopped her as she realized she'd always given the same excuse to her aunt. Her breath hitched in her throat and she struggled to keep her voice stable. "Well, I'll try. I'd love to see you again." She refrained from admitting seeing Colin again might break the tenuous hold she had on her determination to stay away. He was better off without her, she reasoned. But the old argument lost some of its conviction as Danni went on about how much her dad had changed since she left.

"He kind of mopes," Danni confided. "You know, like he's depressed or something. He tries to hide it but he isn't any good at it. He stares out the window a lot, too, and that's just plain weird, if you ask me."

Erin had to laugh, though she could certainly relate. No matter how hard she tried to exhaust her body during the day, by night, she was staring out at the city streets, looking but not seeing.

"And you'd think he'd be totally happy since he was offered the position of chief of police! I'm not sure if he's going to take it, though."

Erin sat up straighter. "Roger Hampton is retiring?"

Danni sounded bored. "Yeah, something about his health, I guess."

Erin knew the real reason but strangely she didn't fault Roger for his decision. The whole situation had affected everyone in different ways. "Why doesn't your dad want the job?"

Erin could almost hear Danni shrug. "Dunno. He just doesn't want it."

Groaning, she almost asked Danni to put her dad on the phone but seconds before it popped out of her mouth she reined in the impulse. "Well, I guess your dad will do what's best for your family," she said lamely.

Danni snorted. "You haven't seen him lately. He's like a different person."

Erin started to offer some excuse but Danni cut in. "Erin…do you love my dad?"

The question, brutally honest and just like a kid to ask without hesitation, left Erin speechless. Danni pressed on.

"Here's the thing. I think my dad loves you and if you can make my dad happy I want you guys to work whatever it is out so you can be together again." Danni paused, and then her voice dropped to a solemn tone usually reserved for a confessional. "My dad hasn't fallen in love with anyone since my mom…died. I never really thought about it until I realized how he was when he was around you. His eyes got all warm and gooey when he looked at you and I can tell he thinks you're something special. That says a lot in my book. My dad's a pretty good guy. Don't you think?"

The question, delivered with a child's earnestness, hung between them. Finally, Erin answered with a whisper. "Yes. Your dad's one of the best."

Danni seemed to breathe a sigh of relief. "Then why are you still there and not here with us?"

CHAPTER EIGHTEEN

ERIN STEPPED OFF THE PLANE with her heart in her mouth. She had two major tasks ahead of her. One, she had to pick up her father from the hospital; and two, she had to undo the damage she'd created between her and Colin.

It'd been a week since Danni's phone call and two days since she'd quit *American Photographic*. Her father had awoken, groggy and confused as to where he was and began ripping I.V. lines from his body as if they were leeches dining on his blood. Erin almost laughed as she recalled the doctor's account.

"Ms. McNulty, I've never seen a man so strong after lying in a coma for as long as he did. He must have a will of steel!"

Erin had chuckled. If only he knew…

They'd had to sedate Charlie to keep him from splitting open the stitches that were holding his insides together. Erin found it vaguely ironic that after awakening from a coma, he was immediately put under sedation for his safety. But it was just as well—she wanted to be there for him when he received the news Caroline was gone. Somehow she knew he'd take the news better if she were there. She figured if they were to rebuild their relationship, now was as good a time as any. Erin finally understood what Caroline was trying to tell her about the importance of family. Now that she was gone, Erin was determined to make an effort to pick up the pieces of the McNulty clan. Patching her relationship with Charlie was a start. She tried picturing Caroline smiling down at her for her decision but tears were never far behind when thoughts of Caroline entered her mind.

But, even so, the years of anger weren't easily wiped away, no matter the circumstances. She and Charlie were due a very long conversation—and Erin wasn't under any misconceptions on how difficult it would be to quell the angry echoes of their past. But for the first time, she was willing to try.

Quitting the magazine had been relatively easy once she figured out that she had no desire to be Harvey Wallace's No. 1 whipping girl. She was talented and could work anywhere, which was what she planned to do when she returned to freelance work. She had enough in her savings to float for a year if need be, but she wasn't wasting much more time on that issue. Right now, her heart was hammering in her chest at the thought of one meeting.

Colin.

It'd been almost a month since she'd seen him last but it felt like a lifetime. In all that time she hadn't dared to call, though she'd wanted to. It wasn't until Danni's phone call that she realized she was clinging to old habits, when in the end, they'd done nothing but bring her misery.

Still, she couldn't deny the shiver of fear that traveled through her at the thought of seeing Colin again. Would he reject her? Was he angry? She wouldn't fault him if he was but she could only hope he felt the same as she did—anxious to see if they had a future together.

There was only one way to find out.

COLIN HAD HEARD CHARLIE MCNULTY was awake and immediately placed under sedation until his daughter could arrive, but he deliberately stayed away from the hospital. He wasn't so pathetic that he would follow her like some lovesick puppy when she clearly wasn't interested in his affections. But the effort it took to keep from doing just that made him surly. When everyone began giving him a wide berth at the station, he knew it was impossible to push her from his mind.

Gripping the report he was trying to read in his hands, he forced his attention to the words that had become nonsensical as his thoughts wandered.

Suddenly, Leslie appeared at his desk and he nearly snapped her head off when she started talking.

Swearing under his breath, he began an apology but she cut him off. "There's someone here to see you." She moved aside and Erin was there. Sucking in a surprised gasp, he couldn't believe she was standing before him when so many times he'd dreamt of the very same scene, yet woken up alone.

"I'll leave you two to talk," Leslie said before turning to give Colin a glare. "And if you're not in a better mood after this, I don't care if you're the chief or not I'm gonna give you a swift kick in your ass!"

The corners of Erin's mouth twitched at Leslie's comment. "I always liked her," she said, her voice a little breathless.

He wanted to be cold, to tell her there was nothing for her in his heart, but he knew it was useless to try. His hands were trembling as he fought the urge to crush her to him. He swallowed and gave a short nod in response. "How's Charlie?" he asked, searching wildly for neutral territory.

"Ornery as ever," she said. "He took Caroline's death really hard. It'll be a while before he can say her name without turning away so no one can see his tears."

"And you?" He barely got the words out, afraid of what her answer would be. He wasn't sure if he could stomach the thought of Erin moving on so quickly.

"I quit *American Photographic*," she replied. When his eyes widened in surprise, she added, "And I'm thinking of moving out of San Francisco."

Thoughts of a new relationship flew to his mind and he fought to keep the bitterness out of his voice. "I'm happy for you."

She took a hesitant step closer. "Are you?"

"Of course, Erin," he said, finding the scent of her skin distracting. "Your happiness is important to me."

"Good." Suddenly, she wound her arms around his neck and his arms automatically closed around her, drawing her close. She looked up at him and her eyes roamed his face as if he were the most beautiful man she'd ever seen. "Because I've discovered I'm most happy—" she pulled his head down to press her lips to his "—with you."

EPILOGUE

COLIN SMILED AS HE WATCHED Erin critique Danni's latest batch of photos. Butterscotch had adopted Danni and never left her side, despite her slow gait. To her credit, Danni never got frustrated with the old girl and had even put a new dog bed for Butterscotch in her room.

Colin couldn't help but swell with pride as Erin delivered genuine praise over the fledgling attempts. Erin looked up and caught his smile, returning it with a blinding one of her own.

He didn't think it was possible but each day she became more beautiful. She rolled her eyes at him whenever he told her so but he could tell she enjoyed hearing it, especially when she felt ungainly and awkward as her belly continued to protrude with their expected twins. He loved to rub her stomach and watch as his unborn children moved under the taut skin. Erin complained that they were using her kidneys as punching bags and her bladder as a trampoline but the comment was delivered with an excited twinkle in her eye. They decided to name the babies, both girls, after Caroline and Rose. When

Erin had approached him with the suggestion, he'd hugged her close, believing it was only fitting. In their own way, the two ladies had brought Erin and Colin together. He hoped both were finally at peace.

Charlie was coming over for dinner, and though Erin's relationship with her father wasn't typical, it worked for them. He was a crusty curmudgeon, but Erin had discovered the soft underbelly he'd been trying to protect all those years and his blustering was mostly an act these days. In fact, Charlie was keeping busy carving a double cradle for the girls. He said the project kept him going when the bad times hit.

And there were bad times. Times when grief bowled him over and the temptation to drink returned but Erin was always there for him. Erin had insisted Charlie move out of that falling-down shack and into Caroline's house, which he did but not before giving her an earful about how he liked where he was and didn't want to leave. In the end, he agreed to move and secretly, Colin believed that Charlie was glad to get away from the memories locked behind those old walls. Somehow, Erin had known that and managed to push without making Charlie feel railroaded. Her insight and generosity of spirit never ceased to move Colin. She was one amazing woman.

And she was all his.

"Just what are you grinning about, Chief?" Erin asked playfully, coming to slip her arms around his waist as much as her burgeoning belly would allow.

He gazed into the startling blue eyes that had taken hold of his heart at their very first meeting and nearly melted at the love cascading through his body.

"Just wondering how I got so lucky," he answered, placing a sweet kiss on the tip of her nose.

Erin's stare drifted over to Danni, who was busy fiddling with her camera, and her hand slid over her stomach in a caress. She closed her eyes and when she opened them again, they were shining with happiness. "Me, too."

* * * * *

Design Tip of the Day

Ambience is everything. Imagine eating a foie gras at a luncheonette counter or a side of coleslaw at Le Cirque. It's not a matter of food but one of atmosphere. Remember that when planning your dining room design.
—Tips from *Teddi.com*

"Now that's the kind of man you should be looking for," my mother, the self-appointed keeper of my shelf-life stamp, says. She points with her fork at a man in the corner of the Steak-Out Restaurant, a dive I've just been hired to redecorate. Making this restaurant look four-star will be hard, but not half as hard as getting through lunch without strangling the woman across the table from me. "He would make a good husband."

"Oh, you can tell that from across the room?" I ask, wondering how it is she can forget that when we had trouble getting rid of my last husband, she shot him. "Besides being ten minutes away from death if he actually eats all that steak, he's twenty years too old for me and—shallow woman that I am—twenty pounds too heavy. Besides, I am *so* not looking for another husband here. I'm looking to design a new image for this place, looking for some sense of ambience, some feeling, something I can build a proposal on for them."

My mother studies the man in the corner, tilting her head, the better to gauge his age, I suppose. I think she's grimacing, but with all the Botox and Restylane injected into that face, it's hard to tell. She takes another bite of her steak salad, chews slowly so that I don't miss the fact that the steak is a poor cut and tougher than it should be. "You're concentrating on the wrong kind of proposal," she says finally. "Just look at this place, Teddi. It's a dive. There are hardly any other diners. What does *that* tell you about the food?"

"That they cater to a dinner crowd and it's lunchtime," I tell her.

I don't know what I was thinking bringing her here with me. I suppose I thought it would be better than eating alone. There really are days when my common sense goes on vacation. Clearly, this is one of them. I mean, really, did I not resolve less than three weeks ago that I would not let my mother get to me anymore?

What good are New Year's resolutions, anyway?

Mario approaches the man's table and my mother studies him while they converse. Eventually Mario leaves the table with a huff, after which the diner glances up and meets my mother's gaze. I think she's smiling at him. That, or she's got indigestion. They size each other up.

I concentrate on making sketches in my notebook and try to ignore the fact that my mother is flirting. At nearly seventy, she's developed an unhealthy interest in members of the opposite sex to whom she isn't married.

According to my father, who has broken the TMI rule and given me Too Much Information, she has no interest in sex with him. Better, I suppose, to be clued in on what they aren't doing in the bedroom than have to hear what they might be doing.

"He's not so old," my mother says, noticing that I have barely touched the Chinese chicken salad she warned me not to get. "He's got about as many years on you as you have on your little cop friend."

She does this to make me crazy. I know it, but it works all the same. "Drew Scoones is not my little 'friend.' He's a detective with whom I—"

"Screwed around," my mother says. I must look shocked, because my mother laughs at me and asks if I think she doesn't know the "lingo."

What I thought she didn't know was that Drew and I actually tangled in the sheets. And, since it's possible she's just fishing, I sidestep the issue and tell her that Drew is just a couple of years younger than me and that I don't need reminding. I dig into my salad with renewed vigor, determined to show my mother that Chinese chicken salad in a steak place was not the stupid choice it's proving to be.

After a few more minutes of my picking at the wilted leaves on my plate, the man my mother has me nearly engaged to pays his bill and heads past us toward the back of the restaurant. I watch my mother take in his shoes, his suit and the diamond pinkie ring that seems to be cutting off the circulation in his little finger.

"Such nice hands," she says after the man is out of sight. "Manicured." She and I both stare at my hands. I have two popped acrylics that are being held on at weird angles by bandages. My cuticles are ragged and there's marker decorating my right hand from measuring carelessly when I did a drawing for a customer.

Twenty minutes later she's disappointed that he managed to leave the restaurant without our noticing. He will join the list of the ones I let get away. I will hear about him twenty years from now when—according to my mother—my children will be grown and I will still be single, living pathetically alone with several dogs and cats.

After my ex, that sounds good to me.

The waitress tells us that our meal has been taken care of by the management and, after thanking Mario, the owner, complimenting him on the wonderful meal and assuring him that once I have redecorated his place people will be flocking here in droves (I actually use those words and ignore my mother when she rolls her eyes), my mother and I head for the restroom.

My father—unfortunately not with us today—

has the patience of a saint. He got it over the years of living with my mother. She, perhaps as a result, figures he has the patience for both of them, and feels justified having none. For her, no rules apply, and a little thing like a picture of a man on the door to a public restroom is certainly no barrier to using the john. In all fairness, it does seem silly to stand and wait for the ladies' room if no one is using the men's room.

Still, it's the idea that rules don't apply to her, signs don't apply to her, conventions don't apply to her. She knocks on the door to the men's room. When no one answers she gestures to me to go in ahead. I tell her that I can certainly wait for the ladies' room to be free and she shrugs and goes in herself.

Not a minute later there is a bloodcurdling scream from behind the men's room door.

"Mom!" I yell. "Are you all right?"

Mario comes running over, the waitress on his heels. Two customers head our way while my mother continues to scream.

I try the door, but it is locked. I yell for her to open it and she fumbles with the knob. When she finally manages to unlock and open it, she is white behind her two streaks of blush, but she is on her feet and appears shaken but not stirred.

"What happened?" I ask her. So do Mario and the waitress and the few customers who have migrated to the back of the place.

She points toward the bathroom and I go in,

thinking it serves her right for using the men's room. But I see nothing amiss.

She gestures toward the stall, and, like any self-respecting and suspicious woman, I poke the door open with one finger, expecting the worst.

What I find is worse than the worst.

The husband my mother picked out for me is sitting on the toilet. His pants are puddled around his ankles, his hands are hanging at his sides. Pinned to his chest is some sort of Health Department certificate.

Oh, and there is a large, round, bloodless bullet hole between his eyes.

Four Nassau County police officers are securing the area, waiting for the detectives and crime scene personnel to show up. They are trying, though not very hard, to comfort my mother, who in another era would be considered to be suffering from the vapors. Less tactful in the twenty-first century, I'd say she was losing it. That is, if I didn't know her better, she was milking it for everything it was worth.

My mother loves attention. As it begins to flag, she swoons and claims to feel faint. Despite four No Smoking signs, my mother insists it's all right for her to light up because, after all, she's in shock. Not to mention that signs, as we know, don't apply to her.

When asked not to smoke, she collapses mournfully in a chair and lets her head loll to the side, all without mussing her hair.

Eventually, the detectives show up to find the

four patrolmen all circled around her, debating whether to administer CPR, smelling salts or simply call the paramedics. I, however, know just what will snap her to attention.

"Detective Scoones," I say loudly. My mother parts the sea of cops.

"We have to stop meeting like this," he says lightly to me, but I can feel him checking me over with his eyes, making sure I'm all right while pretending not to care.

"What have you got in those pants?" my mother asks him, coming to her feet and staring at his crotch accusingly. "*Baydar?* Everywhere we Bayers are, you turn up. You don't expect me to buy that this is a coincidence, I hope."

Drew tells my mother that it's nice to see her, too, and asks if it's his fault that her daughter seems to attract disasters.

Charming to be made to feel like the bearer of a plague.

He asks how I am.

"Just peachy," I tell him. "I seem to be making a habit of finding dead bodies, my mother is driving me crazy and the catering hall I booked two freakin' years ago for Dana's bat mitzvah has just been shut down by the Board of Health!"

"Glad to see your luck's finally changing," he says, giving me a quick squeeze around the shoulders before turning his attention to the patrolmen, asking what they've got, whether they've taken any statements, moved anything, all the sort of stuff you see on TV, without any of the drama. That is, if you don't count my mother's threats to faint every few minutes when she senses no one's paying attention to her.

Mario tells his waitstaff to bring everyone espresso, which I decline because I'm wired enough. Drew pulls him aside and a minute later I'm handed a cup of coffee that smells divinely of Kahlúa.

The man knows me well. Too well.

His partner, whom I've met once or twice, says he'll interview the kitchen staff. Drew asks Mario if he minds if he takes statements from the patrons first and gets to him and the waitstaff afterward.

"No, no," Mario tells him. "Do the patrons first." Drew raises his eyebrow at me like he wants to know if I get the double entendre. I try to look bored.

"What is it with you and murder victims?" he asks me when we sit down at a table in the corner.

I search them out so that I can see you again, I almost say, but I'm afraid it will sound desperate instead of sarcastic.

My mother, lighting up and daring him with a look to tell her not to, reminds him that *she* was the one to find the body.

Drew asks what happened *this time*. My mother tells him how the man in the john was "taken" with me, couldn't take his eyes off me and blatantly flirted with both of us. To his credit, Drew doesn't laugh, but his smirk is undeniable to the trained eye. And I've had my eye trained on him for nearly a year now.

"While he was noticing you," he asks me, "did

you notice anything about him? Was he waiting for anyone? Watching for anything?"

I tell him that he didn't appear to be waiting or watching. That he made no phone calls, was fairly intent on eating and did, indeed, flirt with my mother. This last bit Drew takes with a grain of salt, which was the way it was intended.

"And he had a short conversation with Mario," I tell him. "I think he might have been unhappy with the food, though he didn't send it back."

Drew asks what makes me think he was dissatisfied, and I tell him that the discussion seemed acrimonious and that Mario looked distressed when he left the table. Drew makes a note and says he'll look into it and asks about anyone else in the restaurant. Did I see anyone who didn't seem to belong, anyone who was watching the victim, anyone looking suspicious?

"Besides my mother?" I ask him, and Mom huffs and blows her cigarette smoke in my direction.

I tell him that there were several deliveries, the kitchen staff going in and out the back door to grab a smoke. He stops me and asks what I was doing checking out the back door of the restaurant.

Proudly—because, while he was off forgetting me, dropping by only once in a while to say hi to Jesse, my son, or drop something by for one of my daughters that he thought they might like, I was getting on with my life—I tell him that I'm decorating the place.

He looks genuinely impressed. "Commercial customers? That's great," he says. Okay, that's what he *ought* to say. What he actually says is "Whatever pays the bills."

"Howard Rosen, the famous restaurant critic, got her the job," my mother says. "You met him—the good-looking, distinguished gentleman with the *real* job, something to be proud of. I guess you've never read his reviews in *Newsday*."

Drew, without missing a beat, tells her that Howard's reviews are on the top of his list, as soon as he learns how to read.

"I only meant—" my mother starts, but both of us assure her that we know just what she meant.

"So," Drew says. "Deliveries?"

I tell him that Mario would know better than I, but that I saw vegetables come in, maybe fish and linens.

"This is the second restaurant job Howard's got her," my mother tells Drew.

"At least she's getting *something* out of the relationship," he says.

"If he were here," my mother says, ignoring the insinuation, "he'd be comforting her instead of interrogating her. He'd be making sure we're both all right after such an ordeal."

"I'm sure he would," Drew agrees, then looks me in the eyes as if he's measuring my tolerance for shock. Quietly he adds, "But then maybe he doesn't know just what strong stuff your daughter's made of."

It's the closest thing to a tender moment I can expect from Drew Scoones. My mother breaks the spell. "She gets that from me," she says.

Both Drew and I take a minute, probably to pray that's all I inherited from her.

"I'm just trying to save you some time and effort," my mother tells him. "My money's on Howard."

Drew withers her with a look and mutters something that sounds suspiciously like "fool's gold." Then he excuses himself to go back to work.

I catch his sleeve and ask if it's all right for us to leave. He says sure, he knows where we live. I say goodbye to Mario. I assure him that I will have some sketches for him in a few days, all the while hoping that this murder doesn't cancel his redecorating plans. I need the money desperately, the alternative being borrowing from my parents and being strangled by the strings.

My mother is strangely quiet all the way to her house. She doesn't tell me what a loser Drew Scoones is—despite his good looks—and how I was obviously drooling over him. She doesn't ask me where Howard is taking me tonight or warn me not to tell my father about what happened because he will worry about us both and no doubt insist we see our respective psychiatrists.

She fidgets nervously, opening and closing her purse over and over again.

"You okay?" I ask her. After all, she's just found a dead man on the toilet, and tough as she is that's got to be upsetting.

When she doesn't answer me I pull over to the side of the road.

"Mom?" She refuses to meet my eyes. "You want me to take you to see Dr. Cohen?"

She looks out the window as if she's just realized we're on Broadway in Woodmere. "Aren't we near

Marvin's Jewelers?" she asks, pulling something out of her purse.

"What have you got, Mother?" I ask, prying open her fingers to find the murdered man's ring.

"It was on the sink," she says in answer to my dropped jaw. "I was going to get his name and address and have you return it to him so that he could ask you out. I thought it was a sign that the two of you were meant to be together."

"He's dead, Mom. You understand that, right?" I ask. You never can tell when my mother is fine and when she's in la-la land.

"Well, I didn't know that," she shouts at me. "Not at the time."

I ask why she didn't give it to Drew, realize that she wouldn't give Drew the time in a clock shop and add, "...or one of the other policemen?"

"For heaven's sake," she tells me. "The man is dead, Teddi, and I took his ring. How would that look?"

Before I can tell her it looks just the way it is, she pulls out a cigarette and threatens to light it.

"I mean, really," she says, shaking her head like it's my brains that are loose. "What does he need with it now?"

REQUEST YOUR FREE BOOKS!

2 FREE NOVELS PLUS 2 FREE GIFTS!

HARLEQUIN®

Super Romance®

Exciting, emotional, unexpected!

YES! Please send me 2 FREE Harlequin Superromance® novels and my 2 FREE gifts. After receiving them, if I don't wish to receive any more books, I can return the shipping statement marked "cancel." If I don't cancel, I will receive 6 brand-new novels every month and be billed just $4.69 per book in the U.S., or $5.24 per book in Canada, plus 25¢ shipping and handling per book and applicable taxes, if any*. That's a savings of close to 15% off the cover price! I understand that accepting the 2 free books and gifts places me under no obligation to buy anything. I can always return a shipment and cancel at any time. Even if I never buy another book from Harlequin, the two free books and gifts are mine to keep forever.

135 HDN EEX7   336 HDN EEYK

Name	(PLEASE PRINT)	
Address		Apt.
City	State/Prov.	Zip/Postal Code

Signature (if under 18, a parent or guardian must sign)

Mail to Harlequin Reader Service®:

IN U.S.A.
P.O. Box 1867
Buffalo, NY
14240-1867

IN CANADA
P.O. Box 609
Fort Erie, Ontario
L2A 5X3

Not valid to current Harlequin Superromance subscribers.

Want to try two free books from another line?
Call 1-800-873-8635 or visit www.morefreebooks.com.

* Terms and prices subject to change without notice. NY residents add applicable sales tax. Canadian residents will be charged applicable provincial taxes and GST. This offer is limited to one order per household. All orders subject to approval. Credit or debit balances in a customer's account(s) may be offset by any other outstanding balance owed by or to the customer. Please allow 4 to 6 weeks for delivery.

HSR06

Silhouette®

SPECIAL EDITION™

Logan's Legacy Revisited

**THE LOGAN FAMILY IS BACK
WITH SIX NEW STORIES.**

Beginning in January 2007 with

THE COUPLE
MOST LIKELY TO

by

LILIAN DARCY

Tragedy drove them apart. Reunited eighteen
years later, their attraction was once again
undeniable. But had time away changed
Jake Logan enough to let him face his fears
and commit to the woman he once loved?